OPERATION MEDINA
THE CRUSADE

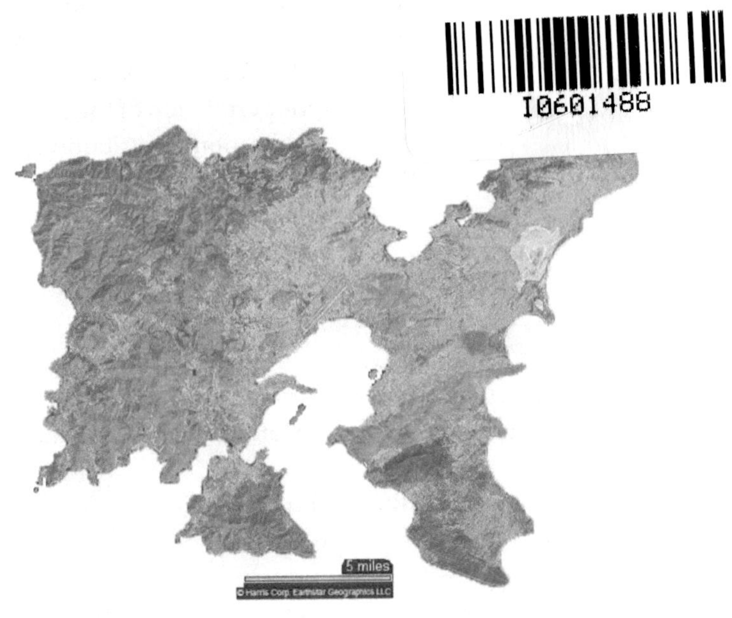

George Mavro

TotalRecallPress.com
www.totalrecallpress.com

TotalRecall Publications, Inc..
1103 Middlecreek
Friendswood, Texas 77546
281-992-3131   281-482-5390 Fax
www.totalrecallpress.com

Copyright © 2012 by: George Mavro
ISBN   978-1-59095-664-9
UPC   6-43977-36648-1

Printed in the United States of America with simultaneous printings in Australia, Canada, and United Kingdom.

FIRST EDITION
1   2   3   4   5   6   7   8   9   10

Dedication

This book is dedicated to the air force security force members who have given their lives for their comrades and the call of duty.

About the Author

The author is a 24 year air force, security force veteran. He served over 22 years stationed in Europe, eight of those in Greece. He holds degrees in Government and International Relations. He presently lives in Florida with his wife and two sons.

About the Book

The second book of the series Operation Medina, The Crusade, opens up with the Greeks retreating on all battle fronts from the Turkish onslaught. The U.S. has dispatched an expeditionary force consisting of a fighter squadron and a small USAF Security Force to assist the Greeks. As the Americans join the fight against the Turks, they begin to exact a heavy toll on the enemy. The Greeks manage to stabilize their Albanian and Macedonian fronts, yet are unable to halt the Turks, who continue to push them back. As the tide of battle begins to turn against General Kemal, he plans a final act of madness. A daring plan is formulated involving a simultaneous attack from both air and land to stop the madman from carrying out his deadly scheme. If the plan fails, the Americans will use the only other alternative left to stop him, a B-2 bomber with a nuclear payload which could lead to a nuclear showdown with other Islamic states. With the odds stacked highly against them, the allies must find a way to stop Kemal and avert a nuclear holocaust.

Prologue

White House Situation Room
19May, 1300hrs EST

President Bill Davis took another swig of his coffee; God knows he needed the caffeine after staying awake most of the night monitoring the events on the other side of the world. Ever since the crisis broke out, the National Security Council had remained in session. His head felt like it was about to explode from a raging headache that only got worse as more bad news came in. United States military airpower had been severely crippled in Western Europe after the terror attacks at Ramstein Air Base and the missile attack on the US aircraft carrier that had been visiting Greece. The Greeks were in full retreat, having been attacked from all sides and the situation looked hopeless. The only bright spot had been on the island of Limnos, where by a stroke of luck, a lone Hellenic navy missile boat had attacked and destroyed a Turkish convoy carrying the heavy weapons for the Turkish invasion force. So far the military situation on the island remained up in the air. The Greeks were still holding, but barely.

"Mr. President."

"Yes, General McDugan," the President replied to the Air Force Chief of Staff.

"I just received a report that the 526th arrived in Greece and while en route intercepted and stopped an enemy raid on the

City of Thessaloniki. They shot down most of the raiding force with no losses."

"At least there's one bit of good news, General. That's why they are there."

"Sir, we are getting a live feed from Istanbul," said Admiral Henderson, the Chief of Naval Operations.

The President looked up at one of the large LCD TV screens that covered the walls of the situation room. He could see a large building that had partially collapsed and was smoking. The Turkish commentator identified it as the Turkish Ministry of Defense. The reporter continued to say that it had been hit by several cruise missiles suspected to have been launched by the criminal American regime and that there had been some loss of life of innocent civilians working inside.

"Innocent, my ass. The bastards are not mentioning anything about the terrorist attacks on our forces or of their use of WMDS on the Greeks. They are calling the unprovoked attack on Greece a war of liberation for the Muslims under Greek domination," said the President.

At that moment General Coleman, head of the JCS, walked into the room with the Secretary of State.

"Mr. President, I just got off the phone with Mr. Samarakis, the Greek Prime Minister."

"What did he have to say, Tom? Is it bad?"

"First of all, he thanked us for dispatching the 526th; they saved the day by destroying a raiding force that was headed for Thessaloniki, Greece's second largest City. The Greeks are hard pressed. They lost many pilots from the surprise WMD attack and most of their air assets are assisting the army with ground attack support, thus they have very few assets to spare for air defense. The ground situation is bleak. The Turks tore a big hole in the Greek defenses with the surprise WMD attack. The Hellenic army is falling back, but in order and making the enemy pay for every meter. The Port City of Alexandroupolis will fall soon. This will give the enemy a port for supplies. The nation is mobilizing, but at this point, the enemy has been slowed, but can't be stopped. The only positive news is that the Albanian and Macedonian fronts have been stabilized for the time being. He is asking for any and all assistance we can provide. They are desperate!"

"Thank you, Tom. Tell the Greek Prime Minister that more aid will soon be on the way. We need a couple of days to organize and get resources in place. Tell him I am sending General Coleman to Athens to meet with his Greek counterpart and come up with a strategy. Also reiterate that Greece has the full support of the United States. This madman Kemal must be stopped!"

"Yes, Mr. President."

Chapter 1

The Greek-Bulgarian Border
2031hrs, 19 May

From a military observation post situated atop a windswept hill a few kilometers from the border, President Nikolovich peered through a spotter scope at the long column of refugees that were streaming into Bulgaria. Looking through the scope, what he saw in the fading light reminded him of news clips of the Bosnian-Serbian war. The look of anguish and despair could be seen clearly on the faces of the refugees who had fled their homes, most with only the clothes on their backs.

"General Petrov. How many refugees have crossed into Bulgaria so far?"

"I would estimate around fifty thousand, Mr. President. Thousands more are pouring in every hour, sir, as the Turkish advance continues to gain more ground." As if to reinforce what the Army Chief of Staff had just said, the rumble of heavy artillery could clearly be heard coming from the southeast.

"Have any Greek Army units crossed the border?"

"Only a few thousand soldiers, Mr. President. The Greeks fight until practically wiped out. Any survivors usually disperse into the hills to continue the fight as guerrillas."

"Have we had any serious incidents with the Turks, General?"

"There were a couple of minor incidents where Turkish troops, pursuing retreating Greek units, crossed our border. Fortunately, they were dealt with without serious incident. But on a more serious note, Mr. President, there have been several incidents of individual Turkish soldiers looting, murdering and raping refugees within sight of our border patrols. In some of these incidents, our troops intervened and there was some shooting."

"I haven't heard of any official protests from Istanbul, General."

"And you probably won't, sir. These incidents were dealt with by my district Commander, General Pavlovich. He spoke personally with the Turkish commander of the Ali Pasha infantry division which is operating in this area. He assured us that he would better control his troops' behavior in the future."

"I don't put much faith in a Turk's promise when it deals with controlling their soldier's conduct against helpless refugees. The Turks have been known for their brutality throughout the centuries."

"That is true, Mr. President. Our own people suffered under their rule for over four centuries. We will continue to aid the refugees as much as humanly possible."

"Yes, General, please see to that. Now, on another note. What do you make of the present military situation? Will the Greeks be able to stop them?"

"It's still too early to make a concise assessment. But it looks rather bad for them. Alexandroupolis fell this morning and

Kommotini will probably fall to the Turks some time tomorrow morning. The bulk of the Greek army is retreating westward, mostly in an orderly fashion. Those units that are being sacrificed in rear guard actions are making the Turks pay for every meter of territory."

"But when will the Greeks make an attempt to stop them, General?"

"I believe that the Greeks will make a stand in the foothills, west of Kavala. If the Turks break through this line," the General hesitated for a moment, "then the road to Thessaloniki is wide open and all of northwestern Greece will be lost to them."

"Kavala! That already gives half of Thrace to the Turks,"

"The Greeks cannot do otherwise, Mr. President. The surprise chemical attack decimated most of their front line units manning their border defenses, leaving the way open for Turkish armor to pour through. Think of it as a break in a dam, sir. Once the water starts pouring through the break, it gets larger until the whole dam eventually crumbles. That is exactly what happened to the Greek front line on the Evros River. Their only hope is to delay the Turks long enough to mobilize their reserves. Don't forget, sir, a large bulk of their army is tied up fighting the Albanians and Macedonians. Not that the Albanians or Macedonians are a real serious threat, but they are using up men and material that could be better used elsewhere. To sum it up, Mr. President, except for a few minor successes on and around Limnos, the war isn't going very well for Greece."

"What about the Americans, General? I heard that some aid is starting to arrive."

"Unless a massive effort is made and I doubt the Americans have the will or ability at this point to do this, their small trickle of aid will not prevent the inevitable."

"Well, that sure sums it up in a nutshell, General Petrov."

"And after their victory against the Greeks, will Bulgaria be next, General? We don't even possess half the modern military equipment that the Greeks do. Can we trust the Turks? Or are we next?"

"I wish I knew, sir. You said it yourself; General Kemal said that we have nothing to fear, as long as we remain neutral."

"I know what I said, General, but I would rather trust the devil himself," replied President Nickolovich, slightly agitated at the General's referral that he would be responsible if anything went wrong.

"We will not be caught by surprise, sir. Our armed forces are deployed in their defensive positions and remain on full alert. I have also ordered the issuing of chemical gear to the troops just in case the Turks decide to use these weapons on us."

"That is good, General Petrov. Just be sure we are ready to implement our contingency plan if we have to."

"Everything will be ready, Mr. President."

"Let us leave this dismal place. I have seen enough of this human tragedy."

Mavrovouni Foothills
2230hrs, 19 May

After a hard day of trudging through grueling mountainous and heavily wooded terrain, the 3rd Macedonian Mountain regiment had finally arrived at its intended destination. Colonel Mihalovic, promoted to full Colonel for his success at Doirani, had immediately ordered the unit to dig in. By late evening, the regiment had established a defensive line on the eastern tree lined slopes of the Mavrovouni foothills, twenty kilometers northeast of the city of Kilkis. Except for a few minor skirmishes with disorganized Greek National Guard patrols, the passage through the mountains had been relatively uneventful.

With nightfall and the possibility of attack, Colonel Mihalovic had spent the past hour and a half inspecting his front line fighting positions. Happy with what he'd seen, he headed for the command post to find Major Ziad. Hearing footsteps, he turned around.

"Sir, there is a classified message from division headquarters for you."

"Thank you, Corporal."

Taking the envelope from the messenger, he continued along the unlit path toward the command post, stopping only momentarily at his tent to read the message. Closing the tent flap, he turned on his flash light, the red lens giving out barely enough light for him to read the message. Opening the envelope, he began reading the message:

SECRET

FROM:

HEADQUARTERS   MACEDONIAN   EXPEDITIONARY
FORCE

DOIRIANI, GREECE

TO: COMMANDING OFFICER 3RD MACEDONIAN
MT. REGIMENT

ENEMY   RESISTANCE   ALONG   THE   FRONT   IS
BEGINNING   TO   STIFFEN.   ACCORDING   TO
RECENT INTELLIGENCE REPORTS THE ENEMY IS
MASSING TROOPS AND ARTILLERY IN KILKIS.
EXPECT AN ENEMY COUNTERATTACK POSSIBLY
BY MORNING. ALL UNITS HAVE BEEN ORDERED
BY CENTRAL HEADQUARTERS SKOPYE TO HOLD
THEIR   POSITIONS   AT   ALL   COSTS.   OUR
ALLIES' DRIVE IN THRACE CONTINUES
UNABATED. IT IS ESSENTIAL THAT WE TIE UP
THE   ENEMY'S   RESERVES   AS   LONG   AS
POSSIBLE TO HELP OUR ALLIES CONTINUE
THEIR OFFENSIVE TILL FINAL VICTORY IS
ACHIEVED.

The news was nothing unexpected for Colonel Mihalovic. He had known that sooner or later the Greeks would recover from their initial shock and react forcefully to the Macedonian intrusion. So far they had been lucky, but he was almost positive that their luck would soon run out. Leaving the tent, he walked the short distance to the command post. The sentry at the entrance immediately recognized him and rendered a salute. Entering, he noticed Major Ziad chastising two young Lieutenants and from what he could hear, it concerned the improper positioning of their platoon's 82mm mortar. One of the Lieutenants spotted the Colonel and called everyone in the tent to attention.

"Please, everyone as you were."

"Good evening, sir. I was just briefing these two officers on the correct procedures in setting up the 82mm mortar."

"Excellent! We must quickly prepare our positions. I believe the enemy will attack some time tomorrow morning,"

"I have inspected some of the fighting positions. They are coming along superbly. You can pass this on to the men, Major"

"I will, sir. They will be happy to hear that."

The Colonel gestured to the two young officers. "Go back to your platoons and make sure that all your fighting positions are completed and that your men are properly fed and rested by midnight. Remember gentlemen. Your main responsibility is to take care of your men. If you do that, they will always take care of you,"

"You are dismissed."

After the two young officers had departed the tent, the Colonel put his arm around Major Ziad's shoulders and led him out of the tent and away from where anyone could hear them. "Take it easy on them my old friend, remember we were young once."

"I know, sir. Such mistakes could cost us dearly."

"You are right, but don't worry. I have ordered Sergeant Baktiar to check all the positions later this evening. He will make sure everything is done correctly."

The Major grinned. "I should never underestimate you."

"We must be ready, Major. Our test under fire may be rapidly approaching. Here, read this message from headquarters."

The Major took his red lens flashlight and quickly read the message in the dim light. "I fear they're probably correct, sir. Our scouts have also reported large concentrations of enemy troops with heavy guns massing around Kilkis."

"I' m afraid that our army's advance has been halted by the Greeks. According to earlier dispatches, many units are beginning to face stiff enemy resistance," said Colonel Mihalovic.

"That was to have been expected, sir. But the 3rd Mountain Regiment has so far met its objectives and so has most of the army. We have been successful in drawing off large amounts of the enemy's reserves and we have even seized a good chunk of their territory.

"Let's hope that we can keep some of it. Skopje has ordered

us to hold our position at all costs."

"Our soldiers will fight, sir."

"I don't doubt that, my friend. But it would be pointless if our army was annihilated in the process. I do intend to hold this position as long as humanly possible and then pull back into the mountains. I don't intend to sacrifice the lives of our soldiers or become a sacrificial lamb for our Turkish allies nor for those fools in the capital."

Major Ziad looked at the Colonel skeptically for a moment. "You're right, our country will need its army to keep the politicians in line and . . ." The sound of incoming shells caused both men to instinctively dive for cover. The peacefulness of the night was momentarily torn asunder by the bright flashes and loud explosions of heavy caliber shells landing all around them. Fortunately, the violent artillery barrage lasted only a couple of minutes. Just as suddenly as it had started, it stopped and the night was silent again, save for the screams of the wounded and dying. The two officers stood up and brushed themselves off. The chemical stench of high explosives hung in the air all around them. Several shrubs that had been set afire by the shelling were quickly put out before the fire spread. Fortunately, it had rained recently. Had it been summer, the forest would have been a dry tinder box and the fires would have quickly spread with catastrophic results for the Macedonians.

"I believe those were 203mm shells. This is only a small taste of what is to come," said Colonel Mihalovic. The rumble of artillery fire could again be heard several kilometers away, hitting another sector.

"Harassment fire. They want to keep us awake all night so we will be exhausted by morning when and if they attack us."

"Go and see to our wounded Major. I will first check on the rest of our positions and afterwards get something to eat. We must make sure that our fighting positions are dug deep enough to offer some type of cover for the troops. Tomorrow will most likely be a very busy day for us."

"Yes, sir. Take care. May the prophet watch over us, my friend," mumbled the Major as his Commander and friend disappeared into the darkness.

Chapter 2

Limnos

0030hrs, 20 May

Eleni lay resting atop a dirty old mattress on the floor of an old abandoned sheep herder's hut, situated in a rocky mountain hillside. Petros had left her there to sleep while he had gone out to search for food. For the past two days, they had been moving deeper into the island's rugged interior to escape the advancing Turkish army. Her first night out had been a terrible experience. The weather had been stormy. Soaked and chilled to the bone, she had slept alone in a small cave used by the local goat herders, while Petros had gone back to the hotel to bury his wife. When he safely returned the next morning, they continued their trek into the island's interior.

Throughout most of the day, they had passed empty villages and scores of terrified refugees trudging in various directions, all with one thing in mind, to escape the Turkish onslaught. Scores of bodies littered the roadsides, victims of air attacks or the intermittent shelling that rained down on the helpless refugees. The stories of murder and mayhem that Eleni heard from many of these hapless people only strengthened her resolve to keep on going. Hungry and alone, she wondered what would become of her. She thought of Yiannis; was he still alive, or was he somewhere at the bottom of the Aegean Sea with his boat and crew?

The sudden sound of movement coming from outside jarred her back to reality. "Oh my God, it's the Turks," she whispered under her breath. If it had been Petros returning, he would have called out her name. Taking the small pistol that Petros had left her, she moved toward the front door, determined to take a few of the enemy soldiers with her, before turning the gun on herself. Silently she waited by the door, the noises growing closer. Suddenly, from behind her, came the sound of someone stepping on broken glass.

"Oh, no!"

Before she could bring the gun around, she was grabbed from behind, the pistol taken from her and a hand was clamped over her mouth. Eleni hoped for a quick death as she saw the glint of a blade.

"It's a woman!" said her surprised assailant in Greek. The soldier relaxed his hold and removed his hand from her mouth.

"Please don't hurt me," she said trembling with fear.

"Don't worry, miss," said a short well-built man who had stepped through the door that she'd been watching. The man was in his mid-twenties and dressed in camouflage battle dress. He wore a beret and the insignia of a First Lieutenant on his shoulder epaulets. He shinned a small red lens flashlight into her face.

"Vangelis, let her go," said the officer.

The soldier immediately let go of Eleni. "No one will hurt you, you're safe now, miss."

"Thank God. I thought you were the Turks," said Eleni, visibly relieved.

The handsome young officer smiled and offered his hand. "I'm Lieutenant Kostas Genetakos, Commander of the first platoon, second airborne company. We've been patrolling this area for the last few hours. We haven't encountered any enemy patrols, but that doesn't mean that they're not around."

"Oh, please excuse me. I haven't introduced myself. My name is Eleni Manolakos"

"That's perfectly all right considering the circumstances. Vangelis must have given you quite a scare. He's gotten very good at sneaking up on people, especially on Turkish sentries."

"Yes, he did," said Eleni, causing a shiver to run down her spine as she remembered the glint of the knife.

"Do you live around here, miss?"

"No. I am from Athens. I was here visiting my fiancé who is in the navy. His name is Yiannis Vassiliou. He commands a missile boat and was dispatched here to monitor the Turkish maneuvers. We were staying at a hotel near Mirina, owned by a former shipmate of his. During the attack on Mirina, the Turks came and murdered the hotel owner's wife. I was hiding in a closet, but they found me. I, I, killed one of them, he was only a boy," she said as tears began to stream down her face.

"Petros, the murdered woman's husband, showed up a couple of minutes later and killed the two soldiers that were trying to rape me. We've been on the run ever since. He brought me here for safety and went out looking for food."

The Lieutenant pulled out a tissue from one of the flaps attached to his web gear and handed it to Eleni.

"Thank you," said Eleni, wiping the tears from her eyes.

"Where is your fiancé now?"

"I don't know,"

"He was out all night on patrol with his boat, the Hydra, when the war broke out. I hope they're all right."

"I wish I could help you, but I don't have any information on the navy. But I can offer you some food. It's not the best, but it's filling."

"Right now I'll eat anything. I'm famished."

Lieutenant Genetakos reached into his BDU pockets and pulled out a package of MREs (meals ready to eat) and handed it to Eleni.

"Thank you very much."

"Sit down and eat your food. You're safe here."

"I'm worried about Petros. He's been gone a long while"

"I'm sure he's okay. He'll show up."

While Eleni was eating her MRE in the dim light provided by the small flash light given to her by the Lieutenant, two soldiers walked in with an individual at gun point.

"Petros!" she yelled, jumping up and giving him a hug.

"You're okay. I was worried sick. What took you so long?" The Lieutenant, observing that Eleni had recognized the individual motioned for the soldiers to lower their rifles and leave.

"I ran into a couple of Turkish patrols a few kilometers back and had to double back the long way. I was found by the Lieutenant's men about a kilometer from here."

"At least they weren't the enemy. I am Lieutenant Genetakos," he said, holding out his hand to Petros.

After both men had finished their introductions and Petros had something to eat, Lieutenant Genetakos got down to business. "Eleni tells me that you're from this island and that you were a former naval officer."

"That's correct. I retired a couple of years ago as a Lieutenant Commander."

"That's excellent," replied Lieutenant Genetakos. "The Prime Minister has issued an order mobilizing all males from the ages of nineteen to fifty-five."

"Meaning?"

"It means that you've been recalled to active duty."

"You're not funny, Lieutenant. I don't see any ships around here right now."

"Look, we need your help. You know the island, my men don't. Will you help us?"

"I just can't leave Eleni by herself."

"Don't worry. She'll be safe at our main base of operations. We'll take her there."

Eleni, who had been listening to the conversation the whole time, spoke up. "Don't worry about me, I'll be all right."

"I'd be glad to help. I have a score to settle with these bastards."

"Thank you, sir."

"You can cut the sir crap, Lieutenant."

"Now, on a more serious matter, Kostas. What's the news on the war?" Are we winning or losing?" asked Petros.

"I can only tell you what I know and that's not very much."

"Anything is better than nothing," said Eleni.

"Well the Turks aren't winning the war, at least not here on Limnos. From the information provided by some of the prisoners that we have captured, they had expected the island to fall quickly after the surprise chemical attack. That didn't happen. On the contrary, the garrison manning the anti-aircraft defenses at the airport survived intact and repelled the initial enemy airborne assault. Suffering heavy casualties in both men and material, the Turks were forced to withdraw. Had they captured the airport, they would have been able to fly supplies and reinforcements in and the battle for Limnos might have been lost. The spirited defense of the airfield bought the time we needed to reorganize our command and defense structures that had been decimated by the chemical attack. The garrison there has since been reinforced with men and some of our surviving armor. The Turks have launched repeated attacks on the airfield, but we're still holding it. Fortunately, the enemy still lacks the heavy guns and tanks needed to secure the island."

"We've been very lucky then."

"More than lucky, my friend. Our navy intercepted and sank the ships carrying the heavy vehicles for the invasion force, but how long the status quo will last, God only knows. Right now, the Turks control most of the coastal areas, but all their attempts to advance into the island's interior in force have been beaten back. Now and then, they shoot a few of their smaller caliber guns at inland civilian targets and mostly kill innocent people for the terror effect, but do little damage otherwise. Fortunately, most of the male civilian population of the island had been issued old surplus M1 rifles years ago and have formed territorial guard units. Some of these units have linked up with regular army units to fight the enemy or have formed guerrilla bands to harass the enemy. We've run into some during our patrols.

"What about their air power?" asked Petros.

"It's difficult for them to pinpoint and accurately strike targets in hilly and mountainous terrain. Their pilots are scared of our stinger missiles to venture close in, so they drop their bombs from altitude. They tear up a lot of ground, but usually miss their targets. If they manage to land armor and heavy artillery, we'll be finished in a few days."

"Let's pray that our navy doesn't let them."

"I'm with you on that, Petros. Now we need to get moving. Our base of operations is about eight kilometers from here."

Xanthi-Kommotini Highway
0410hrs, 20 May

Riding in the back of a duce and a half truck filled with wounded soldiers, Warrant Officer Mihalis Manakos pondered the events of the last couple of days. It had all seemed like a horrible nightmare to him. But at least in a nightmare, once you woke up, it was over. This one only got worse. Looking back in the direction of Kommotini, he could no longer hear the thunder or see the flashes of explosions from the shells that had been raining down on the city. The eerie silence could only mean one thing. The city had fallen to the advancing Turkish army, not that it hadn't been expected, only a company of sappers and a battalion of infantry had remained to delay them. He was now glad that he had fled the city before it had been encircled by the enemy. His original intentions had been to stay and fight, but Athens had decided to abandon Kommotini to its fate. When this afternoon, a string of shells had taken out the makeshift police station and had killed almost everyone inside, he had jumped on the first available vehicle heading west.

Mihalis was amazed at the speed and ferocity of the Turkish attack, which had caught everyone by surprise. Orestiada, Alexandroupolis and Kommotini had quickly fallen. Mihalis wondered what city would be next, Xanthi? When would these bastards be stopped? While he pondered all these questions in his mind, the sound of approaching helicopters, coming out of the southeast, abruptly interrupted his thoughts. Looking up, he could see tracers reaching skyward from the numerous military vehicles that were on the road, toward the as of yet, unseen enemy.

"Damn! Everyone out, we're sitting ducks," he screamed.

The roar of cannon and rocket fire filled the night as the enemy attack helicopters let loose their deadly loads on the vehicle and refugee packed road. Grabbing one of the lesser wounded soldiers, Mihalis jumped out of the truck, down the slight road embankment and into the trees that lined the road. Spotting a clump of boulders, he dived behind them only seconds before the gunships passed overhead, spewing death and destruction all around him. When the helicopters had completed their deadly work and left the area, Mihalis got back up on his feet and surveyed the devastation the attack had caused. He could hear cries for help coming from all around him. With the help of the light, generated by several burning vehicles, what he saw made him sick to his stomach. The road had been turned into a slaughter house, strewn with the bloody, broken bodies of refugees, mostly women and children that had gotten caught in the open during the attack. Several hundred meters from where he was standing, he could see the burning remains of one of the helicopters that had gotten shot down by a stinger missile. *At least the bastards didn't get off scot free, he thought to himself.*

Mihalis noticed the truck he had been riding in. The vehicle had taken a stream of 30mm cannon shells that had transformed it into a pile of junk. Running over to it, he climbed up and looked inside. He immediately jumped back down and stumbled to the side of the road where he fell to his knees and vomited. The inside of the truck had been transformed into a charnel house of blood and torn bodies. Mihalis quickly recovered his composure when he heard the sound of tracked vehicles coming from the east. *If it's the enemy, we're all dead, he thought,* waiting for the approaching vehicles to manifest themselves. A few seconds later, one of the vehicles came out of the shadows. It was a tank, bearing blue and white Hellenic army identification markings on its turret. Mihalis, for the moment, relaxed.

The heavy M-60 main battle tank came to a stop behind the destroyed truck Mihalis had been riding in. Its commander dismounted and approached the scene.

"Do you need any help? We have a spare first aid kit that you could have."

"No. Everyone in there is beyond help," gesturing to the smashed truck.

"Nonetheless, some of the other injured might." Taking the first aid kit from the tanker, Mihalis called out to one of the soldiers helping the wounded. The soldier walked over, took the kit and thanked them. The tanker, having done his small part in helping with the injured, walked back toward his vehicle.

"Hey, aren't you going to stick around to protect us in case the Turks show up?"

"Sorry, we can't stay. We've been ordered to link up with what's left of the brigade on the outskirts of Xanthi."

"Can I bum a ride? No use hanging around here."

The tank commander thought it out for a few seconds. "Sure, I can use another loader. We lost our loader this morning. He was caught outside during an artillery barrage."

"I'm willing to learn."

"I'm Lieutenant Markos Kapsis," the tank commander said,

holding out his hand.

"I'm Warrant Officer Mihalis Manakos, of the former Kommotini police department."

"We heard the news of the Muslim uprising in the city. I heard that it was really bad and that lots of people were killed."

"Yes it was pretty bad. And there were a lot of good people killed," said Mihalis as he once again thought about that night almost forty-eight hours ago.

The tank commander climbed aboard the vehicle. "Let's get moving, climb aboard." A minute later the huge armored beast had disappeared into the night.

The Northern Aegean
20 May, 0743hrs

While the Hydra sped toward harm's way, Lieutenant Commander Vassiliou nervously paced the boat's bridge in anticipation of the battle to come. The Hydra and five other missile attack boats were the vanguard of a heavier task force following several miles behind. The Greek fleet was sallying forth on its first major offensive operation of the war.

What had prompted the Greek moves were intelligence photographs gathered by U.S. satellite and TR1 reconnaissance flights the day before, of Turkish naval movements in the bay of Izmir. The photos showed three tank landing ships taking on armor and self-propelled howitzers. There were several major warships standing by in the harbor that would probably serve as their escorts. Intelligence speculated that the Turks were going to make a major effort to reinforce their beach head on Limnos with the tanks and heavy artillery needed to secure the island. When the Greek pentagon in Athens had received this information, they immediately assembled a strong naval task force to intercept and destroy this convoy at all costs. The Greek task force would sortie out, after it was ascertained by intelligence that the Turks had sailed.

Later that day, high altitude satellite surveillance of the bay of Izmir had become impossible because of heavy cloud cover. A subsequent low level flight by an RF-4 reconnaissance plane over Izmir, reported that the ships had sailed before all radio contact with the pilot had been lost. Later in the evening, additional confirmation of the enemy task force's departure had come from the submarine Poseidon which was patrolling the straits of Izmir. It had picked up the sounds of many screws on its sonar, but was chased away by ASW helicopters before it could get close enough to investigate. Alerted to the convoy's approximate whereabouts, an intercept had been attempted during the night by explosive laden, high speed Panagopoulos class attack boats (a modern version of the Bourloto fire ship). Sallying from the island of Lesbos, rough seas and heavy fire from the escorts had prevented the small high speed boats from penetrating the escort umbrella and getting to the transports. Still, they had managed to ram and seriously damage one of the escorting Frigates. The loss to boats and crews had been heavy. High winds and the heavy concentration of enemy warships in the area had prevented rescue boats from picking up many survivors. It would now be up to the Hydra and the rest of the task force, which was proceeding at full speed, to intercept and destroy the enemy convoy.

"Sir, message from Captain Tassiou. Enemy detected twelve miles east of Agios Efstratios, heading due north, speed fourteen knots. All units will come to a heading of forty-two degrees to intercept the enemy."

"Understood, Mr. Faniou, probably seen by one of our spotters on the island."

"We'll be in missile range in twenty minutes," reported Lieutenant Mavridis.

"And probably be on their radar screens before that, Takis."

Yiannis picked up the phone and rang CIC.

"Anything on the ESM, Mr. Tassakis?"

"Nothing yet, sir. They too, must have their radars on stand-by," replied the EW officer.

"Thank you, Mr. Tassakis. Keep me posted." Yiannis turned to his friend. "This is going to come down to who finds whom first and shoots."

"Or who loses his cool first and goes active and is seen by the other guy."

"They definitely know we're out here looking for them. Where the hell is the air cover promised to us?" said Yiannis.

"Without air cover, we don't stand a chance. We'll be blown out of the water by an air strike before we even get in range."

"Don't worry Yiannis, they'll be there. Trust the air force."

"I sure hope so, Takis."

Thirty Thousand Feet above the Northern Aegean
0748hrs, 20 May

High above the Aegean Sea, Logan and the rest of his squadron were nearing their intercept area. An orbiting USAF E3D AWACS bird, one hundred miles to the west, had detected a flight of Turkish aircraft on an intercept course to the Greek task force, which the 526th had been assigned to provide air cover for. The AWACS immediately vectored the 526th to intercept and destroy the enemy planes.

"Falcon One to all pilots, stand by, we're being painted," said Logan, his threat indicator suddenly coming alive.

"Break, break, inbound missiles!"

Jamming the throttle into full military power, Logan pulled back on the stick, hitting the chaff and flare buttons at the same time. The F-16 went into a vertical climb, the Gs forcing him into his seat. Luckily for him, one of the inbound missiles that had been tracking his plane went for the decoy instead, its proximity fuse detonating the warhead behind him. His wing man wasn't as lucky. His plane disappeared in a cloud of yellow and black smoke after taking a missile hit.

"Falcon One to Bravo and Charlie flight leaders, take out the escorts. Alpha and Delta go for the bombers."

While the American fighter formation was splitting into two groups, the enemy SU-27 Flankers, heavily laden with anti-ship missiles headed for the deck, determined to get within missile range of the Greek ships. With the escorts preoccupied, Logan's flight tore into the Flankers. Spotting a Flanker several thousand feet below him, Logan hit the weapons select switch bringing his radar out of standby. The radar locked onto the nearest target that was the SU-27. The symbol on the HUD, (heads up display) went to air to air guns display and he followed the swinging dot. When the dot had centered on the target, Logan squeezed the trigger, sending a burst of 20mm cannon shells into the enemy plane. The Flanker exploded into a bright ball of fire when the shells ripped into its fuel tanks. Five hundred meters in front of him, another Flanker erupted into flames hit by cannon fire and dove into the sea.

"I got him!" yelled Wendy over the radio.

Logan smiled, "scratch another Jihadi" he mumbled under his breath, doing a three sixty roll at the same time. Coming back to the level flight position, the corner of his eye caught a Flanker, low at his four o'clock position, making for the deck. "Shit. I have to get the bastard before he gets into missile range," he muttered as he nosed the F-16 down. The chirp warning on his AL 69 threat indicator went off and the symbol of a Mig-29 appeared on his six o'clock position. He was being tracked on radar. The Mig fired a short range A-8 missile. Logan hit the flare dispenser and pushed the throttle to the stops. The Gs slammed him into the seat as this time he put the fighter into a tight loop, reversing into his attacker. The F-16, with its tail pipe turned away from the missile, caused the guidance head to lose its heat source and go for the flares. From hunter, the Mig had become the hunted. Logan eased off the throttle and hit the weapons select switch to air to air missile mode. His HUD instantly came alive and he achieved a lock on the Mig. Pressing the firing button, he sent an AIM-9M up the Mig's tail pipes. Out of control, the enemy pilot pulled his ejection handle and was shot out of the doomed fighter. Without hesitating, Logan hit afterburner and went after the escaping Flanker. Switching on his radar, he painted the flanker at eighteen miles on the deck and directly ahead. Knowing that the enemy plane would soon be in missile firing range, Logan hit his weapon selector and brought up an AIM-120 AMRAAM missile. When his HUD indicated a lock, Logan pressed the firing button. The missile quickly accelerated to Mach 3.

The Flanker pilot, preoccupied with achieving a firing solution and launching sequence, had heard his warning buzzer sound of a missile lock. He waited till the last second possible before taking evasive action, but he was too late to avoid the AMRAAM that blew him out of the sky, but not before he had launched his two anti-ship missiles on a bearing attack toward the Greek ships.

Northern Aegean Sea
0803hrs, 20 May

With their radars still on stand-by mode to avoid detection by the enemy's ESM equipment, the Hydra and her other sister boats had been unaware of the air battle that had taken place forty miles to the northwest. The calm was suddenly shattered when the ESM operators detected the SU-27's launch of its two anti-ship missiles. It would now only be a matter of minutes before their fate would be determined.

With the enemy missiles rapidly closing, Captain Tassiou ordered his missile boat squadron to immediately begin evasive action. The enemy pilot had launched his missiles on a bearing attack. The missiles would proceed to the last known coordinates of their targets. Once in the last known vicinity of the Greek warships, the missiles' radars would begin a target search. The Greek boats' only salvation would be to increase their distance between them, providing fewer targets in the sector for enemy missile radars to lock on.

"Incoming missiles, six miles, ETA 1 minute," shouted the ECM officer.

"Stand by to fire off chaff and flares," said Commander Vassiliou.

"ETA, thirty seconds."

"Fire off chaff and flares."

The two AS-14 Kledge missiles had entered their target box and had gone to active search mode. One of the missiles had immediately locked on to the Troupakis, Captain Tassiou's boat. The Troupakis fired off more chaff and flares to deflect the missile. In a last ditch effort, her Emerlik 30mm cannon opened fire. A second later, there was a bright flash followed by a loud boom that echoed across the waters. The Kledge slammed into the small missile boat. Almost immediately, smoke and flames could be seen pouring from the stricken boat as she rapidly lost headway. The other missile had plunged harmlessly into the sea confused by the chaff.

"Aren't we going to help them?" Lieutenant Mavridis asked his friend who was looking at the burning boat, a few miles astern."

Before Lieutenant Commander Vassiliou could say anything, he was interrupted by Ensign Tassakis.

"Sir, have multiple contacts, distance twenty-five miles, bearing 010 degrees, speed twenty knots. They're on a northerly heading and their radars have just gone active."

Yiannis pondered his next move.

"Any word from the Troupakis?"

"None, sir. You're the senior officer and in command now. Captain Tassiou is probably dead. We don't have much time; we are in their missile envelope."

Yiannis looked back at the burning Troupakis that was fading astern.

"Mr. Faniou, radio the other boats, stand by to attack. Send an immediate message to the flag ship; Troupakis hit by missile, Captain Tassiou feared dead, assuming command of flotilla. Enemy detected at twenty-five miles. Preparing to attack, signed Lieutenant Commander Vassiliou. Hurry and send it!"

"Yes, sir," said the communications officer.

Yiannis picked up the phone to CIC. It was picked up by Takis, who had assumed his post. "Takis, stand by to launch on bearing attack on the enemy convoy."

"Roger, Yiannis."

"Sir, message from the flagship Elli. Your message acknowledged. We'll be following up on your attack. Good luck. God be with you, signed Admiral Karrayiannis."

"Thanks, Mr. Faniou."

"Sir, picking up enemy radar emissions. We're being painted."

"Mr. Faniou, send message, fire at will."

"Aye, aye, sir."

Almost in unison the four surviving Combattante missile boats fired off their complement of four Exocet missiles a piece. Within the span of twenty seconds, sixteen missiles were winging their way toward the Turkish convoy.

"Helmsmen, get us out of here, fast!"

"Sir, the enemy has also fired. I have six high speed contacts heading this way. ETA four and a half minutes," said Ensign Metaxas who was filling in on the radar.

"Thank you, Mr. Metaxas."

Twenty miles to the east, the two Turkish MEKO class frigates patrolling the western flank of the convoy had detected the Greek missile launch and had immediately activated their air defense systems. When the missiles were ten miles distant, each of the frigates fired off their complement of eight Sea Sparrow air to air missiles at the incoming Exocets. The Sea Sparrows were only able to shoot down ten of the sea skimming missiles. The rest of the Exocets continued on their programmed course, their internal radars locking on to the nearest available targets in their path. Two of these targets were the MEKO class frigates. With only their point defense guns left to protect them from the incoming missiles, the frigates were sitting ducks.

Only one of the Frigates, the Sultan Ahmet, was able to shoot down one of the two missiles with her Seaguard point defense guns. The other Exocet struck her amidships. It detonated under her torpedo mounts blowing them into the water and damaging one of her diesel engines directly below the explosion. Fire spread quickly throughout the lower decks. Her sister ship, the Badar Khomeini, named in honor of the Ayatollah Khomeini and father of the first Islamic revolution, was hit by two of the Exocets, one of them exploding in her missile storage room. She went up in a huge ball of fire and smoke.

After the battle, one of the Turkish ASW helicopter pilots that had seen the ship hit, reported that she had sunk in less than a minute's time. The remaining missiles sped on toward the center of the convoy, their radars seeking targets. One of them locked on to the Firtina, a small Dogan class missile attack boat. She fired off chaff and flares in desperation, but the missile wasn't fooled. It struck her missile launcher, subsequently setting off the four Harpoons that were stored inside. The blast destroyed most of her superstructure, killing everybody that was topside.

The last two Exocets locked on to the Savastepe, an Adams class guided missile destroyer that had been conducting anti-submarine sweeps. As the missiles closed on the destroyer at over five hundred miles an hour, her port side Phalanx point defense came alive and began spitting out a wall of shells in front of the Exocet. Two hundred meters from the ship, the missile ran into one of these shells and exploded, spraying the ship with hundreds of lethal fragments, killing seven crewmen. The other missile was lost for a split second by the Phalanx system's radar. By the time it was reacquired, it was too late. The Exocet slammed into the Sevastape's port side, just under her bridge and detonated inside the ship's CIC. With fires spreading in her lower decks and her CIC destroyed, she was effectively out of the battle.

Yiannis' command wouldn't escape unscathed. Six Harpoon missiles had been fired toward them by two of the escorts. The small boats raced through the waters, widening the distance between them and firing off chaff, hoping to decoy the missiles. Unfortunately, not all the missiles were fooled. Two of the Harpoons locked on and hit the Lascos, virtually blowing the small boat out of the water and killing everyone on board. One of the missiles was decoyed away by the chaff fired by the Starakis, another struck the Arliotis and detonated in her engine room, killing everyone inside and rupturing her hull plates. The other two continued on their bearing until they ran out of fuel and crashed into the sea. The price had been heavy for the missile boat squadron. Half of the boats had either been sunk or severely damaged and over one hundred of their crew members had been either killed or wounded. Their sacrifice though, had not been in vain. They had opened a large gap in the western flank of the enemy escort umbrella, which was immediately exploited by the Greek task force commander. Within minutes after the attack, several Hellenic Navy Aegean Seahawk helicopters, armed with Penguin anti-ship missiles, raced into the gap, opened by the missile boats. The helicopters, zigzagging low over the wave tops looking for targets, quickly found and engaged the two Kartal class attack boats that had been sent to close the gap. Having no standoff anti-air defense capabilities, the Kartals were no match for the missile armed choppers. In a mere minute, both Kartals had been turned into burning wrecks.

With the entire western flank of the Turkish convoy now wide open, the main Greek task force which had closed the range opened fire with a barrage of anti-ship missiles. In a brave effort to save their charges, the surviving three escort vessels positioned themselves between the transports and the oncoming missiles. In desperation, they fired off their remaining Sea Sparrows, which did succeed in shooting down many of the Greek missiles. Enough of them got through to decide the battle's outcome. Only one of the destroyer escorts had been able to fire her complement of Harpoon missiles before she herself was struck by three Harpoons which broke her in half.

With the escorts gone, the transports were left virtually undefended. Each of the three LST's was hit by at least two missiles, turning them instantly into burning wrecks. One of ships exploded a few minutes later in a spectacular display of fireworks when the flames reached the ammunition stored aboard several vehicles. The other two were abandoned by their crews and sinking. Of the Turkish missiles, only one, a Harpoon, succeeded in penetrating the Greek task force's missile defenses. It slammed into the destroyer Kimono's bow section. When the smoke cleared, fifteen feet of her bow section, up to the water line, was missing and ten of her crew had been killed. The battle had lasted less than twenty minutes.

Historians would later name this naval action, the second naval battle of Limnos. Another battle, given the same name, had taken place between Greek and Turkish Dreadnoughts in the same area, almost a century earlier. The small, but well trained and equipped Greek fleet, had taken on a superior Ottoman navy and swept it from the Aegean. That battle had also resulted in a resounding victory for the Hellenic navy and had eventually influenced the outcome of the first Balkan war. Once again, the Hellenic navy had given its nation a major victory in its hour of need.

Piges Airfield, Northern Greece
0848hrs, 20 May

Master Sergeant George Pappas popped two 600mg Motrins into his mouth and took a swig of water from his canteen as he walked out of the command tent. He had a splitting headache and was exhausted, having spent the last twenty-four hours supervising the construction of his Air Base Ground Defense flight's fighting positions. Having to sit through the Captain's asinine staff meeting had not helped his headache any. His time could have been spent more constructively, such as getting some needed rest. Instead, he spent the last hour listening to the Captain's bullshit on how it was every NCO and Officer's responsibility to ensure that the troops shaved, shined their boots and maintained proper military courtesy. The asshole had done a post check on a couple of his flight's fighting positions during the morning stand to. The Captain was now pissed off, because the sloppy airmen, as he called them, had not saluted him. Needless to say, he had received an ass chewing by the Captain for it. Obviously, the pompous bastard hadn't yet realized that there was a real war going on. Well, the troops would salute him next time he came to their front line positions, he would make sure of that. And hopefully, an enemy sniper would be watching and blow the idiot's head off, once he realized he had an officer in his sights.

Fortunately, the morning out brief hadn't been a total waste. They had received an intelligence briefing from an English speaking Hellenic Air Force officer and some important news had been disseminated. He had admitted that the war was going rather badly for Greece, at the moment. The city of Kommotini, one hundred kilometers to the east, had fallen to Turkish mechanized units, early last night and now Xanthi, a city forty kilometers to the east, was being threatened. This was bad news, he wondered if the Turks would be knocking on their doorstep before long. His flight, which was guarding the eastern approaches to the airfield, would have to bear the brunt of any attack. Luckily, the sector had been reinforced this morning with a company of Greek infantry. The Greeks had set up three 90mm recoilless rifles and several Dragon antitank positions, covering the eastern approaches to the airfield. A couple of his own fighting positions had been augmented with

50 caliber machine guns. The Greeks had even brought along several 120mm heavy mortars to augment the American 81mm mortars. Additionally, the field had been ringed with Artemis 30 and other types of anti-aircraft batteries to provide defense. Even with the additional reinforcements and fire power, he knew that they couldn't hold out very long against a determined enemy attack without additional reinforcements.

Exhausted, but fully awake, George began walking toward the direction of where his flight was deployed. *I guess I'd better go get some shuteye now that it's still relatively quiet, he thought.* Several minutes later, he left the built up area of the main base behind him as a loud wail of a siren cut through the morning air.

"What the hell is that?" he mumbled. When he saw several Greeks running to what looked like recently dug trenches, he remembered what the siren meant, air raid imminent! Stopping for a moment, he reached to his left side where his gas mask case was. Opening the case, he pulled out the mask and put it on. The Turks had used gas once, what would stop them from using it again? Satisfied that his mask was on securely, George began running toward his flight's sector. After running about a hundred and fifty meters, he was out of breath. *There's no way I'll make it back to the flight with all this crap I'm wearing. I'd better find a shelter, he thought.* Spotting one about two hundred meters away, George began running. Before he had even covered half the distance, he heard the firing of anti-aircraft guns and the whine of jet engines coming out of the east. "Shit! So much for the fifteen minute air raid warning we were supposed to have," he said out loud. Looking for someplace quick to take cover, he saw a nearby clump of trees and took off running.

The deafening roar of a low flying jet at full military power tore through his ear drums. Looking up, he saw an F-16, only a few hundred meters away, release its bomb load. Reaching the trees, he hit the ground just as the world around him erupted in a cloud of earth, fire and flying metal. Luckily, the trees had shielded him from most of the blast and shrapnel. After the debris had stopped falling, he got back up on his feet. One of the bombs had landed only thirty meters away. The explosion had shredded and uprooted most of the tress in the little clump. He looked over to where the air raid shelter had been; all that remained of it was a bomb crater, after having taken a direct hit. What surprised George the most was the sight of the enemy fighter that had dropped the bombs. It had crashed just five hundred meters from where he was standing.

"That's strange. I don't hear any bomb explosions nor the aircraft guns firing any more. What the fuck's going on?" he mumbled to himself. His answer was quick in coming. The loud roar of two F-16s buzzing the field made him dive for cover. Hearing no explosions, George looked up and saw the planes making another pass that culminated in a victory roll. Then he saw their USAF markings and realized what had happened. The Calvary had arrived in the form of the 526th Black Nights which had saved their asses.

Piges Airfield
1030hrs, 20 May

When the mission out brief had been completed, the room was called to attention and Logan dismissed his pilots. After this morning's successful mission, he had given most of the pilots, except those standing alert, the rest of the afternoon off. They all needed a break; if they weren't flying a mission, they were standing alert duty. For good measures, he had put everyone on thirty minutes recall which meant they could go no further than Kavala. Picking up his leather flight jacket, Logan headed for the door.

"Sir, may I have a word with you?" asked Captain Barnes.

After their little run in at the Ramstein O club, except for duty related items, he had kept his conversations to a minimum with her. "Sure, Captain. What's on your mind?"

She waited until everyone had cleared out of the room.

"Sir, I would like to apologize for what I said to you back at Ramstein. I finally realized what you meant about inexperienced pilots. I really grew up a lot during these last couple of days."

"Wendy, I'll be the first to admit that I was proven wrong and I thank God for that."

"Why thank you, sir," she said cracking a big smile.

"How would you like some lunch. The Greeks told me of a nice cozy little tavern on the outskirts of Kavala. Colonel Kazas has provided me with a jeep and it's only a twenty minute ride."

"Well, I don't know. I'm pretty tired."

"Come on, we all need a break."

"Oh, what the hell. I am hungry. Let's go try the local cuisine. I'll meet you back here in fifteen minutes. I'd like to freshen up some."

"Okay, sure. I'll go get the jeep."

Chapter 3

Mavrovouni foothills, seven kilometers north of Kilkis

1043hrs, 20 May

Master Sergeant Markos Bihrakis quickly went over his pre fire checklist for the third time. He didn't want anything going wrong with this particular fire mission. Markos was glad that his battery had been selected to fire the opening salvos of the offensive that would destroy the Skopyian invaders. Less than a half hour ago, the battery of twelve M-109A5, 155mm self-propelled howitzers had been given their fire mission from division. Markos had entered the coordinates into his TAC fire computer. He wasn't too sure where the target area was, but he suspected that it was somewhere in the Mavrovouni foothills. Their fire mission would last twenty minutes, but in that short time span, they would deliver over fifteen tons of high explosives into the enemy positions.

Glancing at his watch, he saw that they had thirty seconds to go before opening fire. The thought of his family in Thessaloniki suddenly crept into his mind. He hadn't heard from them since the war's outbreak. Rumors had spread throughout the unit that there had been heavy air raids on the city with many civilian casualties. He prayed that his family was safe.

"Prepare to open fire," he said into the intercom to his crew.

"Fire!" The twelve guns in the battery fired simultaneously, sending their deadly loads almost eighteen kilometers down range.

Colonel Mihalovic had just finished having a cup of coffee in the command post and was about to leave on his morning post checks when he heard the whine of incoming shells.

"Incoming! Take cover," he screamed diving back into the sandbag covered command post. "It's started," he mumbled to himself. *One direct hit and we've all had it, he thought,* as the ground around them shook from the explosion of heavy caliber artillery shells. Miraculously, except for a few nearby misses, the command post survived the twenty minute bombardment intact. When the shelling had stopped, Colonel Mihalovic got up quickly to his feet.

"Alert all our posts, the enemy will probably be attacking in the next few minutes!"

"Sir, no answer from posts four and five," shouted the command post duty officer as he tried to get the two sites on the field phone.

"Most likely the shelling has cut the lines. Send a runner to check on their status immediately. If they've been knocked out, we must immediately send reinforcements to that sector at once. If those positions are gone, we're left with a large gap in the lines"

"Sir, posts six and seven report engine noises directly in front of them."

"Those particular fighting positions have less than a two hundred meter clear zone of fire. If four and five have been knocked out, they won't have any supporting fire on their flanks."

"Sir, posts six and seven report that they've sighted at least two Leonidas armored fighting vehicles, supported by infantry."

"Order the mortars to open fire and send a squad with RPGs to reinforce those positions immediately!" yelled Mihalovic.

"Sir, position six is coming under fire from the enemy APCs(armored personnel carriers). Seven hasn't been spotted yet," said the command post telephone operator.

The two Leonidas fighting vehicles, under the cover of smoke, had advanced to within a couple of hundred meters of the Macedonian positions. The soldiers manning post six had fired off their RPGs prematurely and missed. Now it was the Greeks' turn. One of the fighting vehicles, outfitted with a GIAT 90mm cannon, swung its gun toward the direction of the Macedonian position and fired. The shell exploded a couple of meters to the front of the opening sending up a cloud of dirt and steel fragments, striking the Macedonian machine gunner full in the face. The soldiers occupying the adjacent position, seeing that the APC was preoccupied with their comrades, seized the opportunity to attack. Two of the four Macedonians manning position seven, grabbed their RPGs and climbed out the entrance. Standing up, they both aimed their weapons and fired at almost point blank range at the APC. Both of the rockets were on target. The RPGs hollow shaped charges punched through the thinly armored APC, causing it to explode into a fireball when its 90mm ammunition was set off.

The first shells of the mortar barrage ordered by Colonel Mihalovic finally began arriving. The high explosive shells started landing amongst the Greek infantry following several meters behind the APCs, quickly forcing them to seek cover. The crew of the remaining Leonidas APC spotted the two Macedonian infantry men that had killed their comrades. Bringing the coaxial 7.62mm machine gun quickly to bear, the gunner let off a burst. This cut the two soldiers down in their tracks as they tried to distance themselves from the vehicle. In despair, the surviving Macedonians in fighting position seven opened up on the Greek APC. The driver of the Leonidas put his vehicle in gear and stepped on the throttle. The heavy APC lurched forward toward the Macedonian fighting position. A lone infantry man emerged and attempted to launch an RPG, but was quickly gunned down by the machine gunner. A few seconds later, the APC rolled over the make shift bunker crushing everyone inside.

With the destruction of these two fighting positions, a small breach was opened in the Macedonian defense belt. Receiving no further suppressive fire from the Macedonian positions, the Greek infantry that had been taking cover from the mortar barrage, surged forward and charged through the gap created in the Macedonian lines. Many fell to the continuing barrage of mortar shells, but they continued to push forward. The reinforcements that Colonel Mihalovic had dispatched finally reached the affected area and clashed with the Greeks. The surviving Leonidas APC, which had strayed far ahead of its infantry support, suddenly found itself surrounded by the Macedonians. It managed to gun down several of its attackers before it was also dispatched by several RPG hits.

Feeling that victory was now within his grasp, the Greek battalion commander committed his reserve company to the battle. This was too much for the Macedonians to withstand and they began falling back. With the situation rapidly deteriorating, Colonel Mihalovic sent Major Ziad with further reinforcements to try and stabilize the situation. Standing calmly over the command post radio, he could hear Major Ziad issuing orders to his squad leaders to counterattack. When Ziad asked for further reinforcements, he temporarily turned the request down. Mihalovic was sure that this had been only a company size probing attack. If he committed the rest of his limited reserves now, what would happen when the Greeks attacked in real strength?

"Sir, Major Ziad requests permission to pull back to our second line of defenses," said the radio operator.

Mihalovic had in fact heard the call over the radio. "Tell him permission granted and that another squad will be sent to reinforce those positions" He knew that his friend would not request a pullback unless the situation was really bad. He would not sacrifice his soldiers' lives needlessly.

"Yes, sir."

Having received the pullback order, the Macedonian defenders gradually disengaged and began an organized retreat toward their next line of defenses, several hundred meters to the rear. Thinking that the Macedonians had broken and run, the Greek infantry mistakenly charged ahead. When they reached the second line of the Macedonian positions, they were met by a hail of withering machine gun and grenade fire. Unable to advance any further without heavy casualties, the Greeks pulled back, leaving a score of bodies in front of the Macedonian positions. Upon hearing the news that the Greeks had been halted, Colonel Mihalovic breathed a little easier. He knew that this was only a temporary respite. The Greeks would come back and next time they would attack in sufficient strength to finish the job. The assault on his unit's positions had only been a probe and a rather successful one at that.

In the distance, the Colonel could hear the sound of heavy artillery fire which meant that other parts of the line were being attacked this very moment. They would have to use the temporary break given to them to prepare for the next round which was sure to come soon. Looking up, he saw Major Ziad enter the command post. The look on the Major's face told him that things hadn't gone very well.

"Sir, we've stopped them for now. They have pulled back approximately seven hundred meters from our positions. They will be back in strength, I'm sure of that."

"Yes, I'm sure they will, my friend," said the Colonel.

"All our positions have been reinforced with all the additional men and equipment I could scrounge. The men are working, as we speak, to harden them as much as possible before the next round."

"Good! The troops performed excellently. You can pass that on to the men."

"I will, sir. They will appreciate that."

"What was the butcher's bill?"

"At last count, sir, twenty-five killed, fifteen wounded and three missing. Three of the wounded are serious and are not expected to live." The Colonel winced at the bad news.

"And this was only a probing attack! What happens if they attack in battalion strength?"

"We'll hold them as long as possible and then withdraw into the mountains," said Major Ziad.

"Yes, Major. That will be the only recourse open to us or we'll face complete annihilation."

"At least their armor can't follow us into the mountains."

"Now let us prepare a little surprise that I have in mind. It will buy us a little precious extra time," said Mihalovic.

Ten Kilometers North of Igoumenitsa
1216hrs, 20 May

The new command center for the Albanian expeditionary corps had been established by order of their Commander and Chief in an abandoned house, ten kilometers from the front lines. General Hoxa had left his own bunker in Argyrokastron so that he could personally take control of combat operations in the Igoumenitsa sector, due to what he deemed incompetence by his commanders. The offensive which had begun two days ago to capture the port city was beginning to falter, partially due to a massive influx of enemy reinforcements and mainly to the ineptness of his commanders to act quickly and decisively. His main body was now stalled a couple of kilometers outside the city. The loss of Igoumenitsa would deprive Greece of a major port on her west coast. Despite some early setbacks, not everything had gone badly. Ioannina had been captured yesterday after very heavy fighting. However, the Greeks were now counterattacking in that sector. Hopefully with the capture of Igoumenitsa, some of the pressure on Ioannina will be relieved.

General Hoxa glanced at his watch. The operation he had planned to take the city would commence in fourteen minutes. This attack had to succeed. He was committing most of his reserves in an attempt to smash through the Greek defense line. A failure would be a catastrophe to his battle plans.

"Sir, your transport has arrived and is waiting outside," said the General's aid.

"Thank you, Colonel Zog."

The General followed by his aid, stepped out of the command post and into a waiting BTR-50 armored car. Ten minutes later, they arrived at a make shift observation post, atop an abandoned three story warehouse near the front lines, only a couple of kilometers from the city. Peering through an observation scope, the General could see a grayish pall of smoke hanging over the town from the many fires started by the artillery bombardment. The General looked at his watch again, it was twelve thirty.

"Sir, the attack is beginning, there they go," said one of the staff officers looking through a set of binoculars.

The General peered through the observation scope and saw his armor moving out of their hidden positions. Over thirty T-62s and a sprinkle of T-54 tanks in three vee formations, followed by more than a dozen BTR-40 and BTR-50 armored personnel carriers were heading toward the Greek lines. The Greeks responded with artillery fire. Once the Albanian armor had advanced within five hundred meters of the Greek positions, five Hellenic army M-48A5 medium tanks dashed out of a grove of olive trees to meet them. In less than a minute, five Albanian tanks were burning, victims to the superior laser sighted 105mm gun of the M-48A5s. Nonetheless, technology wasn't enough to offset numerical superiority. Outnumbered almost six to one, three of the Greek tanks succumbed to multiple shell hits by the 115mm guns of the T-62s. The surviving M48A5s turned and retreated toward the Greek lines with the Albanian armor in hot pursuit. Having entered the Greek defense perimeter, the Albanian armor began to fan out and engage a string of block houses that the Greeks had set up in abandoned buildings with direct tank fire. From one of these buildings, two MILAN anti-tank missiles fired out of a second story window and knocked out two of the several T-62s that were engaging a nearby target. Other Albanian tanks had seen the missile launches and began pumping HE rounds into the two story structure. The front of the building quickly disintegrated from the high explosive shells, killing the anti-tank gunners. Hoxa, watching his tanks punch their way through the Greek defense line, sensed that a major victory was within his grasp.

"Sir, helicopters!"

"What! Where?" screamed General Hoxa.

"There, sir."

The General swung his scope toward the direction that his aid was pointing to. He counted ten specs that were rapidly growing larger, flying in from the direction of Corfu Island, twenty-five kilometers to the west. He suddenly felt the bile rise to the top of his throat, barely restraining himself from losing the contents of his stomach. He knew that those gunships spelled disaster for his armor, now caught in the open. The helicopters flew in low over the harbor and made a pass over the city. Having received their final directions by the forward air controllers, the gunships turned toward the front lines. As the helicopters drew closer, the General could discern a star on their fuselage.

"They're American! Where the hell did they come from?"

"Sir, they're AH-64 Apaches, tank killers," said his aid.

"I know what they are, you idiot!"

"Our armor is out in the open, they will be slaughtered. We must call them back!" said one of the staff officers almost in a state of panic.

"It's too late, you fool!" replied General Hoxa. "We are committed!"

The American Apaches, part of the aid package promised to

the Greeks by the U.S. President, had flown to Corfu from Germany via Italy the previous night. For security reasons, they had been hidden under camouflage netting and securely guarded in the island's interior, out of public view and that of any Albanian agents. Greek intelligence which had taken notice of the heavy Albanian armor build up, had speculated that the Albanians would soon be committing themselves to a major drive to capture Igoumenitsa. The Greeks had kept the helicopters in reserve for the proper moment when the Albanians would begin their attack and commit their armor. When that moment finally did arrive, the American aircrews which had been waiting next to their fueled and loaded gunships jumped in and took off for the short ten minute flight to Igoumenitsa.

The Apache gunships made their appearance on the battle field at a very crucial moment in the battle for this key city. Armed with tank busting Hellfire missiles, they caught the Albanian armor in the open, without the benefit of any anti-aircraft protection. In a matter of a few minutes, the enemy armor was cut to pieces by the Apaches. In sheer desperation, the BTRs attempted to deploy their infantry to counter the helicopters with shoulder fired SAMs. But the soldiers never had a chance; most were cut down by the gunships' 30mm chain guns and 2.75 inch rockets. After expanding most of their ammo, the gunships lined up in formation and turned for home. As the last Apache departed the battle field, a lone Albanian infantry man that had been thrown from his BTR when it was hit by a Hellfire, stood up and fired his SAM-7. The missile hit the helicopter's transmission housing, severing numerous hydraulic lines. The Apache pitched out of control and crashed into the ground exploding in a ball of fire, killing all aboard. With their armor destroyed, the back of the Albanian attack was broken. Those few APCs that did survive the helicopter onslaught retreated back toward their lines, their commanders choosing to withdraw, realizing that it was suicidal to proceed any further.

General Hoxa, who had just personally witnessed the failure of his attack and the destruction of most of his armored reserve, was furious.

"The cowards are retreating!" No one replied to the General's comment. "This is only a temporary setback. We will dig in right here until we can resume the offensive. No one will retreat!" said General Hoxa.

"But sir, we just lost most of our armor and several hundred men. We should pull back to more defensible positions," said one of his battalion commanders.

Enraged at the officer's audacity in daring to contradict him, the General drew his service pistol and promptly shot him.

"I will not tolerate any dissension or defeatist talk from any of my officers!" he said, shaking with rage.

"Get that traitorous scum out of my sight," he ordered, pointing to the body. The two guards dragged the body away. Still holding the pistol in his hand, he stared at the other officers present.

"Now gentlemen, you will obey my orders and hold your present positions at all costs or until told otherwise. We will not fail our Turkish allies. Any commander withdrawing without my permission will be shot! Is that understood?"

Not expecting an answer or any further discussion, the General put the gun back into its holster.

"Come Colonel, I must return immediately to Army Headquarters in Argyrokastron."

Kavala, Greece
1300hrs, 20 May

"Lunch was delicious, Jack," said Captain Wendy Barnes as she sipped some more of the pine resin flavored Retsina wine from her glass.

"I told you, Wendy. Kazas assured me the food would be good."

"You sure could have fooled me. From the outside, this place looks like a total dive. The only thing it has going for it is the view and the food, of course," she said.

"The view of the city and the bay is excellent, as for the decor, it looks out of the 1950s," said Logan.

"Yeah and that's probably when it was last painted," Wendy added.

Both of them laughed at her pun. Jack, I'd like to walk around the waterfront."

"Sounds like a good idea. Parakalo, ton logariasmo (Please the bill)," he said in broken Greek, having picked up the phrase from one of the pamphlets on survival Greek that everyone had been issued prior to their departure for Piges.

"Would you like anything else, sir?" asked the man that had served them, in heavily accented English.

"No, thank you. Your bifteki (Spicy hamburger steak) and Tzaziki were excellent."

"Yes, they were really great," added Wendy.

"Thank you," said the old man. "I'll tell my wife."

"I'd love to get the recipe from you some day," said Wendy.

"You mean you can also cook, besides fly?"

"I know a lot more than you think, Colonel," she said jokingly.

"You are welcome to have the recipe, any time." said the old man.

"What about the bill?"

"Please, everything is on the house. You brave American pilots are here to help defend my country. This is the least I can do to show our gratitude."

"Why thank you, we are honored by your hospitality," said Logan, not wanting to refuse and insult the old man.

"I wish I were younger so I could fight the Turks. My son is a soldier. His unit was stationed near the border. We haven't heard from him since this terrible war began."

"Hopefully the war will end soon and he will come home."

"I pray every day for this war to end and for his safe return."

"Let's go," said Logan as he got up to leave.

"May God be with you," said the old man.

"Very nice old man, I hope his son makes it."

They both climbed into the jeep." You still want to go down to the water front?"

Her eyes lit up. "Sure!"

"Let's go then."

"You're a sweetheart," she said. As they snaked through the small winding streets toward the harbor, they passed several military convoys containing tanks and soldiers heading east. "Things are going bad for them on the land war, Jack."

"Yes, the Turks are closing in. Last reports had their advance columns only thirty miles from the base. Any closer and we'll soon be within artillery range."

"The problem is that the Greeks are fighting on too many fronts," she pointed out.

"They're well aware of the problem. Kazas told me that the Greek army began a limited offensive this morning, with the objective of knocking Macedonia out of the war. According to intelligence briefs, I think they will be successful. Afterwards, they can concentrate on the real threat," he added.

Just as they arrived in the city's busy waterfront zone, the wail of air raid sirens screamed through the harbor area.

"God damn it! Just what we need," he blurted out, quickly stopping the jeep so he and Wendy could exit and seek shelter. Anchored in the harbor, were several transports and warships, *a target rich environment for a bomber pilot, he thought.*

"Let's get away from here! This is obviously their target, evident by the half submerged wrecks left by earlier raids."

They had only run about a block when several anti-aircraft batteries along the water front opened up. They both stopped in their tracks and looked skyward.

"Here they come!" he yelled, pointing to several growing specks coming in low from the sea. There were six enemy planes in all. "Shit! They're old F-4E Phantoms, probably carrying a shit load of bombs, too." Suddenly, the loud roar of jet engines in full after burner ripped through the air as four sleek F-16's passed overhead.

"Yeah! Our alert birds, the Calvary to the rescue," she said loud enough to be heard over the roar of the jet engines.

"Get the bastards!" screamed Logan. Each of the four F-16's fired a missile at the approaching enemy planes. The Turkish pilots who had detected the American planes immediately began counter measures, but three of the American missiles found their targets. The three remaining enemy planes dropped to almost sea level and began their bomb run. A thousand meters to shore, the lead plane suddenly exploded, hit by a missile fired from one of the warships anchored in the harbor. The other two continued on their run.

"Get down!" screamed Logan at Wendy who just stood there mesmerized at the approaching bombers. He knocked her to the ground, covering her body with his, just as the Turkish Phantoms released their bomb load. Seconds later, the two remaining F-4s met the same fate as the rest of their flight. Hit by AIM-9s fired from the F-16s, they plowed into two apartment buildings, adding to the carnage that they had already unleashed. Luckily for Logan and Wendy, most of the bombs had landed in the dock area, so they had caught only the tail end of the blast wave. He felt as if someone had kicked him in the head. When Logan's head finally began to clear, he could no longer hear the firing of the anti-aircraft batteries. What he did hear was the wail of emergency vehicle sirens and the screams of the injured and dying. *So this is how it feels to be on the receiving end, he thought.*

"Wendy!" he shouted. He was still lying on top of her. He felt her body tremble beneath him. Logan slowly began to get up.

"Wendy, are you hurt?"

He slowly helped her up. She was sobbing. "I, I never realized how horrible it could be. Flying up there, you never get to see up close what your bombs can do to people. There is no glory in this!" She looked around her at the rubble and the bodies that littered the street.

"No Wendy. We rarely get to see firsthand the death and destruction that we cause. The glory of being a fighter pilot quickly wore off when we were ordered to bomb the broken remnants of Sadaam Hussein's Republican Guards, trying to retreat from Basra during the second Gulf war. They called it, the highway of death. We killed thousands. I participated in the slaughter."

"Oh Jack. Please hold me." He put his arms around her. She looked into his eyes. Her lips touched his. For a moment, they both forgot the war.

"Voithia, voithia!" Logan let go of her and looked towards where the cry was coming from. A young woman was crawling out of the debris of a nearby building that had taken a hit. Much of her clothing had been torn off by the blast and she was covered in blood, having been cut by flying glass. She ran toward them, "Voithia!"

"Jack, I think the word means help." The woman grabbed Logan and pulled him toward the wrecked building.

"Voithia!"

"I am sorry, I don't understand Greek," said Logan

"My baby is inside. Please help me," she said in broken English."

They both ran toward what remained of the apartment building.

Before he could enter, he was stopped by a man exiting the demolished structure. He saw Logan's U.S. flag patch on his flight suit. "Mister, there is an unexploded bomb inside. Get away, it could explode any second," said the man as he turned to run. Logan could hear the child inside the rubble screaming for his mother.

"He's right, Jack. Let's wait for the army bomb disposal units."

"Please, help my baby," said the woman.

"I don't believe the Turks are using time delay bombs. It's probably a bad detonator, a dud. I'm going inside."

"Jack, please be careful."

"I will. What's your child's name?"

"Antonis," replied the hysterical woman.

"Wendy, keep her here," he said as he prepared to enter the partially demolished apartment building. One of the bombs had come through the roof, sheared through an apartment and exploded as it exited the front of the building, bringing the entire front face of the structure down. Slowly making his way to where the staircase was, Logan gradually climbed up the rubble covered steps toward where the child's cries were coming from. Reaching the top, Logan paused to catch his breath. He could hear the child's cries coming from the other end of the hallway. "I wonder where that unexploded bomb is. What a time to find out if the Turks are actually using delayed action munitions," he said to himself. Walking to the other end of the hallway, he entered the ruined apartment. Part of the inside wall had collapsed, exposing it to the outside. Pushing a fallen China cabinet aside, he proceeded toward the bedroom where the cries were coming from, but was suddenly stopped short of his goal by a four foot gap in the floor. He had found where the unexploded bomb was. Logan looked down. Two floors below, Jack could see the protruding tail fins of a five hundred pound, general purpose, and high explosive bomb.

The bomb had gone through the building's roof and tore through two floors, miraculously without detonating. By some wonder the child, a five year old little boy, had not been hurt.

"Mamma!"

"Don't worry, Antonis, I'm here to help you," Logan said to calm the child. *He doesn't even understand me, he thought.* But the child heard his name and stopped crying. Logan looked around for something to bridge the gap. Finding an overturned wardrobe cabinet, he ran to it and ripped off the door. Logan put the door over the hole. It barely fit.

"Come to me, Antonis," said Logan, motioning with his hands. Logan noticed a funny chemical odor coming from the hole. *I wonder what that is, he thought.* The terrified child did not move. Logan fell to the floor and partially crawled onto the door.

"Come, Antonis, for God's sake. Your mamma is waiting for you."

"Mamma," said the child.

"Yes, Mamma," Logan nodded his head to the terrified child. "Come, hurry." With that, the child crawled on to the door and gave his hand to Logan. He grabbed the little boy and slowly crawled backward to safety. Taking the child in his arms, he ran out of the apartment and made his way down the stairs as quickly as possible. Exiting the building, he was greeted by cheers from a throng of people that were gathered a couple of hundred meters away. Reaching the crowd, he handed the child to his mother who was now weeping with joy.

"Thank you, mister. You saved my baby."

"It was nothing."

"You're so modest," said Wendy.

Suddenly, a tremendous explosion rocked the waterfront, causing everyone to dive for cover. The apartment building that Logan had just exited had been completely reduced to a pile of smoking rubble. He now realized what that funny odor inside the apartment had been. It was the bomb's chemical detonator. Getting back up, he looked at Wendy and began laughing."

"What's so funny, Jack Logan? You could have been killed."

"I guess the enemy is using delayed action munitions after all."

"Very funny. Let's get the hell out of here."

"I agree. Let's see if the Jeep is still in one piece," said Logan.

A couple of minutes later they had found the Jeep. Except for a broken windshield and a few dents caused by flying debris, the Jeep was none the worse. Brushing the broken glass from the seats, they climbed inside.

"Jack, you're a real hero. Let me give you your reward."

"And what is that?"

"This." She reached over, put her arms around him and gave him a long kiss.

"I need to be a hero more often. I like these kinds of rewards."

"I had something better in mind, but I don't think there are too many hotels operating right now in this town."

"I'll take a rain check."

"Let's get out of here; it's getting too hot here for my liking," he said. Jack put the jeep in gear and drove away from the shattered waterfront and past the many fire trucks and ambulances that were beginning to arrive.

Mavrovouni Foothills
1440hrs, 20 May

After the first Greek attack had ended, Colonel Mihalovic and his soldiers had worked nonstop throughout the morning and early afternoon improving and reinforcing their new fighting positions. Except for an occasional bout of nuisance shelling, the 3rd Macedonian's section of the line had been relatively calm. That was soon to change. The Macedonian's lack of ammunition had kept them from keeping up a sustained bombardment of the Greek positions, thus enabling the Greeks to quickly consolidate their gains and prepare for a new attack.

While he toured the unit's front line positions, Mihalovic could hear the deep throated roar of diesel engines emanating from the enemy lines just over a kilometer away. He surmised correctly that the Greeks had brought up additional armor for their next attack. Mihalovic had earlier radioed headquarters requesting reinforcements, but was curtly told that none would be forthcoming. They would have to manage on their own resources. The General had said that the whole front line was under enemy pressure and every unit was screaming for reinforcements that were simply not available. Mihalovic knew that a crisis was brewing for the tiny Macedonian army. The idiots in Skopje had bitten off more than they could chew. He wondered how many more lives would be squandered before this foolishness ended.

"Incoming, take cover!"

Hearing the warning and the whine of incoming artillery

shells, Colonel Mihalovic dived into the nearest fighting position just as the first shells hit, sending up large clumps of dirt. He landed on one of the soldiers occupying the position. "What the hell is wrong with, oh excuse me sir, I didn't know it was you," said the startled soldier, once he saw that it was his commander who had landed a top of him.

"That's okay son, I should be apologizing for dropping in like this," he said, brushing the dirt from his uniform.

"Let's all hope that one of those shells doesn't decide to drop in unexpectedly on all of us," said one of the other soldiers that was also occupying the fighting position, bringing a laugh to all those present.

For the next fifteen minutes, high explosives rained down on the area. Many of the Macedonian soldiers taking shelter in the fighting positions tried to make themselves as small a target as possible, huddling in the corners of their trenches. Others prayed that one of those shells landing outside didn't have their name on it. When the barrage finally lifted, an eerie silence hung over the smoke filled woods. Colonel Mihalovic slowly exited the fighting position and looked all around him in the blasted forest. He was joined by other soldiers from adjacent positions. Luckily from what he could tell, casualties had been light. The bloody and dismembered bodies of several soldiers caught outside during the shelling, littered the shell packed woods. Looking at the splintered tress and the crated ground, he wondered how many would survive this day's action. The crack of a tank gun and the high pitch whine of an incoming round broke the temporary silence. Picking up his portable radio, Colonel Mihalovic spoke into the radio mike.

"Cobra One to all units, implement plan Alpha." Plan Alpha called for the reinforcement of the front line positions with additional RPG gunners to help deal with the enemy's armored threat. When he gave the order to activate the plan, the gunners left the protection of their holes and deployed to hastily created positions that provided only light cover, to await the arrival of enemy armor. After issuing the order, Colonel Mihalovic ran to an adjacent fighting position where Major Ziad was located to discuss their next course of action. Major Ziad saw his Commander running toward him, while dodging the enemy tank fire.

"Sir, you must head back to the command post, the unit can't afford to have anything happen to you."

"Nonsense, my position is here with my men. There are other officers that can run the Regiment if something happens to me."

Seeing that the Colonel would not be swayed on the matter, the Major gave in. "If you insist on staying, then at least take some cover and stay in one of the fighting positions."

"All right Major, I'll do that. After you, my friend," said Colonel Mihalovic pointing the way.

From inside the roughly constructed fighting position, they could feel the rumble of the enemy vehicles as they neared the Macedonian lines. The rumble was frequently interrupted by the loud crack and boom of tank guns as they poured shells into the Macedonian positions.

"Well this is it, my friend. If we don't stop them, we must pull back into the mountains if we are to salvage anything," said Colonel Mihalovic.

Before Major Ziad could answer, the field phone inside the fighting position rang.

"Colonel, it's observation post one. They report ten enemy armored vehicles approaching their position and heading this way."

"What is their make-up, Sergeant?"

"Six tanks and several APC's which probably contain infantry, sir."

"They're attacking in company strength. I hope our RPG gunners maintain their cool and don't fire prematurely."

Mihalovic's hopes were quickly crushed, when he heard a whoosh, followed by a loud explosion, as an anti-tank round struck the leading M48A5 tank, wrecking its right track. The iron monster hurt, but not dead, lashed out at its attacker who tried to scramble to safety. A burst of machine gun fire cut him down before he had run ten meters. The rest of the tanks, alerted to the ambush, began spraying the ground around them with machine gun fire. Very few of the RPG gunners were able to fire off their weapons before the heavy machine gun fire killed them outright or drove them to deeper cover. Most of the RPGs did little to no damage to the heavily armored tanks. Only one of the gunners was able to score a lucky hit on one of the AMX-10 personnel carriers, following a hundred meters behind the tanks. The rocket pierced the vehicle's thin armor just below the turret and exploded, killing everyone inside.

"Sir, observation post one reports two vehicles destroyed. The rest are continuing the attack."

"Our only hope now is the mine field," said Major Ziad.

"There they are, they're entering the mine field," said one of the soldiers manning the bunker.

Both officers looked out of the firing slit just in time to see one of the enemy tanks, no more than a few hundred meters away, set off a mine. The enemy tank ground to a halt, having lost one of its treads. Almost immediately, another explosion rocked the woods as another tank set off a mine with the same results as the previous one. The rest the vehicles following behind came to an abrupt halt, not wishing to share the same fate.

"Sir, we've stopped them!" said Major Ziad.

"Yes, but for how long?"

Ziad worriedly looked at his commander and friend. "Sir, now that we have a temporary respite, please return to the command post. It serves no purpose for both of us to stay here."

"I guess you're right. I'll make a run for it."

"Be careful."

The Colonel upholstered his service pistol, climbed out the back of the position and began making his way toward the command post. The stalled enemy tanks could neither go forward nor backwards, but neither could anyone get close enough to engage them with anti-tank grenades. Those that tried were quickly cut down by their machine gunners.

"Major, observation post one reports a strange looking tank like vehicle approaching their position."

"What's so strange about it?" inquired Major Ziad.

"Well, sir. They said it has a roller with long chains on it, attached to its front. The chains are beating the ground."

"It's a mine clearer! Notify the command post immediately." said Major Ziad.

The M48A5 tank, which had been outfitted for mine clearing, had been waiting behind the Greek lines when it was called to clear a path through the Macedonian mine field and get the stalled attack moving. When the mine clearer reached the stalled vehicles, it pulled out in front and began clearing a path for the rest to follow. Within a few seconds of starting to clear a path, its beating chains struck and set off a mine. Several more explosions followed as the mine clearer continued its slow but steady pace forward, beating the ground before it. Colonel Mihalovic, who upon reaching the relative safety of his command post, was briefed on the latest development. Picking up the field phone, he spoke to Major Ziad.

"What is the status of the enemy vehicles, Major?"

"They have brought a mine clearer and are clearing a path through our mine field. They will shortly be through."

"Damn it!"

"Sir, I urgently request mortar fire support. It will keep the enemy infantry inside their APC's, but probably set off the rest of the mine field. But at this point, what does it matter?"

There was a few seconds of silence before Colonel Mihalovic

answered. "Do your best, my friend. You will have your mortar fire support."

The enemy mine clearer had reached a point, three hundred meters from the Macedonian positions, when the first mortar shells began to land.

"There's our requested barrage, sir," said the machine gunner.

"Well at least the mortars will keep them from deploying their infantry," said Major Ziad.

"Major! Observation post one reports ten additional APCs, escorted by three Leonidas II fighting vehicles approaching." Major Ziad suspected that the APCs were full of infantry. He didn't want to admit it, but the situation was rapidly deteriorating.

"Tell the observation post to evacuate."

"Yes, sir."

"Sir!" yelled the machine gunner in panic. "They're almost through our mine field." The mine clearer had reached a point, only two hundred and fifty meters from the Macedonian positions, when a solitary RPG gunner stood up and fired his weapon. The rocket hit the mine clearer's chassis, destroying several sprockets, immobilizing the vehicle. Before the soldier had taken more than five steps, he was cut to shreds by a burst of 7.62 mm machine gun fire from one of the other tanks. His sacrifice had turned out to be in vain, the Greek vehicles had cleared the mine field. The Macedonian mortar barrage that had kept the enemy from deploying their infantry, now seized fire, for fear of hitting their own soldiers. With the apparent lull in the shelling, the Greek M-113 and AMX-10 APCs dropped their ramps and deployed their infantry. The dismounted infantry troops quickly fanned out and took positions behind the other advancing armored vehicles. Several of the Greek infantry men were felled by the heavy fusillade of Macedonian machine gun and grenade fire, but as a whole, the Macedonian fire was proving ineffective. One by one, the Macedonian positions were silenced by the superior enemy fire.

In the command post, Colonel Mihalovic could hear the continuous calls for reinforcements coming over the radio and field phone.

"Sir, Major Ziad is on the line, he requests immediate reinforcements to prevent an enemy break through."

"Give me the field phone."

"Major, what is your situation?"

"Critical, sir. I need reinforcements. The enemy is breaking through our lines. We can't contain them much longer. All I have left is the two OTO MELARA pack howitzers to slow the enemy tanks."

"Major, they're almost on top of us!" screamed the machine gunner.

There was a loud crack and a boom as one of the concealed 105mm pack howitzers, set up for anti-tank support, fired on one of the advancing tanks. The thirty eight pound HEAT round, traveling at over 1270 feet per second, struck the lead tank at virtual point blank range. The enemy tank came to a sudden halt, its turret popped open and two surviving crew men jumped out. Before they could stand up, they were hit by a burst of machine gun fire by Major Ziad's gunner.

The Colonel heard the gunner's warning over the land line and the loud explosion of the enemy tank being hit.

"Major, are you all right?"

"We're okay for now, sir. It was very close. One of the OTO MELARA gun crews just saved our ass. I wish I could now do the same for them."

Ziad could hear the enemy fire, which had shifted toward the position of where the howitzer was deployed. He knew that the exposed gun crew would not survive very long under such a barrage.

"I will dispatch our last reserve company. Use them as a rear guard to buy us some time. We are pulling back."

"I understand, sir. We will do our best." They all heard another crack and a boom, followed by a muffled explosion as one of the enemy APC's went up in flames. It meant that the Otto Melara gun crew was still alive and fighting.

"I know you will. We will see you in the mountains. May Allah be with you always," said Colonel Mihalovic.

Everyone in the command post who had heard the conversation looked at their commander with disbelief.

"Sir, are we pulling back?" asked the command post duty officer.

"That's correct, Lieutenant. Issue the withdrawal orders immediately. Anything that can't be carried or quickly dismantled, destroy it. We don't have much time. The enemy has broken through our defenses." As if to clarify the Colonel's point, enemy tank shells began landing outside.

"What about our wounded?"

"We'll leave the seriously wounded behind. The Greeks aren't uncivilized. They will take care of our wounded. The walking wounded will come with us."

"Yes, sir."

After issuing the withdrawal orders through the command net radio to anybody that was still listening, the duty officer grabbed his code books and ran toward the exit. The last man out, pulled the pin of a grenade and tossed it inside.

Three kilometers east of the Nestos River Bridge 1640hrs, 20 May

The nine remaining tanks of what was left of the Hellenic army's 26th armored brigade lay hidden in thick bushy scrubs, five hundred meters north of the Xanthi-Kavala highway. During the past twenty-four hours, the brigade had been involved in several rear guard actions, helping buy time for the bulk of the Hellenic army to retreat westward. Due to the intense nature of the fighting, casualties had been extremely heavy. Now, the 26th was all that stood between the enemy and the vital Nestos River bridge.

Warrant Officer Mihalis Manakos rested against the turret of the M-60A3 tank, savoring a cigarette, while the rest of the crew lay on the ground trying to get a couple of minutes of precious sleep. During the past twenty-four hours, they had been fighting nonstop, one rear guard action after another. Their only break had been to get some fuel during the night from one of the brigade's tanker trucks, and grab some more ammunition. They had started the night before with fifteen tanks, after linking up with the remnants of the 26th a few kilometers east of Xanthi. Now only nine remained.

Mihalis had been quickly accepted into the crew and instructed in the basics of servicing the 105mm tank gun. At first, he had found it difficult to distinguish between the types of tank shells the M-60 carried, but under the guidance of Lieutenant Kapsis and the rest of the crew he had caught on fast. Not that he really had a choice. His first test under fire came late that same night when the brigade fought a delaying action against a battalion of Turkish armor in the streets of Xanthi. That swift and violent action had been an eye opener for Mihalis. The ten Turkish and six burning Greek tanks left behind had introduced him first hand to the speed and violence of high tech war. Sitting there savoring his cigarette, Mihalis now thought it a miracle that they were all still alive. Most of the credit for that miracle had to be given to Lieutenant Kapsis, their tank commander. His skill and leadership had molded the crew into a well-honed fighting machine. He was proud that he was now part of this crew. The Lieutenant had even given him a compliment on his new found abilities as a tank gun loader.

Lieutenant Kapsis popped his head out of the tank's turret and woke the crew.

"Wake up guys. We have work to do. The enemy has been spotted. They're only a few minutes away. Let's prepare a nice reception for them."

Nestos River Bridge
1650hrs, 20 May

The army engineer nervously glanced at his watch. He had just heard over the radio that the enemy advance column was only a few kilometers away. The job of placing the demolition charges that would drop the span into the river was taking much longer than he had expected. The Hellenic Army's High Command was hoping the bridge's destruction along with the river, swollen by spring rains and melting mountain snows, would slow the Turkish advance and buy them the needed time to prepare their new defense line. The last retreating Greek units had crossed the bridge twenty minutes before. Captain Manos knew that except for a few tanks left behind as a rear guard, there was nothing else to stop the enemy from seizing the bridge.

"Captain Manos!"

"What is it, Andreas?" Captain Manos asked his driver who was sitting in their M-113 command vehicle, a few meters away.

"Sir, message from Captain Stavros commanding the armored unit guarding the approaches to the bridge."

"What did he say, Andreas?"

"He said that the enemy has been sighted, less than three kilometers from here."

"Jesus! We need at least twenty minutes to finish planting the charges," he said out loud.

"Relay to him that we need twenty-five minutes to finish our job."

"I will, sir." But Captain Manos didn't hear him. He was too busy thinking that a catastrophe of gigantic proportions was in the making as he ran toward the bridge to speed up his demolition crew.

Chapter 4

Ambush Site, Three Kilometers East of the Nestos River Bridge

1655hrs, 20 May

In less than a minute of having received warning of the approaching enemy tanks, Lieutenant Kapsis' crew had prepared their vehicle for combat. Their tank, like the rest of the units, had been one of several hundred M-60s the Hellenic army had received from America to modernize their inventory. During the early 90s, the U.S. as a signatory of the Conventional Forces Reduction Treaty in Europe had been required to dispose of thousands of armored vehicles to fulfill its treaty obligations. Rather than destroy the perfectly serviceable equipment, the U.S. had given or sold it for next to nothing to its allies. Hundreds of older or semi obsolete tanks, artillery and various other armored vehicles had been disposed of this way. Greece and Turkey had been the largest recipients of this aid.

The M-60A3 tank, though old and almost obsolete, if compared with some of the later generation Main Battle Tanks like the Leopard 2 in both the Greek and Turkish arsenals, was still a potent fighting unit. Upgraded by the Hellenic army with laser optical sights, a fire control computer and with its 105mm high velocity gun, it was a match for any armored vehicle in the Turkish inventory. Standing in the tank's open turret, Lieutenant Kapsis observed the other M-60 tank crews preparing their vehicles for the upcoming engagement. When everyone had checked in ready, Captain Stavros gave his last set of instructions to his commanders over the command net.

"Panther leader to all units. We'll stay hidden in this olive grove. Train your guns on the road and don't shoot until I give the order. We'll wait until the MILAN and DRAGON gunners lose their loads. This should distract the enemy and draw their attention to the anti-tank gunners. That's when we'll hit them."

Just to make sure that his units had understood the order, the Captain had every commander acknowledge his transmission. Surprise would be essential. A mistake by one of them would most likely prove fatal to all of them. If the Turks, by chance, had helicopter support, surprise wouldn't really matter, they would all die. While they waited for the appearance of the numerically superior enemy, the thoughts of everyone had turned to survival.

"How long are we hanging around here, Lieutenant? Those engineers are going to destroy that bridge. It would be a bitch if they blow it before we crossed over," said Sergeant Nicolaou, their driver.

"Don't worry about the bridge, Nicolaou. They haven't finished laying the charges. The engineer's commander just radioed requesting that we hold the Turks for twenty minutes so they can finish planting the explosives."

"Holy shit!" said Nicolaou, starting to consider swimming across the Nestos a better prospect than facing an entire Turkish armored division.

The Lieutenant alerted his crew. "Here they come, four APC's on the road heading west,"

"Everyone hold your fire, they're reconnaissance vehicles. We want to save our warm welcome for the main body," said Captain Stavros over the radio.

Suilliman Armored Division, Xanthi-Kavala road 1658hrs, 20 May

Brigadier General Karakoglou stood imposingly atop the turret of his Leopard I tank, scanning the empty highway and farmland ahead of them. For the last couple of hours, except for a few stragglers that had been promptly dealt with, there had been no sign of any organized Greek resistance. His scout vehicles were almost a thousand meters ahead of the main body, checking the road for signs of the enemy. The division's leading elements were only a few kilometers from the Nestos river bridge. His orders, personally given by General Kemal, were to seize that bridge intact, if at all possible, and establish a bridgehead on the other side. The latest aerial reconnaissance had indicated that the bridge was still intact. He knew that the last retreating elements of the Greek army had crossed the bridge less than an hour ago. He would personally lead the attack and do his utmost to capture the bridge. It was now a race against time.

His lead elements were now less than three kilometers from the bridge, but alarm bells were going off in his head. All his years of experience told General Karakoglou that this calm was too unnatural. He was positive that the Greeks were up to something. They wouldn't give up such a strategic bridge without a fight. Yet, maybe this time his hunch was wrong. The Suilliman division's drive through Thrace had succeeded beyond his wildest expectations. They had chalked up victory after victory, smashing every obstacle that the enemy had thrown in their path. Unfortunately, the cost in men and material had been heavy. The division was presently operating at 70 percent efficiency. The wear and tear on equipment was becoming very apparent, with vehicles beginning to break down. His troops were exhausted, but they would keep up the pressure and press forward until the ultimate and total defeat of the infidels was achieved.

From the corner of his eye, the General caught a streak of light from the tree line, seven hundred meters distant. The object that he guessed correctly to be an anti-tank missile, flew over his tank and struck another fifty meters to his right. The Leopard I instantly stopped dead in its tracks, blowing its turret, ten meters into the air. Unfortunately his hunch had been right.

"Wolf leader to all units. Under fire from the tree line, one o'clock," he yelled over the command net.

Two more tanks, this time behind him, also fire balled, struck by the wire guided Dragon anti-tank missiles coming from the tree line.

"Wolf leader to all units, saturate the tree line with gun fire. Alpha company, deploy on the threat." Peering through his binoculars, the General could see Alpha Company deploying toward the tree line while his tanks fired into the area.

26th Armored Brigade
1700hrs, 20 May

The ambush which Captain Stavros had set for the Turkish armor had gone off extremely well. In the opening volley, three enemy tanks had been knocked out by his DRAGON anti-tank gunners, before the enemy had even realized what hit them. Once the surprise had worn off, the enemy quickly regrouped and began pumping heavy fire into the grove of trees where the gunners had set up. Fortunately, the only damage caused by their shells was to the forest. The anti-tank gunners had already departed the area. Their explicit instructions were to fire off a volley and retreat across the bridge. The Hellenic army could not, at this stage, afford to lose trained DRAGON gunners and equipment to brave but useless efforts.

It was now the Greek tanker's turn to bloody the enemy. Observing that the Turks were occupied with the anti-tank gunners, Captain Stavros decided that now was the time to strike. He keyed his radio mike.

"Okay men, now's our chance, choose your targets. Ready, fire!"

Nine guns fired almost in unison, nine Turkish armored vehicles died. The 105mm armor piercing rounds fired at a distance of only eight hundred meters, easily punched through the armor of the unsuspecting enemy vehicles. Six tanks and three APC's had been knocked out before the Turks had even realized what hit them.

"Panther leader to all tanks, advance on the enemy."

With Captain Stavros taking the lead, the nine M-60s charged out of their hiding places in a Vee formation.

"Load APDS," screamed Lieutenant Kapsis.

Mihalis grabbed the fifty pound shell and shoved it into the open breach which closed automatically, almost catching his hand in the process.

"Gunner, tank, left," said Lieutenant Kapsis.

"Identified," replied the gunner.

"Fire!"

"On the way, Lieutenant." The loud boom of the gun firing echoed through the open commander's hatch as the tank rocked from the recoil. The enemy tank, less than six hundred meters distant, took a direct hit and ground to a stop, smoke pouring out its hatch. A lone figure climbed out of the now burning tank, its clothes on fire. A burst from their 7.62 mm coaxial machine gun put him out of his misery.

"Gunner, tank, one o'clock. Load with APDS and hurry." The enemy tank, which was only a couple of hundred meters away, was just starting to traverse its turret toward them.

Mihalis, fortunately for all of them, had already shoved the shell into the breach when the order to load came.

"Up!"

"Identified!" The Turkish gun was almost level with them.

"Fire!"

The M-60's spoke first. The shell fired at point blank range, struck the Leopard I just under its turret, causing the tank to blow up in a ball of fire as the ammo cooked off.

"Armored personnel carrier, ten o'clock, five hundred meters. Load HEAT."

Mihalis grabbed the high explosive anti-tank round and went through the loading process.

"Up!"

"Target identified."

"Fire!"

The tank rocked from the recoil. The spent shell casing automatically ejected out of the breach and fell onto the floor of the turret. Five hundred meters away, a BMP 2 loaded with Turkish infantry fire balled.

"Sir, there are too many of them!" yelled the gunner in panic.

"Shut up and keep shooting until I tell you otherwise."

By now, the advancing Greek tanks had reached the main road and cut across the Turkish column. The surrounding landscape was littered with the hulks of burning tanks and APC's, a credit to the skill and gunnery of the Greek tankers. Lieutenant Kapsis knew that his gunner was right. There were just too many enemy tanks. This was a battle that they could not win. They had demonstrated that given the right circumstances, the enemy could be defeated. The Turks were not invincible.

From his commander's perch in the turret, Lieutenant Kapsis saw at least two dozen more enemy tanks approaching from the east. In less than a minute, they would be in gun range. It was time they got the hell out of there.

"Tank, three o'clock!" yelled the gunner.

Lieutenant Kapsis dropped into the turret and closed the hatch. He watched an enemy tank, in horror, through the commander's periscope as it was coming out from behind a burning vehicle. The smoke from the burning tank had prevented them from seeing the other tank until it was already on top of them. The enemy armored vehicle fired at Captain Stavros's tank from a range of two hundred meters, virtually point blank. The M-60 blew its turret in a fiery explosion. The enemy Leopard I suffered a similar fate a few seconds later, hit by at least two shells from the surviving Greek M-60s. Lieutenant Kapsis suddenly realized that with Captain Stavros dead, he was the senior surviving officer and therefore now in command. He keyed his radio mike.

"Panther leader to all units, withdraw toward the bridge. I repeat, withdraw toward the bridge. We've hurt them enough for one day."

The surviving Greek tanks swung to the right and headed toward the Nestos Bridge.

"Let's get the hell out of here. Driver, give her all she's got."

"I'm with you sir," said the driver.

The M-60's V-12 diesel roared with power when Sergeant Nicolaou buried his foot in the gas pedal. Counting the remaining M-60s as they disengaged from the enemy, the Lieutenant discovered that besides Captain Stavros' tank, another one was missing.

"Panther leader to all units, report status." After all the tanks had reported in, he noticed that Panther four was missing.

"Panther leader to Panther four."

"Panther six, four's bought it. Hit by a TOW, fired by one of their APC's."

"Thanks, Panther six. Everyone keep your eyes open for a possible air attack, Panther leader out."

They had been lucky, having lost only two of their number. Lieutenant Kapsis hadn't expected to survive the encounter. He wondered how long their luck would last.

Nestos River Bridge
1709hrs, 20 May

Captain Manos was almost in a state of panic. Nervously he paced up and down the span, occasionally peering over the bridge railing to check on his engineers' progress. He had heard the gunfire a few minutes earlier, suggesting that the rear guard had come in contact with the enemy. At the moment, it was suddenly quiet which meant either the Turks were stopped or the rear guard was dead. If the latter was the case, the enemy was only three kilometers away and probably barreling down on the bridge. His sappers still needed time to finish with the charges. *Damn the bastards at headquarters. They had waited until the last minute to order the bridge destroyed, he thought to himself.* To make matters worse, the proper detonators to set the charges necessary for the bridge's destruction were not with the explosives when they had arrived, causing another couple of hours delay. Peering over the railing, the Captain called down to the Sergeant in charge of the demolition crew.

"Thomas, how much longer?" yelling loud enough to be heard over the roar of the rushing water below.

"At the minimum, fifteen minutes. We're still having some problems with the detonators. It seems the batch they sent us was bad."

"It figures, Thomas. Okay, please hurry and do what you can. The enemy could be here in a few minutes."

Manos wasn't surprised. With the state the army was presently in, it was lucky that they had found any detonators at all. Normally, he and his men would have their own but those were quickly used during the first hours of the war.

"Captain Manos!" He looked up and saw his driver yelling and waving. The Captain ran over to his command vehicle.

"What is it, Andreas?"

"What's left of the rear guard just called in. They request that we wait until they have crossed to blow the bridge. The enemy has been slowed, but not stopped. They figure that we have at the most, ten minutes before the first Turkish tanks show up."

Captain Manos had turned ashen faced at the news. "Are you okay, sir?"

"I'm okay," said the Captain recovering his composure.

"Tell them we need at least another fifteen minutes to finish here."

"Sir, I think you should tell them personally." The faint sounds of tracked vehicles could be heard coming from the east.

The Captain looked up and saw four M-113 APC's followed by several vehicles, approaching the bridge. Fortunately, all bore Greek markings

"It must be the rear guard, sir. The enemy can't be too far behind."

"Andreas, do as you're told and just send the message."

"Yes, sir," said the Captain's driver. But the Captain didn't hear his driver's acknowledgment of the order. He was busy running toward the middle of the bridge.

When he had reached the center of the span, Captain Manos bent over the rail. He saw Sergeant Thomas hanging off a railing, stringing wire. There was less than a meter separating him and the rushing, dirty, brown flood waters of the raging river.

"Thomas!"

"What is it, sir?" yelled Sergeant Thomas, visibly pissed off at being disturbed again.

"You have less than ten minutes to finish the job, or the Turks will cross the Nestos with dry feet!"

Three Kilometers east of the bridge
1712hrs, 20 May

The air was thick with the stench of burning flesh and diesel fuel. Brigadier General Karakoglou surveyed the aftermath of the brief, but costly engagement with the enemy. More than a dozen burning tanks and APCs littered the immediate area. At the cost of only two enemy tanks, an entire armored company had been decimated in less than ten minutes. For some reason unknown to him, his tank was spared destruction when the enemy tanks had ripped through his lead column. Maybe it was Allah's wish that he live to complete their holy crusade against the infidels. He would now turn his full attention to that cause. His forces had to seize the Nestos river bridge intact. The enemy could not be allowed to regroup. General Karakoglou cursed the fools back at headquarters. Had they provided him with adequate air support, this costly encounter might have not happened. His requests for gunships had fallen on deaf ears. He was told the enemy was on the run. Therefore, he did not need any air support. In reality, he knew that was a line of bullshit that they had fed him. The real reason was the air force had pulled back several squadrons for defense of the capital as a result of several enemy air raids. Additionally, enemy air strikes had hampered the flow of fuel and supplies to many front line helicopter attack squadrons. So much for the air force's boast of having achieved air superiority over the Hellenic air force.

"Sir, Alpha and Bravo Companies 31st Armor are awaiting your orders to move on the bridge," said his tank driver.

"Give me the radio."

Alpha Co. 26th Armored Brigade, Xanthi-Kavala Rd. 1715hrs, 20 May

Standing in the open loader's hatchway of their speeding M-60 tank, Mihalis scanned the cloud studded eastern sky. He expected the Turkish air force would be dropping out of the clouds any minute and blowing them to pieces. Especially after the drubbing they had just given their army. They had been lucky so far. Rounding a bend in the road, the tank began to slow. Mihalis swung around and saw that they had reached the bridge. He noticed several APC's and other vehicles belonging to the brigade's anti-tank crews had stopped at the foot of the span. He also observed that there were still several soldiers working under the bridge. Sergeant Nicolaou stopped the tank while the other six remaining tanks took up defensive positions a few hundred meters up the road.

"What the fuck is going on here? Don't those idiots know the Turks are only a few minutes behind us?" said Lieutenant Kapsis, visibly agitated at the engineers' failure to complete laying the explosives. He could see an officer arguing with one of the APC drivers when they pulled up. The officer glanced up and walked toward their tank.

"Let's figure out what the hell is going on?" He climbed down from the turret and approached the other officer who bore the marking of the Hellenic Army engineering corps.

"What's the problem, Captain? My men need to cross this bridge, the enemy will be here in a few minutes," said Lieutenant Kapsis, not bothering to even salute the other officer.

The Captain who appeared to be on the verge of a nervous breakdown, pulled out a pack of cigarettes and lit one in an attempt to calm his nerves.

"Would you like a smoke, Lieutenant?"

"No! However, I would like to find out why those fucking charges haven't been set yet? You asked us to delay the enemy and we just did, losing several good crews in the process!"

"Lieutenant, I'm sorry but we're not finished planting the demolition charges. My, engineers are doing the best they can. Some of the equipment that headquarters sent us is faulty. That's why it's taking longer than usual. My men need at least ten more minutes. I asked the Lieutenant in charge of the anti-tank teams to stay and hold the Turks off until we're finished, but he refused.

"Captain, those men have been fighting nonstop for the last two and a half days. They don't have any more missiles to fight the enemy armor with. They used their last rounds a couple of kilometers back. If it wasn't for them, the Turks would already be here!" Lieutenant Kapsis motioned for the waiting APC vehicles to cross the bridge. The Captain looked on in stunned disbelief as the vehicles began crossing the bridge.

"Don't worry, Captain, we will buy you the extra time you need. Now do your job and blow this fucking bridge!"

"Thank you Lieutenant" Visibly relieved, Captain Manos ran back toward the bridge. When Lieutenant Kapsis had climbed back aboard the tank, he broke the news to his crew.

"I always knew army engineers were fucking worthless," said Sergeant Nickolaou, pissed off at the prospect of having to face an entire Turkish armored division once again.

Broadcasting over the command net, Lieutenant Kapsis briefed the rest of the tank crews of the situation.

"Sergeant, head straight for that slight depression, four hundred meters to the right."

Nicolaou put the tank in gear and the fifty ton behemoth lurched forward. "Panther three to Panther leader. Have three enemy tanks sighted, seven hundred meters southeast."

Before Lieutenant Kapsis could answer, he was interrupted by the crack and boom of two tank guns firing. The Lieutenant looked over to where Panther three was positioned. The tank was engulfed in flames. In the meantime, their tank had reached the position he had pointed out to Nicolaou. The M-60 was now hull down with only part of its turret and main gun showing, giving the enemy gunners a much smaller target to hit.

"Here they come, sir," said Corporal Stamatis, their gunner.

"Stand by to fire, they haven't seen us yet. Gunner, aim for the lead tank."

"Identified, sir."

Suilliman Division, one kilometer west of the bridge
1718hrs, 20 May

General Karakoglou heard the all too familiar boom of tank guns firing. Almost instantaneously, one of the lead tanks, several hundred meters in front of his vehicle, ground to a halt and burst in flames. Several more shots were heard and another two of his tanks were put out of action. The rest of the formation began dispersing smoke, hoping to confuse the enemy gunners. The General knew it was a futile gesture. The thermal imaging sights on the Greek tanks could easily cut through the smoke.

Even with his losses climbing steadily, his determination to seize the bridge did not waver. In fact, he was heartened in the fact that the enemy was making a final stand this close to the bridge. It meant one thing. The enemy tankers were trading their lives for time. The Greeks hadn't finished rigging the bridge for demolition He must act quickly while this golden opportunity still existed.

"Wolf leader to all units. You are to take the bridge at all costs. I repeat, destroy the infidels. If you fall in this glorious Jihad, your place in heaven is assured. Allah is great! Allah Akbar! Driver, forward to the Bridge!"

With the cry of God is great, the Turkish tanks charged forward, oblivious to the cost in lives and equipment. The Greek tankers fought bravely. But courage and determination wasn't enough. The numerical superiority of the Turks began to tell. For every enemy tank knocked out, two took its place. With General Karakoglou leading the assault, the Turks began to win ground and pushed to within five hundred meters of the bridge. One after the other, the Greek tanks were put out of action.

"Sir! I see men running on the bridge, they must be finished planting the explosives," yelled the General's driver.

Without hesitating a moment, the General switched the frequency on the command net radio and called division, ten kilometers to the rear.

"Wolf leader to citadel."

"Go with your message Wolf leader."

"Request immediate priority fire mission on the Nestos Bridge. Set anti-personnel rounds for thirty meter air burst."

"Mission received, Wolf leader."

"Roger, Wolf leader out." General Karakoglou smiled. He knew that an artillery battery had been set up and already had the bridge zeroed in for exactly this type of mission. In less than a minute, the artillery rounds that he had asked for would be arriving.

Nestos Bridge, defensive perimeter
1723hrs, 20 May

With most of his tanks now out of commission, he knew they could not hold the Turkish armor any longer. Lieutenant Kapsis ordered what remained of his command to withdraw across the bridge.

"Nicolaou! Get us the hell out of here! We'll try to hold them from the other side." Sergeant Nicolaou gunned the tank's engine and began backing the vehicle out of the depression. To reach the bridge, less than four hundred meters away, they would have to run a gauntlet of Turkish canon fire. While the tank was backing out of the depression they had so effectively used for cover, Lieutenant Kapsis stole a glance toward the bridge and saw several men running.

"Hey! It looks like they're finished planting the charges. I can see men running."

"Yeah, probably running away," said their gunner.

"Enemy Leopard I, five o'clock," yelled the Lieutenant.

"Identified," answered Corporal Stamatis.

"Fire!"

"On the way." The M-60 rocked with the recoil. The enemy tank took the hit in its engine compartment, causing it to grind to a halt, smoke pouring out its side.

"Load SABOT." Mihalis grabbed one of the fifty pound shells off the rack and shoved it into the open breach.

"Tank, six o'clock!"

The sound of incoming artillery shells caused Lieutenant Kapsis to leave his commander's position on the turret. He closed the hatch and jumped down into the tank. They had reached the main road. Sergeant Nicolaou pivoted the tank around.

The Turkish tank fired first. The M-60 rocked violently. "We're hit," screamed Mihalis in near panic.

"There's no fire and we're still moving. We are lucky, must have been a glancing blow on the reactive armor," replied Lieutenant Kapsis.

"Target identified," yelled the gunner.

"Fire!"

The M-60's gun barked. The enemy tank that was in the process of reloading was hit in the turret and went up in a ball of flame.

"Move it, Nicolaou!".

"I am, sir. It's as fast as she'll go. We have been damaged." A couple of hundred meters to their left, the last of the other surviving Greek M-60s died in a slugging match with three enemy tanks, after killing two of them.

"We're almost there," said Sergeant Nicolaou.

"I hope they don't blow the bridge before we cross it," said Mihalis.

"Oh, my God. The engineers are being massacred," shouted Sergeant Nicolaou, as he saw the dirty puffs of exploding artillery shells above the bridge.

Nestos bridge, west bank
1724hrs, 20 May

Captain Manos watched the mesmerizing battle taking place on the other side of the river. Most of the tanks of the 26th armored brigade had been knocked out. The enemy though had paid dearly. The Greek tankers had fought against all odds, trading their lives for time, so his men could finish wiring the bridge. When he saw Sergeant Thomas and his crew climbing out from underneath the bridge, he knew the tankers' sacrifice wouldn't be in vain. The sound of incoming artillery shells made both men take cover under their APC. Instead of hitting the ground, the shells burst above the bridge, showering the men underneath with thousands of pieces of razor sharp steel. The running men on the bridge were cut to pieces.

"Oh my God! Thomas and the other men are all dead and it's my fault."

"Sir, get a grip on yourself. It's not your fault, this is war! We must blow the bridge now! The enemy is almost on it."

"But the tankers, our men?"

"It's too late, they're all dead anyway. Blow the damn bridge!"

Captain Manos armed the plunger.

Nestos River Bridge
The same time

Lieutenant Kapsis watched in horror through the tank's periscope as the Turkish shells were exploding above the bridge span.

"My God, the engineers are being slaughtered!" he said, as he watched the running men cut down by the lethal shell fragments.

"Oh Jesus, how much longer?" asked Mihalis in panic.

"Don't worry, we made it, we're on the bridge," said Lieutenant Kapsis. All of a sudden, the world around them erupted in a massive explosion as the charges on the bridge were detonated.

Suilliman Armored Division, East side of the Nestos River
The same time

Brigadier General Karakoglou had parked his tank next to the hulk of a destroyed enemy tank, several hundred meters from the foot of the bridge. From this vantage point, he had a clear view of the bridge as he watched the artillery barrage do its deadly work. Only one more enemy tank now stood between him and the bridge and that tank, which somehow lived a charmed life, was itself retreating across the bridge. Victory was finally his, he thought. But before he could fully savor the feeling of success, the bridge disappeared in a cloud of fire and smoke.

"Saytan gavur! (Damned infidel) The damned Greeks have blown the bridge!" he yelled.

The light wind that was blowing from the north began clearing the cloud of smoke and dust that had been enveloping the bridge. Though visibly damaged, the bridge was still standing.

"It's still standing, sir!" said his driver.

"By the grace of Allah, it is!" exclaimed the General. His hopes of victory against the Greeks were once again alive. "Our engineers will have the bridge inspected immediately and any necessary repairs will be made. Hopefully, we will be able to resume our attack in the next few hours. We must inform headquarters of our success at once!"

Mavrovouni Mountains
2036hrs, 20 may

Colonel Mihalovic watched with deep sorrow as the body of his long-time friend, Major Ziad, was lowered in a shallow grave next to some large pine trees, high in the Mavrovouni foothills. His friend had finally succumbed to his wounds an hour ago. The Major had a chest full of shrapnel from a Greek tank shell, while helping a wounded soldier during the enemy breakthrough. He had been carried through the mountains obviously in great pain, refusing to be left behind. The Colonel had attempted to persuade him to remain behind with the other wounded, but the Major preferred to die in the company of his soldiers, rather than fall in the hands of the enemy, even though it might have saved his life. *A true soldier to the very end, thought Colonel Mihalovic,* as his friend was laid to rest in an unmarked grave, far from his home. He wondered if his friend had given his life for nothing, to a lost cause.

As he stood there in silence while the grave was filled with dirt, he mentally went over the day's disastrous events. Their retreat into the mountains had been anything but orderly. Once the enemy armor had penetrated their defense lines and entered the regiment's rear area, their retreat had almost turned into a total disaster. Most of their heavy equipment had to be abandoned. Only the brave self-sacrifice of a few soldiers who threw themselves under the enemy tanks, carrying satchel charges, saved the day. Otherwise, most of the regiment would have been annihilated. Still, they had suffered very heavy casualties. Fortunately, they had been able to save a couple of the field radios and were still able to communicate with headquarters.

The news from the rest of the front was still very sketchy. From what they could gather from the radio, it was not good. The capital, Skopje, had suffered an air raid and the army had been ordered to pull back to better defensible fighting positions in the mountains. *So much for the no withdrawal order, he thought.* What everyone knew, from the highest general to the lowliest private, was that the enemy had given the Macedonian army a severe battering. All they could do now was to dig in, hold their positions and pray for a quick Turkish victory. Otherwise, they were all finished.

Once the regiment had retreated into the mountains, their luck had gotten better. Except for an occasional bout of harassing artillery fire and a few low level buzzes by enemy aircraft, they had been left alone. The Colonel was sure that the enemy knew where they were. The sparsely vegetated mountain side offered few places for his men to hide in and he was sure those planes that had buzzed them earlier were reconnaissance birds. Their last pass had been a half an hour ago. He saw Captain Slovik, his new Operations Officer, approaching in the waning evening light. The Captain, a Christian Macedonian from Skopje, had been his Alpha company commander, but now as the ranking officer, he had succeeded Major Ziad.

"Good evening, Captain."

"Good evening, sir. I'm here to report that Alpha and Bravo companies have completed their forward defense positions. And sir, the men are taking turns sleeping."

"That's good to hear. The men need the rest."

"May I add, sir, we're situated in a very good defensible location. Our right flank is protected by a high cliff and our left flank is protected by a series of deep gullies. We have covered the gullies with machine guns and with some of our remaining mortars," said Captain Slovik.

"The 301st Brigade is situated two kilometers east of here. They should be able to cover any remaining gaps in our defense lines, Captain."

"I sure hope so, sir. We lost a lot of men and equipment today."

"I'm well aware of our situation, Captain," the Colonel said, thinking of his dead friend.

"You've done a good job, Captain. When, and if we ever leave here, I'm putting you in for promotion to Major."

"Thank you, sir."

"I'll be at the command post if you need me."

"Yes, sir."

Colonel Mihalovic returned the Captain's salute and headed for the regiment's new command post that had been set up in a cave in the mountain side that one of the scouts had discovered.

Forty-Thousand Feet over Northern Greece
2148hrs, 20 May

After an exhausting twelve hour flight from Barksdale air force base Louisiana, the twenty-four B-52H bombers of the 917th Bombardment Wing were approaching their target area. The B-52s had been dispatched to Europe, as part of the US President's aid package to the Greeks. Older than most of the air crews which flew them, the giant bombers were still formidable weapons. Each of the huge eight engine planes could carry over twenty tons of ordnance, from conventional iron bombs, anti-ship missiles, mines to nuclear tipped cruise missiles, thousands of miles before needing refueling. Its excellent range and payload capacity made it an ideal weapon system to use for traditional carpet bombing. This technique had been mastered with the venerable BUFF, as its air crews called it, during Vietnam and Desert Storm. Now it was going to be used once again.

Tonight's target for the 917th was a location somewhere in the Mavrovouni mountain range, near the Greek-Macedonian border. The Hellenic Army had begun an offensive earlier in the day to dislodge and destroy the Macedonian invasion force which had seized a sizable chunk of Greek real estate. The American bombers would be dropping their load on suspected Macedonian troop positions and hopefully would blow a hole through them that the Hellenic army could exploit.

"Condor One to all aircraft, two minutes to target," said Colonel Markus, the bomber formation leader over the inter plane net.

"Sir, the latest target coordinates have been downloaded into the targeting computers from the satellite uplink," said the bomber's weapons' officer. Even as they flew to the target, the bombers' computers, which were linked by satellite to the pentagon's command and control center, could be updated in real time with target information obtained by reconnaissance aircraft or by reconnaissance satellite while the bomber was airborne. The twenty-four B-52s had reached their target areas and were now flying under auto pilot, directly linked to the plane's sophisticated targeting computer which would take the plane to its bomb release point. The bombs, which were usually released several miles from their targets, had to be dropped at a precise time and location to hit their mark. This was accomplished by the plane's computer which used data from the military's orbiting navigation satellites to fix the plane's exact position. The computer then took in account the plane's airspeed, winds and atmospheric conditions aloft and plotted the exact time and release point.

"Roger, Joe," replied the aircraft commander. "I hate to be those poor bastards on the receiving end, but they have it coming to them. They started this war."

"How's everything else look? We're coming in enemy fighter range."

"All clear so far, Colonel, nothing on the radar and nothing from the Greek AWACS plane."

"That's good to hear. Just the same, keep your eyes open."

"I will, sir," said Lieutenant Johnson, the bomber's weapons' officer.

Cruising at forty-four thousand feet over the night skies of northern Greece, Colonel Markus thought of home and his family, back in Louisiana. This would be his third war in his twenty eight year air force career. By virtue of his rank and position as squadron commander, he didn't have to go on this mission. He suspected this would probably be his last war and he loved flying the old war bird. So he had jumped at the opportunity to go on this deployment. Looking at the darkened landscape passing underneath the bomber's nose, he wondered how many times this ancient land had been fought over and how much blood had been spilled over it, in just the last century alone, never mind all the past millennia since the Greeks first settled it.

"Opening bomb bay doors," said the weapons' officer.

"Roger, have an "open" light on my panel," said the air craft commander.

"Ten seconds till bomb release, five, four, three, two, one, bombs away."

Each of the B-52s, which was carrying eighty, five hundred pound bombs, released their deadly load and turned for Mildenhall air base, England. Mildenhall, which was another 4 hours of flying time, would serve as their base of operations until their deployment was over. The bombers would be many miles away when the bombs would finally reach their targets.

Mavrovouni Mountains
2058hrs, 20 May

The inside of the large cavern that served as the regiment's command post was bathed in the dim light given out by the battle lanterns. Colonel Mihalovic looked at the eerie shadows made by the light that danced on the cavern walls. It made him think of the old folklore and legends which said the souls of long dead soldiers still walked these mountains at night. He thought of his friend, Major Ziad, and hoped that his soul had entered paradise as Islam promised for all holy warriors, and not wandering these accursed mountains. Unfortunately, he thought many more soldiers' souls would be making that final trip before this war was over. He looked up and noticed that Captain Slovik had entered the command post.

"Sir, all the necessary guards have been posted and reconnaissance patrols have been sent out. So far, no contact with the enemy has been reported from any of our patrols. I find this very odd, Colonel, especially after their successful attack against us this morning. I hate to sound defeatist, but one would think that they would be following up on their success."

"Maybe they are licking their wounds. They did suffer heavy casualties. But knowing the Greeks, I believe that they are up to something. I know the men are exhausted, but we must keep up our guard."

"Don't worry about the men, sir." Everyone inside the cave was suddenly startled by the sudden noise of loud explosions outside the cave.

"They're getting closer," yelled Captain Slovik.

"Everyone get down and cover your ears!" screamed Colonel Mihalovic.

The loud explosions were now almost on top of them. The noise level of the outside detonations had reached an almost unbearable crescendo.

"What in Gods' name is it?" yelled Captain Slovik in terror.

"Bombs," screamed Colonel Mihalovic

The flashes from the exploding bombs lit up the inside of the cave well enough that Colonel Mihalovic could see the terror etched on the faces of his men.

"Look out!" screamed the Colonel as he saw part of the ceiling loosened by the falling bombs giving way.

The warning was too late for one of the soldiers that happened to be underneath the section that gave way. He was killed instantly, crushed by tons of rock.

"It's the end of the world! We're all going to die! I'm getting out of here!" screamed another soldier, gripped by panic.

"Stop him!" yelled Colonel Mihalovic, but the soldier, terrified out of his wits, had already reached the mouth of the cave before he could be stopped. Stepping outside, he only managed to take a few steps before a 500-pound bomb landed just a few meters away. The soldier was picked up by the force of the blast and bodily hurled back inside the cave. His body landed a few feet from Captain Slovik, a bloody mass of torn flesh, barely distinguishable as once being human.

The storm of fire and metal lasted less than a minute, but it had cut a swathe of death and destruction several kilometers long through the Mavrovouni Mountains. Many Macedonian units caught in the hell storm had ceased to exist or were decimated to the point where they were no longer an effective fighting force. Those that had been in the cave and escaped the full fury of the attack had been the lucky ones. The mountain had shielded them from the bombs.

The horrible din of exploding bombs had suddenly stopped and was replaced by a peaceful stillness. Slowly getting up to his feet, Colonel Mihalovic took stock of their situation. Less than a dozen men were all that remained of his command at the moment and some of these men were in no condition to even take care of themselves, much less face the enemy. Hearing a whimpering noise coming from somewhere in the cave, the Colonel shined his flashlight at the source. Curled up against the cave wall was a soldier, shaking uncontrollably from the ordeal he had just experienced.

"Someone help that man! The rest of you, grab some lights and first aid packs and get a rescue party formed."

"My God, sir. I've never experienced anything like what we just went through in my life. What exactly happened?" asked a visibly horrified Captain Slovik.

"Not too many have survived what we just went through and lived to talk about it. What we experienced, my good Captain, was a classic carpet bombing attack. Since the Greek air force has nothing in their inventory capable of doing such a thing, I suspect that we were just bombed by United States Air Force B-52s or B-1 bombers."

"The Americans, sir?"

"Yes, Captain, the Americans. The war is now lost, if not Macedonia herself."

Captain Slovik looked at the Colonel with shock and disbelief. "But sir, our leaders said that the Americans could not deliver enough aid in time to save the Greeks."

"Obviously, the idiots were wrong. Dead wrong," he added. "Please accompany me, Captain."

Both men went outside the cave. Colonel Mihalovic shined his lantern down the mountain, but the drifting smoke obscured much of the beam.

"Sir, your light, the enemy might..," but the Colonel cut him off.

"Don't worry Slovik. There are no Greeks for kilometers out there right now. They would be fools if they were here. The bombers did the work for them."

Even though the drifting smoke obscured much of their visibility, what they did see was enough to cause Captain Slovik to sink in total despair. The landscape had been churned into a no man's land. What they saw reminded Colonel Mihalovic of pictures of World War One, most notably Verdun. The ground around them was churned up and pockmarked with dozens of large craters.

"No one could have survived this hell," said Captain Slovik.

"Now you see reality, Captain. We are finished. The 3rd Macedonian Mountain Regiment has been, for all purposes, annihilated, blasted off the face of the earth."

"Help!"

"My God, someone's alive out there," said Captain Slovik.

"You men come with me. We must hurry, the Greeks will be here by morning," said Colonel Mihalovic.

"Sir! There are several men coming up the hill."

"If it's the enemy, we will offer no resistance. No use getting anyone else killed. The war is over for us!"

"It's not the Greeks, sir. It's one of the patrols I had sent out," said Captain Slovik.

"We were luckier than I thought. We must hurry and find

the survivors and leave this accursed place, time is of the essence," said Colonel Mihalovic

"What are we going to do?"

"Find the remnants of our army and head for home. The war is over for Macedonia. We need to put our house in order."

"Yes, sir," replied a down stricken, but happy to be alive, Captain Slovik.

Chapter 5

Kesan Command Bunker
0015hrs, 21 May

General Kemal apprehensively paced the command post situation room, awaiting word that his forces had broken out of the Nestos River bridge head. Except for this one bright spot in Thrace, the course of the war had taken a turn for the worse. The fleet had suffered a major setback when it had attempted to reinforce the invasion forces on Limnos. Also, several of the navy's subs had been sunk by US and Greek Naval P3 aircraft. He never did have any confidence in the navy; they were too soft, always too afraid to risk their precious ships. Now thanks to these cowardly fools, the army on Limnos was in a desperate situation.

Nonetheless, he could not solely blame the navy for the set back. Victory had been snatched from his very grasp by the accursed Americans. He had grossly underestimated their will and resolve to aid the Greeks. No matter, he would make them pay. The Greeks were in their death throes in Thrace. In another forty-eight hours, they would be begging him for peace. A peace dictated on his terms. He noticed his aid Colonel Azoglou approaching.

"Sir, I have excellent news. The Suilliman armored division has broken out of the bridge head and is on the move westward once again. Brigadier General Karakoglou reports that he is encountering light resistance, both from enemy ground and air forces."

"Thank the prophet," replied General Kemal.

"It seems the Greeks are pulling back and are only attempting delaying tactics, sir."

"Yes, my friend. They are pulling back and saving everything for their final stand. Intelligence believes it will be at the Platamon River."

"Oh sir, I do have some bad news."

"What is it, my friend?"

"We just received a message from Skopje, Macedonia."

"What does it say, Ahmet?"

"I'm afraid Macedonia is finished. Their army, which was holding in the Mavrovouni Mountains, was attacked tonight by heavy bombers, believed to be USAF B-52s. They have lost radio contact with many of their units. Losses are presumed to be very heavy. Skopje has issued a general retreat order for all of their forces in the field. They have ordered what is left of their army to pull back across their borders."

"My God, B-52s! No one could stand up to a B-52 raid unless well dug in, and even then...," said General Kemal, remembering the Gulf war.

"The Macedonians had no type of air defenses available. They must have been slaughtered," said Colonel Azoglou.

"Those damn Americans again! I will teach them a lesson. Have General Karakoglou destroy the airfield where the

Americans are operating from."

"Sir, the planes most likely will have been evacuated to somewhere else. We can just surround and bypass the base till we have finished with the main objective. We need every available resource to crack the enemy defenses at the Platamon River."

"No! Have Karakoglou dispatch a brigade to the airfield. I want that place destroyed and everyone else remaining there. The Americans have been a thorn in my side from the very beginning. I will teach them a lesson."

"I will do as you ask, sir."

Special Forces Base Camp, Limnos
0100hrs, 20 May

It had been a pure stroke of luck for Petros and Eleni, running into Special Forces patrol. Leaving the old hut, they accompanied the soldiers back to their base camp, deep in the wooded Kornos foothills. The journey to the commando's camp had been through some of the island's most rugged terrain, having to bypass most of the island's populated areas that were under enemy occupation. Eleni, bruised and exhausted by the long trek, had immediately fallen asleep when they arrived at the camp. Petros had been impressed with the camouflage job done to make the numerous tents and other temporary structures set up by the soldiers invisible from the air. They had been set up or built to blend in with the forest and surrounding terrain. He was sure Eleni would be safe here.

The mood in the camp was one of optimism and elation. The news of yesterday morning's great naval victory by the Hellenic navy had lifted everyone's spirits and gave them a much needed morale boost. After days of repeated military disasters, there was finally a ray of hope that the Turks could be stopped. Eleni had been awakened by Petros later that morning to be given the good news that Yiannis and his crew had made it back to Salamina. He had become a national hero and had even been decorated by the President. She had been overjoyed at the news that Yiannis was alive and well. Perhaps after this terrible war was over, they might still have a chance to have a life together.

To help pass the time and make herself useful, Eleni had volunteered to help with the caring of the wounded in the camp's makeshift infirmary. Short of drugs and real medical facilities, she did whatever she could to make the wounded soldiers comfortable. She was in the infirmary tent pulling the night shift when Petros had walked in. *She has to be a very brave girl he thought,* as he looked around the tent that reeked of antiseptic and unwashed bodies.

"Eleni, I have some more good news."

"Is it about Yiannis?"

"Yes, as a matter of fact. The Hydra took part in today's naval battle. She came out of it all right."

"Oh, thank God, Petros. I was so worried."

"They're calling the action, the Second naval battle of Limnos, after the first one in the Balkan wars of 1912. The Turks have suffered a major defeat. It was a great victory for our nation."

"Where did you get the news about Yiannis, Petros?"

"We just received it over the wireless from Athens."

"What about the rest of the war."

Petros turned somber. "The war is still going rather badly for us in Thrace. The bright side is in Macedonia and Epirus. The army has stabilized those fronts and is pushing the enemy back."

"But we may still lose the war?"

"Yes, it's still very possible, Eleni. Their conversation was momentarily interrupted by a messenger from the command post.

"Sir, Major Christakos would like to see you."

"Tell him I'll be there in a few minutes."

"Yes, sir."

As the messenger walked out, Eleni gave Petros a questioning frown. "What's that all about?"

"Oh, nothing special, the Major probably has some questions."

"I can figure out that much, Petros. I believe that you're up to something."

"They need some information about certain areas of the island."

"And they probably want you to show them the way there. Petros, please be careful. You're not exactly a young man anymore."

"Don't worry Eleni. I realize that I'm no longer Special Forces material, but they do need my help. I have a score to settle with the bastards, for Anna's sake."

"I know, just don't do anything foolish."

"I promise I won't. Now I have to go"

Eleni gave Petros a hug and a kiss on the cheek. "I'll be waiting for you to return safely. I want you at my wedding."

"You can count on it. I will be there."

A few minutes later, Petros was walking toward the small long abandoned sheep herder's hut the commandos had taken over and were using as their command post. Hidden amongst the trees, one had to look very carefully not to miss it. Walking inside, Petros discerned through the dim light provided by two battle lanterns, Major Christakos and several other officers and NCOs gathered around the hut's only table, looking over a map.

"Ah, good morning, Commander. I'm glad that you're here. Would you like some coffee?"

"It's my pleasure to be of service, Major, and yes I would like some coffee."

Major Christakos took a metal cup off the table and poured some coffee from a thermos that had been resting at the foot of the table.

"Here, Commander, I hope you like it. We liberated this coffee from a Turkish headquarters element near Mirina which some of my men paid a visit the other day." Petros took a sip, savoring the hot liquid.

"Now to get to the point of why I asked for you. We just received another message from Athens, officially confirming your reactivation and appointment to the rank of Commander and your designation as naval liaison to this unit.

Congratulations Commander," said Major Christakos holding out his hand.

Petros was not impressed by the Major's fanfare, but he shook his offered hand out of politeness.

"Now that the formalities are over, let's get down to the business of killing Turks," said Petros rather abruptly. The Major was momentarily taken back by Petros' manner. Then he remembered that this man had a very personal grudge to settle with them.

"Well Commander, as I briefed you earlier, we've received intelligence from Athens, indicating that reconnaissance flights have detected a large enemy supply dump on the west side of Mudros bay, to be more precise, a few kilometers north of Konidos."

"I know the location," said Petros.

"How well?"

"When I was a boy, I used to go swimming and fishing there with my friends. In later times, I'd take my family there picnicking."

"Excellent, Commander. Athens wants that dump taken out. It would definitely weaken the already tenuous foothold that the enemy has on this island and aid those units still fighting. After today's naval defeat, the Turkish navy will be very hard pressed to keep supplying their army on this island. Do you think that you could lead a squad of my men there, through the Turkish lines?" asked Major Christakos.

"There are several small foot paths mainly used by the local goat and sheep herders leading down from the foot hills to the beach. It has been a long time since I've been there and used any of them, but they probably haven't changed much, even after all these years."

"Good! I'll leave you then with Lieutenant Genetakos who will be your second in command for this mission. You two can go over the details. You leave for Moudros within the hour."

Platamon River, ten kilometers West of Kavala, Greece
0150hrs, 21 May

Mihalis leaned on the tank's turret and took a sip from a cup filled with hot coffee, hoping the liquid would take the night chill from his weary body. It was his turn at guard duty, so the rest of the crew could get some needed rest. Wrapping a green army blanket around his shoulders to stay warm, he thought about yesterday's miraculous escape from the Nestos River highway bridge. He was sure God had been watching over them. By all accounts they should have been blown into the river when the charges had gone off. Maybe they would have been better off. At least the bridge would have been destroyed and the enemy delayed for many hours. Instead the bridge had only been damaged. Their engineers would have it repaired in a matter of hours. Mihalis glanced over at where newly promoted Captain Kapsis was sleeping. With Captain Stavros dead, Lieutenant Kapsis had been promoted to take his place. God only knows he earned it. They were all still alive, thanks to his skill and leadership. Mihalis had to admit, the newly minted Captain was one hell of a soldier.

After their escape across the Nestos Bridge, the Captain had ordered them to proceed west, hoping to link up with the rest of the remnants of the 26th armored. They didn't have long to wait. Just a few kilometers down the road, they met up with some of the other survivors of the 26th. Low on fuel and ammo and harassed by enemy shelling, they headed west and eventually ran into a forward support team where they repaired their tank, refueled and replenished their ammo stocks. With their tank in the lead, they continued west through the refugee clogged roads until they had crossed the Platamon River. It was here at the river where the Hellenic army had decided to make its stand and hopefully blunt the Turkish drive. Without having a chance to even rest, the 26th was quickly reinforced and ordered onto the defense line, overlooking the river. The troops had immediately gone to work, helping the already over-worked army engineers who had been working nonstop constructing fighting positions. The unit's armored vehicles were dug in up to their turrets, with only their guns and anti-tank missiles protruding. By late evening, most of the back breaking work had been finished. Their new defense position now consisted of a formidable series of pill boxes, housing anti-tank gun and anti-tank missiles, protected by several layers of mines and anti-tank traps. Taking the first watch, the Captain had ordered the crew to get some rest for tomorrow's pending battle. A rested crew would fight more efficiently.

Mihalis heard the sound of artillery fire coming from the east. He surmised that the enemy must be on the move again. The enemy's delay on the Nestos had only proved to be temporary. Except for a few rear guard elements sacrificing themselves to buy time for the rest of the army, very few obstacles now remained between them and the main body of the Turkish army. Sometime tomorrow morning or early afternoon, there would be a great battle, here by this small river that would decide the fate of Greece. The Hellenic army had committed all of its remaining reserves on this last line of defense. If the enemy managed to break through, the road to Thessaloniki would be wide open. The city would be theirs for the taking. He would fight till his last breath to prevent this from happening. If they lost the battle, they would all be better off dead. Fortunately, not all the news was bad. He had heard that there had been a naval battle off of Limnos and the Hellenic navy had emerged victorious. Maybe, just maybe, there was a glimmer of hope that the Turks might just yet be stopped.

Igia Hospital, Athens
0203hrs, 21 May

Closely watched by the police officer guarding the room, nurse Maria Stathis administered a dose of medication through the IV tube connected to the comatose girl lying in the bed. Looking down at the helpless young woman, all wrapped in bandages and gauze, she knew she should be feeling sorry for her. Instead she felt hatred. She hated the bitch for having her own private room, while hundreds of wounded soldiers and injured civilians had to lie on the corridor floors for lack of space. What made her hate this person ever more so was that she was a Muslim, and not just any Muslim. She was the daughter of the Grand Mufti of Kommotini, or ex-Grand Mufti, since he had been murdered the night before the war. The girl who had been brutally raped and then shot in the head during her father's murder, had been air evacuated to Athens in critical condition. The government had given her the VIP treatment. She had been operated on by the best neurosurgeon in Greece, given a private room and a twenty four hour guard. Instead of thanking the Greek government for this special treatment, her people blamed the Greeks for her father's murder and had risen in open revolt. Hundreds of innocent Greeks living in the city had been killed and the city set ablaze. For all that Maria cared, the little bitch could die and go to hell.

"Are you finished, nurse?"

Maria gave the policeman a dirty look. "Yes I'm finished. You can go back to reading your magazine. I have work elsewhere to do!" she said rather sarcastically.

Picking up her medicine tray, Maria turned to leave the room.

"Father."

Maria thought she heard someone whisper something.

"Father," this time she heard it clearly. Maria turned and looked at Fahtme.

"She spoke. She's out of the comma," said Maria.

Maria ran out of the room, yelling for the doctor. The policeman picked up the phone that was on the table and dialed the special number he had been given. After a couple of rings, someone answered on the other side.

"This is patrolman Tambakakis, posted at Igia hospital. The Mufti's daughter has awakened. She's out of the comma."

"I'll tell the General immediately," said the person on the other end."

Piges Airfield
0222hrs, 21 May

The now all too familiar high pitched whistle of incoming shells made Master Sergeant George Pappas dive for cover behind the wall of sand bags, protecting the entrance to the command bunker. The shells landed about a dozen meters away, showering him with dirt. For the past hour, the airfield had been subjected to sporadic artillery fire. Luckily, most of the shells had landed in open areas causing little damage. Latest intelligence reports placed the closest Turkish units less than twenty kilometers from the airfield. Getting back up, George brushed himself off and walked to the bunker's entrance where he identified himself to the sentry and proceeded inside. Because of his fluency in Greek, he had been chosen to serve as an interpreter. If the choice had been his, he would have rather been out in the base perimeter fighting positions with his troops.

George walked hurriedly down the short flight of stairs and

entered the command post. He had been summoned by Lieutenant Colonel Kazas and he suspected that whatever the Colonel had to say would not be good. He walked through the operations center and went into the conference room where he found Kazas sitting at the conference table with Colonels Logan and Sardis along with several other staff members. He would wait in the control center until they had finished their meeting. Taking off his heavy Keflar helmet and flak vest, he laid it down beside a small sofa and got a cup of black coffee from one of the two pots set up in a corner of the control center. He took a sip of the hot liquid and sat down. While he waited for the meeting to finish, George pondered his situation. He wondered if he would ever see his family in Germany again. At least one of his worries was over. His parents were okay. Colonel Kazas had gotten him a line through to Athens yesterday evening and he had briefly spoken to them.

George looked up. The door to the conference room had opened, the meeting was over. Colonel Kazas emerged from the room and walked toward him. George stood up in the officer's presence.

"Sit down, George. May I join you?"

"Go right ahead, sir. What's going on?"

"Things aren't going well for us in Thrace, George."

"I kind of gathered that, especially with all the incoming pyrotechnics."

"That's the reason I called you here. Athens and Washington have decided to evacuate the fighters to Mikra airfield,

Thessaloniki. We can't afford to lose these planes. If this shelling intensifies, the runway and taxiways will soon be rendered unusable. The planes will become prisoners in their own shelters."

"I realize that, sir."

"I hope you will understand the rest of what I have to say."

George gave the Colonel a quizzical look. He did not like what he just heard. "When do the planes leave?"

"Immediately. The Turks are less than twenty kilometers from the field. The Greek army will not sacrifice any more men and material than already here in place to hold this base. We need every soldier we've got to man the Platamon River defense line," said Colonel Kazas.

"So what's going to happen to all the people and equipment that are here?"

"Within the hour, Hellenic Air Force and USAF transport planes will be arriving to evacuate all essential equipment and personnel."

So that was it, George thought to himself. "Essential, sir?"

The Colonel momentarily hesitated before answering. "George, you are the first, besides Colonel Logan and Sardis to know this. I thought it better that I tell you before you hear it from someone else. Higher Command has decided that only critical personnel will be evacuated by air. Right now, getting mission essential equipment and ammunition out of here have priority. Those fighters will play a crucial part in the upcoming battle that will probably decide the fate of this nation. We are critically short of fighter planes and the techs to service them."

"Which Higher Command has made this decision, sir?"

"Both the USAF and the Hellenic Air Force."

"So we will be left to our fates."

"That's not true, George. The Hellenic army already here will stay and help defend the airfield."

"They're no match for tanks and neither are my Security troops," said Master Sergeant Pappas.

"The airfield will be defended and the enemy delayed as long as humanly possible. Afterwards everyone will withdraw toward the Platamon River. If it helps any, the transports are bringing in more anti-tank weaponry."

"It will help a little, but will not stave off the inevitable. Well, thanks for the information, sir. I'm going back to get my troops ready for the coming battle."

"George, you're leaving on the first transport out. Your language expertise is needed."

"Thank you, sir. I prefer to stay and fight with my men. Besides, I'm not really needed, you speak perfect English."

"You know, Sergeant that I can give you an order to catch that plane."

"You could, sir. But I think you won't." The Colonel looked at George with admiration. He was not the least surprised that his offer was turned down.

"I respect courage and loyalty, George. I wish I were back in the cockpit myself." Colonel Kazas offered his hand. "Good luck, I hope to see you soon at Mikra. Now, will you excuse me,

I have a lot of things to do if this operation is going to go off smoothly."

"Thank you, sir. I got a lot of work to do myself to help prepare a hot welcome for the Turks."

The 526th, Ten Miles South East of Mikra Airfield
0315hrs, 21 May

The eleven remaining F-16 fighting Falcons of the 526th flew westward over the Halkidiki peninsula on a heading for Mikra airfield. As they approached the eastern outskirts of Thessaloniki, Logan's AL 69 threat warning indicator came alive. It was cautioning him that target acquisition radar was beginning to sweep the area. Logan hoped that the Greek air defense network had gotten their IFF transponder codes. All they needed now was a trigger happy gunner adding to their woes. Not that he could blame the Greeks for being overcautious. Thessaloniki had taken a serious pounding by the Turkish air force these last couple of days. Fortunately, the missile gunners left them alone. Their IFF transponder codes were working perfectly.

The flight of jets continued westward, skirting the eastern fringes of the city. For the first time since the war had started, Thessaloniki's inhabitants were enjoying a restful night. There had been no air raids. Logan knew that the enemy's air force had suffered heavy casualties to the city's air defenses, recently bolstered by the addition of Patriot missile batteries flown in from Germany. More than likely, Logan figured that the Turks were husbanding their resources for the big attack on the Platamon River.

It hadn't been only the Turkish air force that had suffered heavy casualties. His squadron had suffered over thirty percent losses in the past couple of days. Many of the losses had occurred yesterday when they had been ordered to destroy the Nestos River bridge after the botched demolition job. Heavy enemy anti-aircraft fire and missile defenses had thwarted their initial attempt to destroy the structure with conventional iron bombs. Only a few minor hits were scored at the cost of three planes. After this high-priced failure, Logan refused to hazard his crews on another attempt. Later in the day, a flight of F-15 Strike Eagles, specially called in from England, using GBU 24 laser guided glide bombs, finally took out the bridge. And that was at the cost of one F-15 and both its crew members. The whole effort had been for nothing. The Strike Eagles had arrived too late to save the day. The enemy had managed to establish a secure bridge head on the other side and was able to bring the rest of their armor across the river by erecting a pontoon bridge.

Ten kilometers from the field, Logan's radio suddenly came alive.

"Mikra control to Falcon leader, we have you on approach radar, 6 miles due east. We will turn on our runway lights. You are cleared to land."

"Roger, Mikra control. Thanks for the assistance." Logan looked out to the west and saw a line of lights surrounded by a sea of darkness.

"There are the lights, everybody. Let's make it quick, we don't need any unwanted company following us in." Logan said. He and his wing man would be the first planes touching down. Lining his plane up with the rapidly approaching runway, he thought of everyone left behind at Piges, a hundred miles to the east. The enemy would be there by morning. Hopefully, they would hold out long enough for relief to arrive. But why was he kidding himself? There would be no relief. The garrison was left to fend for itself. Their only chance would be to retreat westward toward the Greek lines. The decision to abandon them had not been his. Logan had argued against it, to the point where he had been given a direct order by the Greek Wing Commander to evacuate his fighters. He would make the enemy pay, he promised that to all those left behind.

Limnos, Moudros Bay
0340hrs, 21 May

With their faces blackened and equipment taped down as not to make noise, the Hellenic Army Special Forces team silently made their way down the narrow rocky path. With Petros as their guide, they had trudged for three straight hours through the island's rugged country side, passing many enemy outposts and patrols, until they finally reached their destination undetected. Petros halted the team at the edge of a tall cliff that overlooked the bay.

"Here we are, gentlemen"

Lieutenant Genetakos put the night scope to his eye and

scanned the coast line. "There's the dump, about fifteen hundred meters up the beach, right where those lights are. I think that there's also a small ship there."

"Let me see," said Petros, taking the scope.

"You're right. It is the dump and there's a small landing craft offloading supplies. The bastards are bringing in supplies under the cover of darkness."

"We're in luck, Commander. I don't see any portable lights on. Probably scared of drawing an air attack," said the Lieutenant.

"Or they're short on fuel or portable generators," said Petros.

"Although I am sure they have lots of sentries."

"Probably so, Commander. My men can handle them. Once we cut the wire, we'll be in and out in thirty minutes. Can you get us close to them without being seen?"

"Yes, I know a way down but it's very steep. You'll have to carry only the gear you will need," said Petros.

"That won't be a problem. We'll take only the explosives, a few grenades and side arms along. I will leave two men to watch our other gear and cover us with the machine gun."

"Let's hope we don't need it. If we're spotted, we'll be cut to pieces climbing back up the cliff," said Petros.

With Petros in the lead, the commando team began the hazardous climb down the cliff. Fifteen minutes later, they had reached the bottom, emerging less than five hundred meters from the ammo dump.

"Thanks for all your assistance in getting us this far,

Commander. Now we got if from here," whispered Lieutenant Genetakos.

"What do you mean, Lieutenant?"

"You're staying here. It's too dangerous to come with us."

"Listen, Lieutenant. I'm going to get that landing craft. That'll be one less boat that they can use to re-supply their troops."

"Sir, you haven't been trained in the use of these explosives, nor are you . . . "

"In shape?" said Petros cutting the Lieutenant off.

"Lieutenant, I happen to be one of the best swimmers on this island."

"Sir, I don't want to be responsible for anything happening to you."

"Then consider my request an order."

"Okay. If you insist on going through with this," replied the Lieutenant, not wanting to argue with him any longer. After briefly explaining to Petros how the explosive charges worked, the team was ready to go.

"Everyone has their watches synchronized. The charges will be set to blow forty-five minutes from now. Good luck Commander. Remember, if you're not back here when we return, we're leaving without you."

"I understand, Lieutenant. Good luck. May God be with you."

After the team had departed, Petros made his way silently along the base of the cliff toward the water's edge. He thought he heard something. Dropping to the ground, he carefully crawled forward until he heard the same noise. This time he knew what it was; enemy soldiers. Not more than fifteen meters in front of him was a machine gun nest that had been set up to cover the water front. Slowly retracing his steps, he gave the machine gun a wide berth. Fortunately, it was a cloudy night and darker than usual. The enemy soldiers did not see him.

A few minutes later he had reached the water's edge. Quickly stripping down to his underclothes, he secured the explosive charges around his waist and entered the cool water. *Thank God it's almost summer or I would freeze to death, he thought.* Glancing at the illuminated dial on his watch, he saw that he only had thirty-five minutes to complete his task. With a slow but steady stroke, Petros set out for the landing craft, over five hundred meters distant.

Piges Airfield
0400hrs, 21 May

Except for the one hundred and fifty men remaining to defend the airfield and the small group of technicians waiting to board the transport that had just landed, Piges had become a ghost town. During the past few hours, under the cover of darkness, USAF and Hellenic air force transport planes had arrived to pick up personnel and equipment being evacuated to Mikra airfield. Except for some sporadic shelling, the evacuation had proceeded in an orderly manner. Anything that could be usable to the enemy and could not be taken along was destroyed and all cryptographic material had been burned.

Master Sergeant George Pappas sat in his Hummvee watching in silence as the final group of personnel boarded the last C-130 Hercules transport departing for Mikra. During the last thirty minutes, the shelling of the airfield had intensified. The enemy was closing in.

"That plane better hurry up and get moving, the shelling is getting worse," said George.

"That's the last plane out, isn't it, Sarge?" asked Airman First Class Smith, his driver.

"Yes, Smith. I suppose it is."

"So we're being left on our own?"

"No Smith, we aren't being left to fight alone," said George, not wanting to lower the man's morale any lower than it already was.

"The Greek army troops have stayed to fight with us. They've even flown in some more heavy weapons. Don't worry, we'll kick their ass."

Airman Smith smiled. "Yeah, Sarge. We'll kick ass. They won't take this place from the sky cops without a good fight."

"Hey, they've turned the ramp lights off," said George.

"There they go," said Airman Curwin, the Hummer's Mark 19 gunner, pointing at the taxing C-130 transport, visible only by its taxi lights.

"Incoming!" screamed Curwin.

"Everybody, out of the vehicle. Take cover," yelled George.

They rapidly exited the vehicle and dived to the ground for

cover. Hearing a strange whooshing noise, George looked up in the sky and saw several streaks of light diving into the ground. They're rockets. *The Turks must have a multiple rocket launcher system within range of the field, thought George.*

The transport which had continued to taxi through the rocket barrage, suddenly careened off the taxi way and burst into flames. It had taken a 122mm rocket hit in its forward section.

"Shit! The plane's been hit. Everybody back into the vehicle," yelled George.

Gunning the engine, they raced toward the area where the plane had come to rest. Fortunately, the shelling of the airfield had momentarily lifted and they reached the burning plane without further incident. The plane's fuselage had broken in two with the forward section already engulfed in flames.

"We gotta hurry, Sarge, it's going to blow any minute."

George knew that Smith was right. There would be no fire department or ambulances arriving to help any survivors, they were it.

"Smith, Curwin, the tail section. If anyone's still alive, they would probably be in there," said George.

With the help of their flash lights and the dim light given off by the burning forward section they entered the plane's smoke filled tail section. The inside of the rear fuselage was a jumble of twisted metal, smashed cargo pallets and broken bodies.

"Hey Sarge, let's get out of here, there's no one left alive," hollered airman Curwin.

With the help of the dim light given off by the burning forward fuselage, George spotted a body pinned against its seat by a cargo pallet.

"Sarge, let's go."

"Wait a minute, I found someone." Forcing his way passed the pallet, George examined the body and saw that it belonged to a young woman. Checking her pulse, he saw that she was alive.

"Hey guys, come here quick, this one's alive! Rushing to his aid, the two men pushed on the pallet while George undid the girl's seat belt and pulled her from the seat. Except for a large bruise and a small cut to her head, there was no sign of serious injury. Throwing her over his shoulder, they quickly exited the plane.

"Run. She's going to blow," yelled George.

They had gotten halfway to the vehicle when the plane exploded, the blast knocking them off their feet.

"That was close, Sarge,"

"Yeah, Curwin, too close."

As he picked up the girl off the tarmac, he heard a moan . "I think she's waking up."

Reaching the Hummvee, George laid her down in the back of the vehicle and grabbed his first aid kit. Pulling out a bandage, he soaked it with water from his canteen and cleaned some of the blood off the girl's face. She stirred and opened her eyes.

"Oh, my head. Where am I, what happened? Why am I

here?" she said, rather confused.

"Take it easy, you received a nasty bump to your head," said George.

"I was on the plane, it was getting ready to leave." she then noticed what was left of the burning transport and tried to get up. George held her down. "My friends, they were all inside the plane. Where are they?"

"When the plane had started to taxi, it was hit by a rocket. There aren't any other survivors. You were the only one that we rescued."

She collapsed into George's arms sobbing. "Oh, God. All my friends, they're all dead.

"This is how war is. We never really get to see the horrors of it until it strikes home and becomes personal. Like good soldiers, we just load up the planes with bombs and missiles and send them out to do the killing," said George to the sobbing girl.

"Hey Sarge, CSC is on the radio. They want to know if there are survivors and if we need additional help" said Airman Smith.

Even if there had been fire department and emergency medical personnel available, George doubted there was much anyone could have done. Everyone on board had been killed almost instantaneously.

"Tell them there is only one survivor. Everyone else has bought it. There is nothing more that we can do."

"Roger, Sarge. And oh, there is some bad news. Enemy units

have been sighted by Greek army scouts five kilometers from our eastern perimeter."

"Gee, Smith, that's great news! Anything else to report?"

"Nope."

The girl had stopped crying and finally let go of George. "I'm sorry," she said.

"That's okay," said George reaching into his BDU jacket pocket and pulling out a cloth bandage.

"Here, clean up your face," he said handing the girl the bandage and his canteen. "I'm Master Sergeant George Pappas, flight Sergeant for the Security Force unit defending this airfield."

"I'm Sergeant Cindy Hall. I was an F-16 crew chief," she said wiping the remaining blood off her face which George noticed happened to be very pretty."

"Smith, take us to CSC."

"Okay, Sarge."

"Look Cindy, I'm taking you to security control. It's in the underground command bunker and a lot safer there for you."

"But the enemy is only a couple of kilometers away."

"Don't worry. We have enough weapons to hold them off," said George, obviously lying not to put the girl under any more stress.

"That's not what I heard. Please don't let me be captured by the enemy. I heard of some of the atrocities they've committed."

"Don't worry. We won't let them take this place."

"We're here Sarge," said Smith.

"I'll take her inside and be right back."

Walking inside the bunker's entrance, she turned and looked George straight in the eyes. "Please promise me that you won't let them take me alive."

"Look Cindy. I told you not to worry."

"Don't lie to me. I was Colonel Logan's crew chief. I know this base and everyone on it was abandoned to their fate and there isn't going to be any rescue force coming soon."

"Okay Cindy. Since you know the truth, I promise if anything happens, I will be back to get you."

"Thank you."

Entering CSC, George turned Sergeant Hall over to one of the medics so she could have the cut on her head checked.

"Hey Sarge, the Captain wants you, he's back in his office," said one of the duty command post controllers."

"Yeah, he's always in his office," said George.

George went to Captain Halverson's office and knocked on the door. "Come in."

"You wanted me, sir?"

"Yes, Sergeant. What's the status of the plane?"

"There was only one survivor."

"That's terrible. However, that's war." George wondered if this sorry excuse of an officer had even left his office to go outside to get a taste of what war was really like. But George was sure of one thing, the asshole would very soon find out the hard way.

"Yes, sir."

"Sergeant, intelligence reports place the enemy at three kilometers from the base perimeter. I expect an attack within the hour. I will direct all combat operations from CSC. I need you to be up with the troops."

"I plan to be, sir."

"Good. You will hold out as long as possible and then fall back and regroup around the command post. This will be our last line of defense."

"Right, sir." George knew that if the enemy broke through their defense positions, it was all over. There would be no final line of defense. If they were over run, he would try to save as many of his troops as he could and head for the Greek lines.

"Is that all, sir? I must get back to the troops."

"That's all, Sergeant."

Chapter 6

Limnos, Moudros Bay
0420hrs, 21 May

It had taken slightly longer than Lieutenant Genetakos had originally foreseen to infiltrate the enemy ammo dump. Encompassing several acres, the dump had been ringed with two layers of razor sharp concertina wire for security and had been surrounded with portable light units spaced fifty meters apart to provide illumination. Fortunately for the Greek commandos, the enemy was extremely short on fuel. Only every second light unit had been turned on to conserve fuel. As a result, the dump was bathed in a murky light, making it easier for the Lieutenant and his men to enter unnoticed. Initially, everything had gone to plan. Leaving two men just beyond the wire to provide cover, the rest of the team had cut through the concertina barrier, but ran into a mine field. Crawling on his hands and knees, the Lieutenant, using a bayonet, rapidly cleared a path through the mine field to the last wire. Reaching the main wire, he cut a hole, large enough for everyone to fit through.

Once inside the area, the commandos quickly fanned out and began setting the explosive charges amongst the stacked fuel barrels and munitions cases. Just as they thought they were going to pull it off and return home without incident, everything began to rapidly fall apart. One of the Lieutenant's men, while looking for a good place to plant his charges, ran into a sentry that was relieving himself behind a pile of ammo crates. The sentry was quickly and quietly dispatched before he could sound the alarm, nonetheless Lieutenant Genetakos knew that sooner or later the sentry would be missed. Unfortunately for the commandos, it turned out to be a lot sooner than they would have liked.

Sergeant Gilderim walked up to the entrance gate and observed his sentry alert and at his post. He was very pleased. The Sergeant, a strict disciplinarian, had no tolerance for slackers, especially during war time.

"How is it going tonight, Private Abdulla?"

"Fine, Sergeant. Everything is going well. They just finished offloading that boat," said Private Abdulla, pointing at the landing craft at the water's edge.

"It's getting ready to leave. I wish I were on it. This accursed island reeks of death."

"That is defeatist talk, Private. We will crush the infidels."

"Yes, Sergeant!"

"Let me in, I wish to check on the other sentries."

"At once, Sergeant!" said Private Abdulla, as he opened the gate to let Sergeant Gilderim into the dump.

"Who is guarding the back side of the dump?" asked Sergeant Gilderim.

"Private Sadik, Sergeant. He's a good soldier, a farm boy from Balikeshir."

"I'll check on him first," said the NCO.

The commandos had almost completed planting the demolition charges when of the lookouts detected someone approaching.

"Lieutenant, Marios says someone's coming," said Sergeant Iakovou.

"Shit! He'll notice the sentry's missing."

"I'll take care of him, sir."

"Okay, Sergeant. Hurry it up; we'll be finished in a few minutes. Iakovou drew his knife and disappeared in the shadows.

Sergeant Gilderim had reached the back of the dump and there was no sign of the sentry. He was beginning to get annoyed. Private Sadik was supposed to be on guard. He was nowhere to be found. If he found Sadik asleep, he'd shoot him personally and save the army the trouble. The Sergeant poked his head around a tall stack of crates containing 81mm mortar bombs. In the dim light provided by a distant light all unit, he saw Sadik sitting propped up against several ammo boxes. "The bastard's asleep," he said out loud.

"Sadik, wake up," shouted Gilderim at the same time kicking the soldier who in turn toppled over.

Sadik would not be getting up, his throat had been cut.

"My God. The enemy is in the ammo dump!" yelled Gilderim in panic.

He quickly pulled his pistol out of its holster. The Turk's sudden move had caused Sergeant Iakovou who had snuck up behind him to miss his mark. The Turkish NCO dropped the gun and let out a cry of pain at the same time Iakovou's blade gashed his side. Fighting for his life, Gilderim grabbed Iakovou's arm and gave it a twist, causing him to drop the knife. The two men struggled to the ground. Sergeant Iakovou, who had expected an easy kill, was totally caught off guard at the sudden change of events. Now, he too, was fighting for his life.

Spotting his gun, just a short distance away, Sergeant Gilderim dove for the weapon, but Iakovou was able to grab hold of one of his legs. Stopping just short of the gun, the Turk kicked out at Iakovou with his other leg, striking him a glancing blow to the head. Momentarily stunned by the blow, Iakovou let go of the Sergeant's leg. Seizing the opportunity, Gilderim immediately went for the pistol. Iakovou who quickly recovered from the blow saw his knife lying beside him, picked it up and lunged at the Turkish NCO. Sergeant Iakovou landed on top of the Turkish soldier just as he pulled the trigger. The shot reverberated throughout the ammo dump.

Lieutenant Genetakos had just finished planting the last of the charges when they heard the shot. "Jesus! It must be Iakovou. Corporal, get the men out of here. I'm going to check on the Sergeant."

"Let me do it, sir."

"No. Just do as I tell you. Get out of here before it's too late."

"Okay, sir."

With his pistol drawn, the Lieutenant ran toward the vicinity where the shot had come from. Reaching the area, he found both men embracing each other. They were both dead. Iakovou had been killed by Gilderim's shot and the enemy soldier had died by a knife wound to the heart. Since there was nothing that he could do to help Iakovou, he turned and ran toward the hole in the fence only a hundred meters away.

"Halt!"

The Lieutenant turned and fired a shot at the source of the yell and was immediately rewarded by a hail of bullets. He felt a sharp burning pain in his left shoulder as he ducked behind a stack of ammo crates. "Damn it, I've been shot, I'm pinned down and the charges are going to blow in less than twelve minutes. What else can go wrong?" Genetakos mumbled to himself. He had to get out of there fast. Any second now, more guards would show up and he'd be trapped and quickly eliminated. The enemy soldier firing at him was less than twenty meters away, behind a pile of boxes. The Lieutenant pulled a grenade off his ammo harness. What the hell, he thought. If the grenade set off the munitions prematurely, he'd be killed instantly. At least his men had gotten safely away.

Private Abdul was trembling from both fear and excitement. He had detected an enemy saboteur inside the dump and now had him cornered. Help would soon be on the way. This would most likely mean a promotion to corporal and an end to standing guard duty. From the corner of his eye, Private Abdul saw a small round object hit the ground a couple of meters from where he was standing. The object rolled toward him and stopped less than a meter away. Before his brain could rationalize that the object was a grenade, it exploded in a bright flash ripping him to shreds.

"What the hell!" exclaimed a surprised Genetakos who was still holding his grenade.

"Lieutenant! Are you okay?"

It was Corporal Moutis. His men had come back and saved his ass. "Yeah, you dumb son of a bitch, I am over here."

"We'll be right there."

A few seconds later, the Corporal and another soldier were helping the Lieutenant to his feet.

"Let me go, I'm all right."

"You're wounded," said Corporal Moutis.

"It's nothing. The bullet just grazed the shoulder. Anyway, I thought I told you to get the men out of here?"

"When we heard the commotion, the men wouldn't leave without you."

"You're all crazy. But thanks, you guys saved my ass. Now let's get the hell out of here. This place is set to blow in eight minutes and will soon be crawling with soldiers."

Moudros Bay
Same Time

Petros had just finished putting his clothes on, when he heard the gun fire coming from the direction of the ammo dump. *The Lieutenant and his men must have been discovered, he thought.* Fortunately, his short swim to the landing craft had gone off without a hitch. When he had reached the boat which was preparing to get under way, he had attached his one explosive charge on the ship's propeller guards. Not having enough charges to sink her, he planted the explosives on the ship's stern which would damage the screw and immobilize her. As soon as he had finished planting the explosives and had begun his return trip, the craft had gotten under way. It had been a very close call. Had the boat started its engines while Petros had been planting the charges, he would have been cut to shreds by the propeller.

Petros looked at the illuminated face of his watch, less than eight minutes remained till the charges detonated. The shooting had momentarily died down. He prayed that the Lieutenant and his men had made good on their escape. His hopes were quickly dashed when he heard the sound of automatic gunfire followed by a flare shooting skyward. Almost immediately, the surrounding area was bathed in the intense light given off by the parachute flare. Petros dived to the ground, just as the machine gun nest which was situated fifty meters from where he was lying opened fire.

"Damn," he mumbled. The Lieutenant and his men were pinned down. The commandos would either be cut to pieces or killed when the dump went up. He would have to do something quick or his friends would all die.

A couple hundred meters down the beach, the Lieutenant and his men were pinned down by the enemy machine gun. Tracers passed only inches above their heads. They could neither go forward nor backwards.

"Lieutenant, that dump's going to blow in five minutes," said Corporal Moutis.

"I realize that, but we wouldn't get two meters before that gun rips us to shreds."

While the Turkish machine gun was preoccupied with the commandos, Petros grabbed a grenade from his pocket and pulled the pin. Even though the flare had not yet gone out, he stood up and began running toward the gun, thirty meters away. When he was almost half way there, he was spotted by one of the ammo handlers who shouted a warning to the gunner. The gunner immediately shifted his gun and let loose a burst just as Petros flung the grenade. Petros suddenly felt as if he'd been hit by a sledge hammer in the chest. The grenade exploded in a bright flash, silencing the machine gun.

The grenade explosion caught the commandos by complete surprise. They had just been given a new lease on life.

"The gun's knocked out; it must have been the Commander. Let's get out of here fast, the dump's going to blow in a few minutes!"

"Lead the way. We're right behind you, Lieutenant," said Corporal Moutis.

Petros lay there, bleeding in the damp sand, unable to get up. He didn't feel any pain. One of the bullets had severed his spine. *The gun must have been taken out. I can't hear it any longer firing. At least the Lieutenant and his men now stood a chance of getting away, he thought.* Petros faced toward the east. He saw a faint smudge of light on the horizon. It would soon be a new day. He suddenly felt very tired. Closing his weary eyes, he began to drift off. Just before he lost consciousness, he saw Anna. She was smiling and motioning for him to come to her.

When Lieutenant Genetakos heard the grenade go off, he immediately knew what happened. Petros had taken out the gun and saved their ass. They had no time to waste; the dump would blow in a couple of minutes.

"Hurry men, we must head for the cliffs. The rocks will offer us some shelter from the blast."

The commandos had just managed to reach the cliffs and take shelter between the rocks when their charges detonated hundreds of tons of munitions and fuel. The blast was so great that the flash and explosion was seen in Turkey, almost fifty miles away to the east.

Piges Airfield
0510hrs, 21 May

After departing the underground JDOC (Joint Defense Operation Center), George proceeded to the sector where his ground defense flight was deployed. He could hear the enemy artillery pounding the sector the Greek army was defending. Luckily, USAFE/SP headquarters had sent him a heavy weapons team with a jeep mounted 90mm recoilless rifle. Because the weapon had been withdrawn from the Security Forces inventory several years prior, it had taken a couple of days to dig up the guns and personnel still knowledgeable to operate them. He had sighted the guns on each of his flanks.

The 90mm rifle would be effective against anything except a heavy main battle tank. Only a side hit on a heavy tank would have any chance of stopping it. Hopefully, the enemy wouldn't throw too many against them. George had no illusion of achieving a spectacular victory against the Turkish army. That was virtually impossible. If they really wanted to capture the base, a handful of cops and Greek soldiers wouldn't stop them. All they could do was try to exact a steep price on the enemy.

The shooting from the Greek positions had died down to an occasional sporadic shot.

"Hey Sarge, message from JDOC," said the flight radio and telephone operator man.

"What do they want, Simmons?"

"They said the Greeks have successfully repulsed an infantry attack on their positions and have inflicted heavy casualties on the enemy. The Greeks suffered only a few killed and wounded."

"That's a good start for our side. Thanks Simmons," George said to the flight radio operator. "Simmons, notify everyone to stand to. It'll probably be our turn next."

Suilliman Armored Division Headquarters
0520hrs, 21 May

The Suilliman division had halted its drive just eleven kilometers short of the Platamon River to rest and resupply. General Karakoglou was in his mobile command vehicle formulating the division battle plans for the morning attack.

When he was briefed on the failed attack on the enemy airfield, he was livid. This would set back General Guval's timetable for the Platamon offensive. The General wanted the assault on the Platamon river line to commence by mid-morning. He vented his anger on his executive officer, Colonel Nuri, who was with him in the command vehicle.

"Colonel Nuri! I have personally given my word to both Generals Kemal and Guven that the airfield would be in our hands by daybreak. I will not be humiliated by a handful of Greek and American dogs, which are surrounded, outgunned and outmanned! I want that airfield taken immediately and all in the infidels defending it, wiped out to the man! Do you understand me, Colonel?"

"Yes, sir."

"Dispatch the 31st armored Battalion, they'll do the job."

"Sir, those men are exhausted and their equipment needs servicing and maintenance."

"Colonel, you will obey my orders to the letter immediately. We are all exhausted. If you haven't realized, yet, there is a war going on!"

"Yes, General. I will issue the order."

"And Colonel, I want no prisoners taken. This will be an example to the Americans, of what happens to those that decide to ally themselves with the Greek dogs!"

The Colonel gave General Karakoglou a questioning look. "You heard me correctly. No prisoners."

"Yes sir."

Igia Hospital, Athens
0526hrs, 21 May

The hospital room housing the Mufti's daughter buzzed with activity. A string of doctors and nurses hovered over the critically injured girl now that she had come out of her comma. Even though she was still in critical condition, her chances for survival had greatly improved. The Chief of Police and the Minister of Public Order were also present in the room, along with several other high ranking officials. Everyone hoped that the girl would speak and shed some light on the gruesome crime perpetrated against her and her father.

"Doctor, will you do something. She must be able to speak and answer questions. It's vital to the nation that we find out what happened to her."

"General Makarios, as I've told you before, we are doing the best that we can. She has suffered serious injuries, both physically and mentally. The girl is lucky to still be alive," said Dr. Pikoulas.

The girl stirred as the effects of the mild stimulant that she had been given took effect. She opened her eyes for a moment. "Father, where are you?" she said unable to properly focus on the people in the room from all drugs still in her system.

"Fahtme, you are in Athens, at Igia hospital."

"What, what am I doing here?"

"You were injured, I'm Dr. Pikoulas."

"Athens?"

"Yes, Fahtme. Do you remember what happened at your

house?"

"Two men, father. He was shot. I was . . . Oh my god!" The girl began to cry as the realization of what had happened to her began to sink in.

"Fahtme, what happened to you in Kommotini? Who were those men that did this to you?"

"General, please. She can go into shock at any moment. Let me talk to her," said Dr. Pikoulas.

"Doctor, I can't begin to even try to explain to you how important it is to the nation that we find out what really happened to this girl."

"I realize this. But if this girl dies, you will never find out what happened."

"Okay doctor, the show is yours."

"Fahtme, do you hear me?"

The girl stopped crying and tried to focus on the doctor. "Fahtme, this is Dr. Pikoulas. Do you understand me?"

"Yes," said the girl.

"Fahtme, you are safe here. We want to catch the men responsible for hurting you and your father. Do you understand?"

"Ye . . . yes."

"Fahtme, were the men that hurt you, Greek?"

"My father, where is he? He was shot. Can I see him?" She said, not seeming to comprehend the question that had been asked her."

"He is dead, Fahtme," said General Makarios.

"No! I don't believe you," she said, starting to sob once more.

"It's no use, General. She is under much emotional stress and the drugs aren't helping the situation."

"Fahtme, I am General Makarios, Commander of the Greek Police. It is very important that we find the men that murdered your father and did this to you."

The sudden howl of an air raid siren could be heard going off throughout the city, followed by the lights going off in the hospital. "Damn it! They surely picked a time for an air raid," said the General.

"What is that noise?" asked the girl, apparently frightened by the siren and the lights going out.

"I'm here, don't be frightened," said Dr. Pikoulas, as he held the girl's hand.

"It's an air raid Fahtme. We are at war with Turkey. Thousands of people have been killed on both sides," said General Makarios.

"Oh, God. My people," said the girl. The hospital's emergency lights suddenly came on as the backup generator kicked in.

"Fahtme, were the men that did this to you Greek?" the General asked her once again.

"No."

A sigh of relief could be heard coming from the men in the room. "Did you know these men?"

"Yes."

"Were these men Muslims?"

A loud explosion rocked the hospital as a Scud C missile, which had penetrated the city's Patriot missile defense, landed a couple of blocks from the hospital. The girl screamed in terror.

"Fahtme, it's okay. Calm down, please!" said Dr. Pikoulas trying to calm the frightened girl.

"Damn them. That was close," remarked the General.

The girl would not calm down and continued to scream. At one point, she even tried to get up from the bed.

"Nurse, the hypo! Hurry before she hurts herself."

The nurse handed the doctor a hypodermic syringe containing Valium, which he administered to the girl. The drug quickly took effect. "She'll rest now," said the doctor.

"Sergeant, do you have everything on video?"

"Yes, sir," said the police technician, still shaking from the near miss.

General Makarios turned to the Minister of the Interior who had remained silent the whole time.

"I believe Mr. Minister that we might have enough to absolve the Greek government of any connection in this sordid affair."

"It will have to do for now, General. But we really need something more substantial. I will immediately brief the Prime Minister. The recording will be immediately aired over television," said the Minister over the wail of ambulances rushing to remove the dead and wounded from the three story apartment building that the missile had struck.

The General spoke to the policeman guarding the room.

"Patrolman, as soon as she is awake and coherent, you will call my office immediately."

"Yes, sir."

Piges Airfield
0555hrs, 21 May

As the sun rose over the airfield, the tempo of the Turkish artillery barrage on the American positions had intensified. The Air Force Security Forces who were defending the south east sector had gone on alert waiting for the attack that was sure to come. Some of their listening posts located a couple of kilometers from the airfield had earlier reported hearing engine noises. Master Sergeant Pappas had guessed correctly that noises were coming from armored vehicles and had pulled in the listening posts back to base. He was managing the whole American defense operation, even though the Captain was technically in charge.

"Sergeant Pappas, I have a message from the Captain."

"What does he want?"

"He relates that the Greeks have come under heavy artillery fire and we should possibly expect an imminent attack."

"What a brilliant deduction," said George. *The idiot was safe and secure in his bunker issuing instructions, thought George.* "Okay Smith, thanks for the info"

George heard the field phone ring. "Sarge, observation point one has spotted enemy movement five hundred meters in front of their position. Possible enemy scouts."

George looked at his grid map. "Let's send our friends a welcome card. Smith, request an 81mm fire mission at grid coordinates D.4, 3.2. Ten rounds, high explosive."

"Will do, Sarge."

A minute later, the first mortar rounds were on their way down range. The high explosive shells began landing amongst the Turkish infantry squad which had been reconnoitering the approaches to the American positions. When the last mortar round finally landed, only two of the twelve man Turkish recon squad had remained unscathed. In their first contact with the enemy, the USAF Security Force Air Base Ground Defense flight had drawn first blood for the battle for Piges airfield.

31st Armored Battalion, Two Kilometers East of Piges
0605hrs, 21 May

Lieutenant Colonel Murat glanced skyward at the stream of 122mm rockets, winging their way toward the American positions on the airfield. In a couple of minutes, the barrage would end and four companies of tanks and infantry would begin their assault on the airfield. His armored units, along with a company of infantry would hit the American positions and the rest of the assault force would attack the Greek sector. It would be overkill, but his commander wanted the airfield taken in minimum time. He could not understand the military logic behind this decision. The airfield had been abandoned by its aircraft, it could have been bypassed. It posed no threat to the

Turkish army nor did it have any strategic value at this point. His troops needed rest and the equipment needed servicing and maintenance for the upcoming attack on the Platamon River line. He would not question the decision no matter how irrational it seemed to be. One command that he did question though, was the order to take no prisoners. It was one thing to kill your enemies on the battlefield, but to kill defenseless prisoners was murder. Unfortunately, this opinion wasn't shared by the majority of his fellow officers, who considered him too soft and tainted by western ideals. To some extent this was true. During his early years in the army, he had spent a year at West Point as an exchange student. There, he had studied and trained with the Americans and had developed a respect for them and their ways. Nevertheless, orders were orders, no matter how unpleasant. He would carry them out to the best of his abilities.

The artillery and rocket barrage that had been battering the American positions had suddenly lifted. Checking his watch, Lieutenant Colonel Murat observed that it was time to begin the attack. Keying his mike, he gave the order to move over the battalion command net. The twenty Leopard II tanks and various other armored vehicles under his operational control began moving forward.

Piges Airfield, USAF SP Area of Operations
0622hrs, 21 May

Sometime during the night, George had posted himself and

his radio man in one of the larger fighting positions on the line. Technically, he should be in JDOC with the command staff. However, he could better conduct operations personally on the line with his men. Besides, on the front line, he didn't have to deal with the Captain. The artillery and rocket barrage that had been pummeling the American positions had suddenly ceased. George took this as a bad omen. The enemy would soon begin their attack on them. So far, they had been lucky. He had only lost two men when a 122mm rocket had scored a direct hit on their fighting position. He suspected that their luck was about to change. His fears were quickly realized when a series of explosions and small arms fire erupted from the Greek area of operations. It sounded to George that the Greek MILAN anti-tank gunners had gone into action and had scored a few hits.

"Simmons, get on the line with JDOC and find out what's going on."

The firing coming from the Greek zone had intensified. The crack of tank guns could clearly be heard over the small arms fire.

"Sarge, JDOC reports that the Greeks are coming under heavy attack by armored units, accompanied by infantry, possibly company strength. They have so far managed to destroy three tanks. Oh, and that last artillery barrage took out our mortar support."

"Just great, another 3 dead and our fire support gone. Any other bad news?"

"Nope, just that, Sarge."

George knew good and well that his two squads manning the line, armed with only light weapons and a few LAWS, would be no match against a company strength attack.

"Damn it. If they hit us with a dozen tanks, we're all fucked," said George.

"Sarge, observation post one reports that they've sighted armor heading this way."

That was only a kilometer away. "Have them come in, fast."

"Roger."

He would have to get reinforcements on the line fast. "Simmons, give me the mike. Tango one JDOC."

"Go ahead with your message," they replied.

"Observation post has spotted armor coming this way. Attack is imminent. Request that you immediately dispatch the reserve force."

"That's negative Tango one. They are needed to defend JDOC from potential enemy infiltrators."

That was the voice of Captain Halverson. George was infuriated.

"That fucken idiot," he said out loud. "Listen, you stupid son of a bitch." At this point George was yelling into the radio, not caring that it was heard by everyone on the net.

"We probably won't be able to stop the enemy, even with the reserve force. But if you don't dispatch them, we don't stand a chance in hell. And if by some miracle I survive and you haven't gotten a Turkish bayonet up your ass, I will personally shoot you myself!"

"I will dispatch half the force, Sergeant. And when this is over, I will bring you up on charges and make sure you're busted and end up in jail for threatening an officer."

"Fuck you, sir! Tango one out," said George savoring the moment. Anyway, they'd all probably be dead before the morning was over.

George knew they'd be fighting a losing battle. The six men that the Captain was sending from the reserve force were all armed with LAW rockets, but the weapons were virtually ineffective against heavy armor.

"Sarge, the ninety crew has a tank in sight, range 800 meters."

"Have all the other positions hold their. . . ," before George could finish his sentence one of the 90mm recoilless rifles fired. The HEAT round hit the tank dead center on its turret. The tank stopped. But as the smoke began to clear, the steel monster began moving, its turret turning searching for its attacker.

"Sarge, they didn't kill it," shouted Simmons.

"Tell them to aim for the sides. Its' frontal armor is too thick." Before the tank could find the offending gun, the mobile jeep mounted anti-tank gun fired. This time the shell struck the tank broadside, just under the turret. The shell penetrated and exploded inside, killing the crew.

"Sarge, they got the bastard!"

The six men that the Captain had sent drove up in one of grenade launcher equipped HUMMVEES. George exited the rear of the fighting position to go meet them. He recognized

Technical Sergeant Marshall who was leading the reserve force.

"What's up, Sarge?" asked Sergeant Marshall.

"Things aren't looking too good, Joe; we're barely holding our own."

"I didn't realize it was that bad."

"Neither does the Captain," said George.

"Yeah, you really pissed him off. He wanted me to relieve you of duty, but I refused to take your spot. He said he'd put me up on charges, too. I just laughed at him."

"Well, that's good to know. I don't want to start a mutiny, but that idiot is a clueless coward who'll get us all killed. Somebody has to look out for the troops."

"All the troops are behind you, Sarge."

"Thanks, Joe. Now here's the plan. I need your men to take the left flank. When the enemy tanks are in range, shoot your LAWS aiming for their tracks. We can't kill them, but we can stop them. Once you use your LAWS, fall back immediately."

"Gotcha, Sarge. Let's move it, guys."

George turned and gave instructions to the squad's HUMMVEE driver and gunner. "You two, head for that clump of trees, three hundred behind the line and don't fire until I tell you. Now move out."

George jumped back into the fighting position just as some more tank shells began raining on their positions.

"More enemy tanks at seven hundred meters, Sarge," said the machine gunner.

They all heard the distinctive blast of the 90mm anti-tank

gun. The 90mm HEAT round struck the tank's side, entered the engine compartment and exploded. Flame and thick black smoke could be seen pouring out of the tank. Its crew quickly abandoned it, only to be cut down by accurate M-4 rifle fire coming from the American positions. The reserve force which had gotten into position quickly fired off their LAWS at the three remaining tanks. The 60mm rockets struck two of the tanks destroying their tracks. Immobilized, but still dangerous, one of the tanks fired off a burst of machine gun fire, killing two of the escaping LAW gunners. The third tank, unscathed, continued forward until hit by a 90mm shell that ripped into its crew compartment, killing everyone inside. This time luck had run out for the anti-tank crew. A salvo of 120mm shells fired by the two immobilized tanks exploded right in front of the speeding jeep, causing the driver to lose control and roll the vehicle over. Both the driver and gunner were killed instantly, crushed by the vehicle rolling over them.

The enemy infantry which had been following behind the tanks quickly went into action. With fixed bayonets and supported by cannon fire from the two immobilized Leopards tanks, they charged forward. The American positions immediately opened up with a hail of machine gun, fifty caliber and automatic rifle fire cutting down most of the first wave thrown against them. Ordered to exterminate the Americans at all costs, the Turkish NCOs pressed their men forward. One by one, the American positions began coming under direct fire. Slowly but surely, the Turks began gaining ground.

After two of his positions had been knocked out by enemy LAWS, George decided to use his last Ace. Getting on the radio, he ordered the HUMMVEE that had been hiding in the clump of trees to go into action. The gunner quickly opened up, unleashing a deadly stream of high explosive 40mm grenades at the Turkish infantry. Unable to withstand this withering barrage of high explosive fire, the enemy retreated, leaving scores of dead and wounded in front of the American line. Seeing their comrades in full retreat and fearing that the Americans would turn their attention on them next, the two tanks crews abandoned their vehicles, much to the relief of Master Sergeant Pappas. Cheers could be heard coming from the American positions. Unfortunately, their success would be short lived.

31st Armored Battalion
Same Time

The report that Lieutenant Colonel Murat had just received over the command net, had turned his blood to ice. The attack on the American positions had failed. An entire armored company had been mauled and he had no gains to show for it. He had to act immediately. Command would not accept another failure. The price for failure would most likely be a firing squad. He must finish the job before headquarters received the news. Transmitting over the unit command net, he gave the orders for his reserve company to attack.

With his tank in the lead, the twelve tanks of Delta Company surged forward. This time he would have no artillery support to soften up the enemy positions. All of the division's batteries were re-positioning themselves and stockpiling ammunition for the upcoming attack on the Platamon River. He would use brute force to achieve his objective. At least he'd rather die facing the enemy than be shot by his own soldiers for failure.

Piges Airfield, USAF/SP Area of Operations
0651hrs, 21 May

The air force cops had used the small respite to remove their dead and provide first aid to the wounded. The casualties to the sky cops had been heavy, seven killed and three wounded, two seriously. Lacking a doctor, all they could do for the wounded was to make them comfortable and transport them to JDOC where they'd be safer. Without hospital care, the serious cases would probably be dead by nightfall.

It wasn't too long before the sound of heavy gun fire could once again be heard coming from the Hellenic army positions to the northwest.

"Sarge, JDOC says the Greeks are catching hell from enemy armor. It's doubtful if they can hold out much longer."

"Thanks, Simmons."

That wasn't exactly the news George wanted to hear. Another attack by the enemy on his positions and they'd also be finished. He had to quickly consider their options. If the Turks broke through the Greek line, he and his men were screwed. They were trapped. With their backs to the sea and Turks barreling down on them from two sides, they too, would be hammered to pieces. Their only options would be to attempt a breakout and head for the Greek lines at the Platamon River or surrender to the Turks. An option George didn't exactly relish. The high-pitched whine of incoming tank fire interrupted George's thoughts.

"I think this is going to be it for us, Sarge," said Airman Kostner who was on the position's machine gun.

George heard the field phone ring. He put the receiver to his ear. "This is position three, have sighted four enemy tanks, distance eight hundred meters."

George put down the phone and took the radio from Simmons. "Tango one, JDOC."

"Go ahead Tango one."

"Request to pull back. We've sighted four enemy tanks. We have no means at our disposal to stop them."

"Negative Tango one. You will hold your position," said the voice of Captain Halverson.

"George grabbed the transmitter. "Listen you cowardly son of a bitch. We are all going to die here for nothing. Our only chance is to attempt a break out while we still have some means to do so."

"I am ordering you to hold your position."

"Sergeant Pappas, position four reports two more armored vehicles backed by infantry sighted," said Airman Simmons.

This made George's mind up. He would not sacrifice his men's lives for the sake of an incompetent officer.

"Simmons, issue the order for everyone to fall back. We'll meet at JDOC."

"Roger, Sarge."

Before the order could be given, JDOC was on the radio. "Be advised Tango one that the Greeks are falling back. Enemy armor has broken through their line."

"Roger JDOC, we'll also be withdrawing from our positions," said George not waiting for a confirmation from Captain Halverson.

"Sarge, let's get the hell out of here. The enemy tanks are only five hundred meters away," said the machine gunner.

"Okay, grab the radio, and let's move,"

With the pullback order given, the sky cops began falling back toward the center of the base, tossing smoke grenades to cover their withdrawal. Yet even with the smoke screen, many of them fell dead or wounded to the heavy tank and machine gun fire that was still raining down on them. Unable to take their wounded along, they were left where they lay in the hope that they would be given medical attention as stipulated by the Geneva Convention. Unknown to the Americans, the Turks weren't abiding by the Geneva Convention today. When the advancing enemy infantry came upon a wounded American, he was either shot or bayoneted on the spot.

With the enemy hot on their heels, Master Sergeant Pappas was only able to gather up a small group of survivors. They all quickly headed toward the center of the airfield where JDOC was located. Pausing momentarily to catch their breath, the radio man attempted to contact JDOC.

"Sergeant Pappas, I can't get JDOC.

"Maybe their antenna's been damaged," said George.

"I hope that's the problem, Sarge," said Simmons.

"Okay, let's move it. JDOC is just behind those hangers," said George pointing to the structures, two hundred meters away.

"Lawson and Thompson, check out those hangers. We'll cover you, but hurry, we don't have much time."

"Sure thing, Sarge," said Lawson. A couple of minutes later, the two airmen motioned for the rest of the group to come over. When they reached the hangers, George was almost out of breath.

"It's a bitch running with all this gear," said George.

"That ain't the only thing that's a bitch, "replied Airman First Class Thompson. "The enemy beat us to the bunker,"

"Oh fuck. What are we going to do now?" asked Tech Sergeant Marshall.

"My God," said George to himself, suddenly remembering the promise that he had made to Sergeant Cindy Hall.

Both men crawled to the edge of the hanger; George could see a large group of Greeks and Americans with their hands up in the air, lined up against the side of the bunker. Several of the prisoners were being searched by their captors. About a dozen meters away was a BMR-600 armored personnel carrier with a soldier atop the cupola, manning the 12.7mm machine gun. George heard a woman's scream.

"Don't touch me you dirty bastard."

It was Cindy. He saw an enemy soldier dragging her away from the group of prisoners and toward the bunker's entrance. One of the other prisoners attempted to intervene, but he was immediately clubbed to the ground by several rifle butts.

"Sarge, we have to do something," said Morrison.

Before George could answer, one of the enemy soldiers who appeared to be an officer yelled something to the BMR gunner. The gunner nodded and cut loose with his machine gun.

"The bastards are shooting them," yelled Marshall as he jumped to his feet.

George barely managed to grab a hold of him and pulled him back around the corner of the building.

"Wait a minute! If you run out there that gun will cut you to pieces and then get the rest of us. We have to do this right the first time. Now, how many LAWS do we have left?"

"Two," said Marshall.

They could still hear Cindy screaming as she was being dragged into the bunker.

"Listen up, men. I can't ask you to risk your lives just to rescue a girl, but remember those bastards just murdered our friends. We can try to save her and kill all those murderers in the process or turn around and try to escape through their lines."

Marshall was first to reply. "Let's kill the bastards."

"Yeah, let's waste 'em," said Thompson. Everyone nodded in agreement.

"Hand me the LAWS," said George.

"Johnson, I want you to climb up the ladder over there and set up the sixty on the roof. When the first LAW goes off, open up with all you got."

"Okay, Sarge." Wrapping several belts of 7.62 ball ammo over his neck, he slung the machine gun over his shoulder and began climbing the ladder to the hanger's roof.

"The rest of you, once that BMR is knocked out, you run like hell toward the bunker. Shoot whatever moves. We rescue the girl, then hightail it out of here. The rest of them will be here any minute."

Once their machine gunner was in position, George and Technical Sergeant Marshall armed their LAWS.

"Marshall, if I miss, you've got to get the APC, or we're all toast. Remember, they aren't taking prisoners."

"Okay, Sarge."

"Let's do it then."

Holding the anti-tank rockets in their arms, both men ran from the cover of the hanger. One of the Turks spotted the pair and hollered a warning to the rest. The gunner swung his machine gun around to fire, but George let loose first. The anti-tank rocket hit the BMR ripping through the thin armor, killing everyone inside. At that same moment, their machine gunner on the hanger's rooftop opened fire, sending a stream of 7.62mm copper jacketed rounds ripping into the Turkish infantry men. Those not killed outright by the machine gun fire, were shot down by George and his men. Reaching the bunker's entrance, George peeked inside. Everything looked clear. Dropping his

M-4, he un-holstered his 9mm issue Beretta, entered the dim stairwell and proceeded down the stairs, accompanied by two other security troops.

"Watch it!" screamed Airman Kern, as an enemy soldier jumped out of the shadows.

The Beretta barked twice, the shots reverberating in the confined stairwell. The 9mm rounds struck the soldier full in the chest, dropping him to the ground. Reaching the bottom level, they heard another scream.

"She's still alive. In here!" yelled George.

The three of them burst into the command center, Cindy was lying on the ground, her pants had been pulled down and shirt pulled off, exposing her breasts.

"Look out. He's behind the table! But the warning came too late. Several bursts of automatic fire ripped through the bunker. When the shooting was over, the enemy soldier was dead, but so was Airman Kerns. George rushed over to Cindy who was sobbing. She threw her arms around him, "I thought you wouldn't come."

"Are you all right?"

"Yes, I think so. They tried to rape me," she said wiping the tears from her face.

"We have to get out of here. The rest of them will be here any minute."

Cindy put her shirt back on, straightened herself up and picked up Kern's M-4 off the floor.

"I know how to use it. I won't be taken alive by them again!"

"Let's go, "said George, putting his arm around the girl.

Exiting the bunker, they met up with the rest of the squad. "Where's Kern," asked Marshall.

"He bought it," replied George.

"Hey, Sergeant Pappas, I see tanks coming," yelled the sixty gunner from the top of the hanger.

"Hurry up and get down here. We're leaving," yelled George.

"I'll be right down."

31st Armored Battalion
Same Time

With his tank in the lead, Lieutenant Colonel Murat guided the rest of the formation toward the center of the airfield. He should have been happy of his victory, but he wasn't particularly gloating, since he had lost almost two armored companies to achieve it. Nevertheless, it was a success; the remainder of his battalion was mopping up the last remnants of resistance. His troops had taken no prisoners in accordance with the General's wishes. That was one thing he was not proud of. The message he had just received from division had even boasted his spirits higher and relieved some of the recent tension he had been going through. His battalion would not be utilized in the opening stages of the offensive against the Platamon River line. Instead, they would stay at the airfield and await reinforcements and supplies. He could only thank Allah for their good fortune. The unit was severely understrength and the men were totally exhausted. A refit was just what the unit needed.

"Enemy sighted, twelve o'clock atop the hanger," shouted the gunner.

Colonel Murat looked up and saw the man running on the hanger roof top. He was carrying something that looked like a portable anti-tank missile.

"Cheetah one to all units, enemy sighted twelve o'clock! Fire on the hanger."

The loud crack of several tank guns firing almost at once, made the Colonel duck back inside the turret. The section of the hanger where the enemy soldier had been running was simultaneously hit by several shells causing that part of the structure to collapse in a cloud of dust.

"Cease fire, cease fire. Save your ammo, we may need it later," said Colonel Murat over the command net.

Fearing any further losses to his armor from anti-tank traps, the Colonel directed his tanks to halt and ordered his armored personnel carriers forward. Three BMR-600 APCs pulled to the front of the column and disgorged their troops who immediately began deploying toward the hangers. The Colonel took advantage of this temporary halt and lit a cigarette. Taking a deep drag, he savored the thick aromatic smoke of Turkish tobacco. *Perhaps he thought to himself, he just might live to see tomorrow.*

Chapter 7

Piges Airfield
0745hrs, 21 May

George heard the enemy tank fire. His sixty gunner disappeared in a cloud of dust and smoke as the section of the hanger's roof he had been on collapsed after being hit by the tank rounds. George quickly came to the realization that they were virtually surrounded and the possibility of escaping through the Turkish lines was slim. Their only avenue of escape now was toward the sea, a few kilometers to the southwest.

"Sarge, what do we do now? asked Airman Simmons.

George looked at what was left of his ABGD flight. Nine exhausted men and a girl. It wasn't much if they had to fight their way through toward the coast.

"We better head for the beach. It's our only hope to escape. Maybe we can hide out there till night fall and then try to sneak through their lines," said George hoping to boost their flagging morale.

"We're with you, Sarge," said Airman Simmons speaking for the rest of the group.

"Me, too. I won't be captured by those bastards again," said Cindy.

"Let's move it then. Everyone, keep your eyes open. The enemy will be here any minute."

The squad spread out in traveling formation and headed at a brisk run toward the beach. They had not gone more than a hundred meters when someone gave the warning to take cover. Everyone immediately hit the dirt, just as a stream of machine gun bullets tore up the ground around them.

"Now we're really screwed," said Marshall who was sharing the small dirt mound that George and Cindy were using for cover.

George snuck a quick peak above the mound. It instantly drew a stream of machine gun fire. What he'd seen in his brief glimpse wasn't good. A squad of enemy infantry men had come from around the partially demolished hanger and had set up a machine gun. The gun had effectively pinned them down while the rest of the enemy squad began to advance toward their location. If they didn't move or do something soon, they would all be dead in the next few minutes.

As he scanned the area looking for an escape route, George noticed one of the HUMMVEES they had brought over with them, parked beneath a couple of trees not more than a hundred feet away. He could see that it had a MK-19 grenade launcher mounted on the roof. If only they could get to the vehicle, they might stand a chance to get away.

"Marshall, there's our way out," said George pointing to the vehicle.

"Sarge, we'll be cut to pieces before we get ten feet."

"Either way, we're dead if we stay here."

"Since you put it that way, let's go for it."

George yelled out to the rest of the squad.

"Listen Up! When I say now, I want everybody to start shooting. Morris, use your 203 and lob a couple of grenades toward the machine gun. All I need from you guys is to keep their heads down, while we go for the HUMMVEE," said George.

"Okay, Sarge," yelled Morris. Everybody shouted their acknowledgment.

Both George and Marshall quickly dumped their flak vest and helmet so they could run faster. "Are you ready?"

I am if you are," said Marshall.

"Let's do it. Now!"

George heard the loud rapport as the 40mm grenade left the M-203's barrel. When the grenade hit the ground, the explosion was drowned out by the noise of the rest of the squad opening up. Both men took off at a fast run. Fortunately, luck was with them. The 203 grenade had landed within a couple of meters of the gun, showering the gunner with dirt. Unable to see because of dirt in his eyes, the gun fell temporarily silent. The rest of the enemy squad had automatically gone to ground. It was the chance that George and Marshall needed. Reaching the vehicle, George hopped into the driver's seat, while Marshall took the gunner's position and charged the gun. George hit the starter and the engine roared to life.

"We got about a hundred rounds left in the can," shouted Marshall.

George put the vehicle in gear and floored the pedal. The

Hummer took off with Marshall working the gun. The enemy squad was cut to pieces by a dozen high explosive grenades that landed amongst them. George pulled the vehicle up to where the rest of the squad was and everybody quickly piled in. Those not fitting inside held on to whatever they could.

"Tanks!" screamed Marshall from the gunner's position

"Fuck! That's all we need," said George as he began zigzagging all over the road to make themselves a more difficult target for the enemy gunners.

The lead tank fired on the fleeing vehicle at less than half a mile range. The shell zoomed overhead and exploded several meters to the rear, showering the vehicle with shrapnel. George a heard a high pitched scream.

"We lost Martinez, stop the vehicle!" yelled Marshall.

"If I stop, we'll all be killed."

Several more shells zoomed overhead and exploded a dozen meters to the side. Fortunately, no one else was hit. The tanks faded from view as George took a curve. "Hold on!" he yelled.

The vehicle left the paved road and entered a narrow bumpy dirt road surrounded by tall bamboo plants that led toward the beach. George slowed down a bit as not to lose anyone that was hanging on to the vehicle. They finally reached the beach ten minutes later.

"We made it and we just might be in luck," said George, pointing to a Kaiki, a type of Greek fishing boat, anchored just offshore.

Stopping the vehicle at the water's edge, everyone quickly

jumped off and formed a defensive perimeter around the HUMMVEE.

"Hopefully, that's our ticket out of here. We've got fifteen to twenty minutes at the most before the Turks get here. We better get started," said George.

"Do you know how to sail that thing?" asked Cindy.

"My dear, all Greeks are natural born sailors."

George's comment drew a laugh from everyone. "Right Sarge, just don't get us lost like Odysseus," said Marshall.

"Right, wise guy. Take down the MK-19; we might need its fire power. Hey, does anyone know anything about diesel engines?"

"I do, Sergeant Pappas," said Senior Airman Jefferson.

"Before I joined the air force, I used to help my dad work on his equipment on our farm."

"Well Jefferson, there's our ticket out of here, let's get it running."

George and Jefferson quickly stripped to their shorts. Just as they entered the water, a shot rang out. They all hit the dirt.

"I saw somebody moving in the bushes, over there," said Airman Simmons.

"No shoot. I filos, friend, I Greek!"

"Wait. Don't fire," said George. George yelled out in Greek for the person to come out with his hands up. Slowly with his hands in the air, the man came out. He was in his early twenties, of medium build and wearing a Greek Army uniform. Two of George's men went and searched him.

"He's clean, Sarge."

"Who are you? said George to the handsome dark haired young man.

"I'm Sergeant Theodoros Peratos. I was with the Greek army unit defending the base perimeter. The enemy broke through our lines. All my comrades are dead. The bastards took no prisoners.

"How did you manage to get away?"

"I was knocked unconscious by a grenade blast. When I woke up, the Turkish infantry had already passed. They had mistaken me for dead. I want kill all those fucken bastards," said Theodoros in broken English.

"We all do," said Marshall.

"Theodoros, do you have a weapon?" asked George.

"Yes, it's in the bushes. I'll go get it." A few seconds later Theodoros emerged, carrying a G-3 assault rifle and several pouches of ammunition.

"He's bleeding," said Cindy.

"You tend to him. We're going for the boat. Marshall, hurry up and take down that gun. We may need it."

"I only have about seventy rounds left for it," said Sergeant Marshall.

"It'll have to do. We don't have much time. George dove into the choppy water, followed by Jefferson, and swam towards the anchored fishing boat.

31st Armored
0801hrs, 21 May

Lieutenant Colonel Murat peered through the thick acrid smoke coming from the burning BTR at the corpses of the executed Americans. Next to the bodies of the slain Americans, lay the bodies of their executioners. *At least, he thought, his country men died like soldiers with weapons in hand, not shot down like dogs as the Americans had.* The last report he received, had related that the Americans responsible for the destruction of the BTR and the death of his soldiers were last seen heading south. Not that it really mattered, the airfield was secured and the Americans were surrounded and had no place to go. The noose was slowly tightening around them. They would all be dead within the hour. It was time to finish the hunt. He would dispatch a squad to deal with the Americans.

"Cheetah one to Bravo Company, you will immediately dispatch a squad to track down and destroy the Americans. They are believed to be heading south toward the beach. All other units will resume operations," said Colonel Murat over the command net.

"Sir, message from division. We are being immediately recalled to the line. It seems we'll be taking part in this morning's attack," said his radio man while handing Colonel Murat the coded message.

They must all be insane, he thought, as he read the message. He had been told the unit would rest and refit. His men were all exhausted. There was no way they could keep going like this.

"Driver, head for the coast. I want to handle the elimination of the Americans personally."

"Yes, sir!" said the tank driver, as he put the giant metal beast in gear.

Piges Beach
0813hrs, 21 May

George was really beginning to get worried. They were having difficulty in getting the boat's old engine started. If they failed to get it going within the next couple of minutes, their escape attempt would end in disaster.

"How's it going, Jefferson?"

"I've cleaned the injectors, Sarge. I'll be ready to give it another try in a couple of minutes."

"We don't have a couple of minutes, Jefferson. How's the fuel situation?"

"Jesus, I'm doing the best I can. The tank's about 3 quarters full"

"I'm sorry. I know you are, Jefferson. At least we have gas."

George began hauling in the anchor rope. "Don't mind me, Jefferson. We have to get everyone aboard and we don't have time to waste." Jefferson ignored George and kept on working. Once the anchor was in, George tied a line to the bow, jumped into the water and swam to shore. Reaching the shore, he was helped out of the water by Marshall.

"Grab the rope and pull the boat in. We have to get everyone aboard. We have no time to spare, they'll be here soon."

Once the boat was beached in shallow water, George motioned for everyone to get inside. After everyone had climbed aboard, George and Theodoros pushed the boat into deeper water and climbed in.

"Thompson, Jones, grab the oars and start rowing like your life depended on it." Slowly the boat began moving into deeper water, when they were about 500 meters into the bay, Marshall pointed towards the shore.

"I hear engines!"

They could all clearly hear the deep throated roar of the heavy diesel engines in the distance. The enemy would soon reach the beach.

"Jefferson, get the engine started now or we are all dead."

"She's ready to go Sergeant Pappas. Here goes nothing." Jefferson hit the starter. The motor turned over, coughed and spattered to life. Everyone erupted in cheers, but their joy was short lived as the engine sputtered a few times and died.

"Try it again!" yelled George.

"The battery is really low, it might not work."

"If it doesn't, then we're dead anyway," said George.

Jefferson hit the starter and the old engine roared to life. "Yes! She's running, Sarge."

"Give her all she's got. They'll be here any minute!"

Jefferson pushed the throttle all the way forward. Slowly at first, the boat began moving forward and gradually picked up speed. George took the tiller and pointed the bow toward the mouth of the small inlet, less than a mile away.

"Can't this thing go any faster?" asked Cindy.

"This is all she's got. About twelve miles per hour," said George. Cindy didn't look too pleased with the answer. They were still a half kilometer from the inlet when the first enemy tank reached the shore line.

"Jesus! There they are," Marshall pointed to a tank that had reached the beach. The tank fired.

"Everybody down," screamed George.

The first shell struck the water, less than a hundred meters behind them sending up a large plume of water. In the matter of a few seconds, it was followed by a string of shells that straddled the small boat.

"They have our range!" yelled George in panic. He jammed the tiller hard to the right putting the boat into a tight turn, hoping to spoil the enemy gunners targeting.

The next salvo barely missed, sending a large plume of water cascading over the gunwales, causing the boat to pitch up violently. Cindy who had been holding on to the railing lost her grip and was tossed into the water. Sergeant Peratos, who had been sitting next to her, pulled off his boots and dove into the sea to help the foundering girl. George had seen Cindy fall into the water and the Greek soldier who jumped in after her, but if he stopped to pick them up, they would be blown out of the water. Seconds later, the boat had rounded the point and was out of sight of the Turkish gunners. Throttling back to idle, he could see Theodoros struggling to keep the girl above water.

"Franklin, tie that rope end to the stern davit and throw it out as we go by."

"Okay, Sarge."

George yelled out to the Greek soldier telling them what they were going to do. Pushing the throttle to the stops, the small fishing boat surged forward. The enemy tanks which had ceased fire were caught by surprise when the boat reemerged from around the point. It was the opportunity that George had needed.

"Throw it, now!"

Franklin tossed the rope which landed only a few feet from Theodoros and Cindy. They both grabbed the rope and held on for dear life. George put the boat into a hard turn and headed for the mouth of the inlet. The boat was less than a hundred meters from safety when the enemy gunners opened fire. The shell screamed overhead and struck the face of the rocky point sending pieces of rock flying. A few seconds later the boat had reached safety. George throttled down.

"Help them aboard," ordered George.

After both had been helped aboard, they quickly stripped the wet clothes off Cindy who had turned blue from the cold water and covered her with an old blanket, found in the boat's cabin. Theodoros had also stripped to his shorts and hung his wet clothes on the mast next to Cindy's to dry.

"Oh, that water was cold," said Cindy as she pulled the blanket tighter around her.

"You can thank Theodoros for pulling you out of the water or you'd be fish bait," said George.

"Yes, I think I will." Cindy turned, hugged the Greek soldier and gave him a kiss to the lips.

"I owe you my life," she said,

"Let's get moving. We have to get out of here soon, or you all might be sorry you came along," said George pointing to the storm clouds blowing in from the northwest.

"You're getting old, Sarge." Marshall said, loud enough for everyone to hear. The comment brought instantaneous laughter to the rest of the squad.

George smiled. Laughter was a good sign. They could still crack jokes after all they had been through. Their spirit had not been broken.

"Jefferson, hold the tiller. Keep her bow pointed out to sea. Everybody else gather round." George showed them all an old chart that he had found in the boat's small cabin.

"Okay everybody. Here are our choices. We can head this way. Here is the city of Kavala. It's about fifteen miles to the east across this bay," he said pointing to the chart.

"The only problem is, it's within the range of the Turkish guns. If they happen to break through the Greek defense lines, the city will fall. Our other option is to head for the island of Thassos," said George pointing to the smudge of land barely visible on the horizon.

"The Turks, for the time being, have left Thassos alone. We should be safe there."

"I think we should head for the island. I don't want to run into those bastards again," said Cindy. There was a murmur of agreement by everyone present.

"Okay, Thassos it is." George pointed the old fishing boat's bow toward the island, twenty miles away to the south.

Argyrokastron, Albania
0855hrs, 21 May

Throughout the night and early morning hours, what remained of the shattered Albanian army streamed back across the frontier in total disarray. After losing most of their armored reserve in the battle for Igoumenitsa, it was only a matter of time before the rest of the front collapsed. During the night, the main road leading from Ioannina to Igoumenitsa had been cut by armored units from the Greek 21st armored brigade. Thousands of Albanian soldiers had been trapped by the advancing Greek tanks and forced to surrender or face total annihilation. These same soldiers, who days prior stood at the gates of Igoumenitsa as conquerors, entered the same city as prisoners of war. Their captors marched them to the port to await transportation to prison camps being set up on the island of Corfu.

The Greek offensive that had begun during the night had pushed to within ten kilometers of the Albanian frontier. In an attempt to stem the Greek advance, General Hoxa had ordered the remnants of his air force committed to battle. Though successful in temporarily stemming the Greek drive, the Albanian air force, for all purposes, had ceased to exist.

Deep inside his underground command center, the Albanian dictator was pouring over a map of the front. He was desperately trying to find a way to stave off a total military disaster. Present in the room were several other senior officers. General Hoxa looked up from the map.

"General Alia, I want the 14th Infantry brigade to be deployed at Ktismata."

"Sir, the 14th no longer exists."

"What do you mean?"

"They were wiped out in an early morning counter attack against an enemy armored battalion."

"I see," said General Hoxa.

He glanced at the map one more time. "I see that the 9th Infantry battalion is just south of the border. Have them . . .," before he had finished, General Alia interrupted.

"Sir, the 9th surrendered last night. They had been cut off and surrounded by enemy armor."

"What! The traitorous scum surrendered to the enemy while their brothers were bravely dying for the glory of Albania."

"Sir, they were cut off, out of ammo and surrounded by superior enemy forces."

"That is defeatist talk. I had given specific orders that no one will surrender."

"But sir, they would all have been annihilated."

General Hoxa flew into a fit of rage and slapped General Alia across the face.

"You coward! I'm immediately relieving you of command. You are not fit to lead a group of boy scouts! You will fight the enemy as a common soldier."

Alia was trembling from fear. He knew that the General had been merciful with him. He could have been shot.

"General Berisa, you will immediately assume the position of Chief of Staff."

"Yes, sir."

"You will immediately order all units to stand and fight where they are. All territorial Security units will be deployed to the border. We will defend our borders at all costs."

"Sir, some of these units are needed to keep the Greek minority in line."

"We can no longer afford the luxury of babysitting these traitors. Have all their leaders and priests arrested and have ten of them executed as a warning to the others."

"But, sir, world opinion."

"Damn world opinion and do as I tell you!"

"At once, General!"

General Berisa turned to leave. "Berisa, what can be done with the people's Militia?"

"We can probably raise four Brigades within the next twenty-four hours, sir"

"Excellent! Do it and have them deployed immediately. We will stop the enemy at our borders and hold them until our Turkish brothers are victorious!"

General Berisa knew that it would be almost impossible for the lightly armed People's Militia to stop the Greek armored units that would shortly be bearing down on them. However, he feared for his life if he addressed the issue. The war was not going at all as planned. For all practical purposes, they had lost and should be suing for a cease fire. This lunatic was leading them to ruin.

"As you wish, sir.

"And General, see that all commanders are briefed that any talk of surrender will be punishable by death. Inform any unit that surrenders to the enemy that the families of the officers in command will be immediately arrested and executed."

"Yes, sir," said General Berisa, ashamed of himself for not speaking out. He knew only a miracle would save them from this lunatic.

"Now, all of you get out of here and carry out your instructions."

General Berisa and the rest of the staff had just exited the command bunker when the wail of a nearby air raid siren sounded. Berisa turned toward the bunker's entrance that was less than a dozen meters away. He could see most of the other officers running toward the bunker. For some unknown reason, he decided not to go back down and ran toward a small sandbagged trench, a hundred meters from the bunker's entrance. Reaching the trench, the General heard the sound of aircraft coming in from the southwest. Simultaneously, several nearby anti-aircraft emplacements opened fire. He knew the gunners had little chance of hitting the speeding planes with their antiquated equipment. The loud roar of the jets hurt his ears. He looked up and saw three planes flying at an altitude of five hundred meters. From what he knew of NATO aircraft, he identified them as F-15 Strike Eagles. *The bunker must be their target, he thought.* The first plane broke off and turned toward the bunker followed by the other two. He watched as one of the planes released a long shinny object, a bomb. What can one bomb do, he wondered? The large bomb continued its path toward the bunker and then disappeared. A couple of seconds later, the General felt the ground rumble beneath his feet. He watched in awe, as the bunker's twenty ton steel door blew off its fittings and sailed through the air as if it were made out of paper.

"My God! It was a laser guided bomb!" he said aloud. For a moment, he remembered the scenes on TV of the Gulf war. The Americans had destroyed several Iraqi bunkers using special designed laser guided smart weapons that could enter through ventilator shafts. He had just witnessed the use of one of these bunker busting weapons.

The General remained in his shelter while the fighter bombers circled the target area checking on their work. Since there was no need to use another bomb on the bunker, the planes turned for home, their mission accomplished. When the roar of the jet engines faded toward the south, General Berisa stood up and brushed the dirt from his uniform. He began walking toward the bunker. Heavy smoke was pouring from its entrance. The rescue teams that would be going inside to search for survivors began to form up. There was little chance of finding anyone inside alive. Hoxa was dead. The miracle that he had hoped for had just occurred. Hopefully, as one of the few senior surviving army general staff members, he might just be able to end this madness. Conceivably, he could even salvage what was left of the country and the Albanian armed forces.

Northern Aegean, seven miles NW of Thasos
0945hrs, 21 May

With every turn of its screw, the small fishing boat left the Greek mainland farther behind and took its passengers closer to safety. George had kept the old engine at full power until they were safely out to sea before he throttled it back on Jefferson's advice. It would be at least another hour at their present speed before they reached Thassos. With his hand firmly on the tiller, George kept the boat's bow pointed toward the island which was now clearly visible to the south. They had been lucky this far. Looking to the northwest at approaching storm clouds, George suspected they would be in for a major blow. The freshening wind was already beginning to pick up the sea spray, drenching the small boat's passengers. He prayed that they would reach the island before the storm broke.

"I don't like the look of those clouds," said Theodoros to George in Greek, not to frighten the others present.

"Me neither. Looks like a squall brewing," said George.

"A Bourini, the fishermen call it," said Theodoros.

"It only lasts about an hour or two. Unfortunately for us, it can generate up to force nine winds."

"That is all we need," answered George worriedly, looking at the lightning flashes which were getting closer.

"This Kaiki can take it. They are very strongly built," said Theodoros.

"I don't think we will reach shore before the storm breaks,"

"Unfortunately, I think you're right, Sarge. There's a boat heading this way," yelled Marshall, pointing to the east.

George looked eastward and saw the approaching boat. "Theodoros stay outside. You are not wearing a uniform. They will probably think you are a fisherman. Hurry! The rest of you, inside." Those not already in the cabin rushed inside.

"You think they've seen us?" asked Marshall.

"We'll know soon enough. Here, grab the tiller." George went to his pack and pulled out his binoculars and put them to his eyes. "It's a small patrol boat, probably armed with 40mm cannons."

"Large enough to blow us out of the water," said Marshall.

The patrol boat which was on a westerly heading, suddenly made a small course correction and exposed its stern. George saw her flag that was hanging from her mast. Slowly, he put down his binoculars.

"What is it?" asked Marshall.

"They've seen us. She's Turkish."

"Oh, God, what do we do now?"

"The only chance we have is to hit her with the grenade launcher if she comes close enough. With those guns, she can blow us out of the water long before we are in range with our gun. Let's hope they think we're a couple of fishermen out for a catch and leave us alone."

"Fishing, with a war on?"

"Wars come and go in these parts. People still have to eat," said George.

The patrol boat Natalya had been patrolling near Thassos since early morning. Sailing from the captured enemy port city of Alexandroupolis, her orders were to intercept and destroy any enemy shipping plying the waters between Thassos and the mainland. Thassos had not yet been attacked and command wanted to prevent any further supplies and reinforcements reaching the island. So far, her patrol had proved fruitless, until her radar operator had reported a small contact to the west. Her commander, Lieutenant Edin, had ordered the helmsman to change course and intercept the small target. When they had neared enough for visual identification, the target had proved to be a small fishing boat. Edin was disappointed, but his men could have some fun using the small boat for target practice. Not wanting to waste expensive 40mm ammunition for such a small target, he would let his 50 caliber gun crew do the job. At point blank range, the 50 caliber shells would tear the small wooden boat to shreds.

Marshall stood by the covered MK-19 trying not to look scared, but in reality, he was terrified.

"Sarge, they're getting closer."

George observed the approaching patrol boat. He could see the gun crew on the boat's bow operating what looked to be a heavy machine gun.

"Yeah, I can see and I think they mean business," said

George. "Don't fire until I tell you. You have to hit her the first time or we're all fucked!"

"Don't worry, Sarge. We don't have the ammunition to waste anyway," said Marshall.

George waited nervously while the enemy boat closed the range. At a hundred and fifty meters, George gave the order to shoot. Marshall ripped the canvas cover off the gun and immediately opened fire, sending a stream of 40mm high explosive grenades into the patrol boat. Grabbing an M-4, George rushed out and opened fire on the enemy gunners. The first few 40mm shells struck the bridge instantly killing her captain. Surprised, the enemy gun crew which had been awaiting the order to fire began shooting back. George could feel the heavy slugs hitting the boat, but he quickly breathed a sigh of relief when several of Marshall's shells hit the boat's forward section, taking out the enemy gun. After what seemed an eternity, the firing stopped.

"That's all our ammo," said Marshall.

"I don't think we need anymore," said George as he pushed the throttle to full speed.

The patrol boat with flames pouring through its hatchways was almost a kilometer astern when it suddenly exploded in a thunderous roar, as the flames reached its ammunition stores.

"We did it. Sent the bastards to hell," said Marshall.

"Yeah we did. Is anybody hurt?" asked George.

"We're okay. But we're taking on some water," yelled Simmons from inside the boat's cabin.

George thanked God that no one had been hurt in the brief but violent engagement. Unfortunately, his joy was short lived as the boat's engine suddenly sputtered and died.

"God damn it. That's just what we need." said George, rushing into the boat's small cabin.

The inside of the boat's cabin had almost two inches of water on the floor. Pulling the engine hatch covers, George could see water entering from a couple of holes made by the Turkish fifty caliber slugs. They had entered just below the water line.

"Simmons, stuff some of these rags into the holes," said George, handing him an old shirt he had found hanging in the cabin's interior.

"Everybody else, start bailing her out."

"Jefferson, can you get the engine going again?" asked George.

Jefferson looked at the old engine for a moment. "Nope, we're screwed."

"What do you mean?"

"It looks like one of the bullets smashed the fuel pump."

"Can you fix it?"

"Not without a spare and I don't think her previous owner carried one."

"Can't we row to shore?" asked Marshall.

"We'll have to. But we're still pretty far out and the weather is worsening," said George.

"At least the leaks are temporarily plugged. Me and Simmons will take the first turn at the oars," said Marshall.

They had not gone more than a mile before the storm caught up with them. The small boat was now at the mercy of the wind and waves.

"We have to point her bow into the wind or else we'll broach," said George.

"Wait, I have a better idea," said Theodoros.

"Let's have it," said George

"Maybe we can rig that old piece of canvas that's in the cabin supply locker into a storm sail. If it works, we can run with the weather."

"Do you know how to sail?" asked George.

"I used to sail small boats as a hobby before I went into the army."

"Give it a try then." With the help of Marshall and Jefferson, Theodoros quickly rigged the fishing boat's mast with a crude storm sail. Taking the tiller from George, Theodoros found the wind gage. The boat picked up speed.

"We're heading out to sea," said George.

"We don't have a choice; we'll have to run with the weather. It'll blow over in a couple of hours," said Theodoros. Gradually the island of Thasos faded from view, as the small fishing boat was blown out to sea.

Mikra Airfield
1015hrs, 20 May

The atmosphere in the briefing center was tense, as the pilots of the 526th awaited their mission brief. The room was called to attention when Logan and Colonel Kazas entered.

"As you were," said Logan. Colonel Kazas took the podium.

"Good morning, gentlemen. Oh and excuse me, ladies. I know everyone is tired after last night's exodus from Piges. But the enemy attack on the Platamon River line has begun." Kazas walked over to a map hanging from the ceiling.

"The enemy is throwing everything they've got at us and your mission will be to blast them back across the river. Your main targets will be enemy armored vehicles. Your planes have been armed up with Mavericks and Mark 82s, so please put all your ordnance to good use."

"I always loved shooting galleries," said one of the pilots known as Driller.

"So how come you still haven't learned to shoot straight, Driller?" said Wendy breaking the ice and bringing a chorus of laughter from almost everyone in the briefing room.

"Okay everybody, let's get back to business," said Kazas.

"Are there any questions before I turn it over to Colonel Logan?"

"Yeah, I have a question. What about enemy air defenses? asked Cowboy.

"Good question. Intel has learned that the enemy has pulled back what's left of their air force to defend the capital. A couple of squadrons of their fighter bombers did make an appearance this morning over the front but they suffered heavy casualties, thanks to the Patriot batteries your country delivered to us. Be very careful of their triple A. They have brought up several batteries of tracked vehicle mounted ZU-23-4 radar guided anti-aircraft guns to cover their attack. They may be obsolete, but they fire over thirty-four hundred 23mm shells a minute. It is still a very formidable weapon. Additionally, expect to encounter Stinger and Sam-7B shoulder fired missiles. Are there any other questions?"

"Yes, I have one," said Wendy Barnes.

"Any word on the missing C-130 or from our people left at Piges?"

Kazas momentarily hesitated. "I'll answer it, Colonel," said Logan.

"All contact with the field was lost at 0400hrs. It's presumed the plane never made it off the ground. The field fell to the enemy, sometime this morning. There isn't yet any word of survivors."

"We'll make the bastards pay," said Cowboy.

"Excuse me, Colonel. May I say something?" said Kazas.

"Sure, be my guest,"

"Thanks to the aid from your country, we have dealt decisively with both the Macedonians and Albanians. In spite of that, the final battle that will decide the fate of Greece is now upon us. If we lose today, we have lost the war. There is no further retreat. To all of you, whatever the outcome of today's battle, I wish to express the sincere thanks of all the Greek people for your sacrifices and contributions. Good Luck and good hunting!" Kazas left the podium and turned for the door to leave the briefing room.

Logan came to attention. "Room atten hut!"

"Take your seats," said Logan once Kazas had departed.

"I'll only keep you a minute. What I want to tell each and every one of you is that you are all one hell of a bunch of fighter pilots. Let's kick ass for all those left behind at Piges. Let's do it. Ladies and gents, man your planes!"

"Remember Piges!" yelled Cowboy, as everyone left the room and headed for the crew buses that would take them out to the flight line.

Chapter 8

Platamon River Defense Line, 26th Armored Battalion

1025hrs, 21 May

Mihalis Manakos stuck his head out the loader's hatch and looked up at the gray sky. The falling rain drops that pelted his face felt good. It would wash away the acrid smell of burning flesh that still lingered in the atmosphere after the previous shelling. The vicious artillery barrage had rained death on them for almost half an hour. Looking around, Mihalis could see patches of thick, oily smoke bellowing skyward from several vehicles destroyed by the shelling.

"They haven't even attacked yet," said Captain Kapsis who was standing in the commander's hatch and had been watching Mihalis.

"We'll send the bastards to hell, Captain."

"We better, Mihalis. The nation's survival rests on what happens here today. There can be no further retreating."

"Captain, if we all fall here today, I want you to know that I am very proud to have been given the opportunity to have served and fought by your side."

"Why thank you, Mihalis," said Captain Kapsis, rather moved by the comments.

"I am proud to have you as a crew member. If you ever decide to quit the police force, you're welcome on my crew any day. You make one hell of a tanker."

"I don't think so, Captain, I think I'll stay a cop. It's just a tad safer," said Mihalis jokingly.

Before the Captain could answer, both individuals heard the sound of approaching helicopters.

"There!" said Mihalis, pointing to the east at several specks that were rapidly growing larger.

"Enemy gunships!" shouted the Captain, as he pulled back the charging handle of the tank's fifty caliber machine gun and waited till the gunships came within range.

"Captain!" yelled Sergeant Nicolaou. "Division's on the radio. They say to expect an enemy air attack."

"No Shit!" replied Captain Kapsis.

Mihalis stared in horror at the approaching enemy gunships. He counted over twenty before he entered the relative safety of the tank and closed the hatch. The enemy, hoping to force a quick breakthrough of the Greek defenses, had thrown almost their entire remaining force of helicopter attack ships at the Greeks. The Greeks were prepared and waiting for them. Scores of stinger ground to air missiles delivered to the Hellenic army just only this morning by the emergency American airlift, arched skyward. Over a dozen enemy gunships were blown out of the sky in the first volley. Almost immediately, hundreds of antiaircraft guns of various calibers opened fire, putting up a wall of lead in front of the approaching enemy gunships. The enemy attack was over before it had begun. Those few helicopters that had survived the deadly passage fired off their missiles and fled toward the Turkish lines. Very few of their anti-tank rockets found their targets.

"Well everybody. That kind of evened the odds. At least we might have a chance now," remarked Captain Kapsis, after it was all over.

"Hey look! What they are doing?" asked their driver, as he looked across the river.

"I think they are dispensing smoke,"

"Yeah, I think you're right Captain. I can't see them no more. I wonder what they are up to?" said Mihalis.

"Okay everyone, get ready. I think they're coming."

Using the cover of the smoke screen, scores of enemy tanks began fording the shallow Platamon River that separated them from the Greek positions.

"They sure are, sir, and lots of them. I can see them through my infrared sights." said the gunner.

"Okay men, this is it. Let's give 'um hell," said their commander, as the sound of tank gun firing erupted from the Greek lines.

Over the Platamon
1110hrs, 21 May

Looking out of his cockpit to the east, Logan could see plumes of smoke rising over the battlefield. This would be the crucial battle that determined the fate of Greece. The sky this morning was very crowded. The Greeks had thrown whatever aircraft they had available into the battle to help blunt the

Turkish offensive. Most of their fighters, F-4s, F-16s and even A-7s brought out of mothballs, were armed with air to ground ordnance in a last ditch effort to stop the advancing enemy armored formations. A couple of Squadrons of HAF Mirage 2000s flew CAP over the front to protect the bomber force from enemy fighters detected in bound by a HAF AWACS. Suddenly, Logan's radio came to life. They were being vectored by a forward air controller to a section of the front that was coming under extreme enemy pressure. It was time to end radio silence.

"Falcon leader to Falcon flight. We are nearing the target area. Keep your heads up for missiles and triple A," said Logan. His threat indicator began giving warnings of multiple threats in the area. Crossing the Greek lines, he could see dozens of enemy armored vehicles fording the shallow river.

"This is going to be lively guys," said Logan as he switched his HUD to air to ground mode. He was immediately rewarded with a plethora of targets. All around him, the sky rapidly filled with dirty black puffs of anti-aircraft fire. Lining up a tank in his cross hairs, he fired off an AIM 65 Maverick air to ground missile. Seconds later, the enemy tank blew up in a spectacular fireball. Flying parallel to the river, he could see, off in the distance, several columns of tanks and armored personnel carriers beginning to cross the river.

"There's the main force," said Logan over the radio. "Let's see if we can slow them down and give them a lesson they'll never forget. Logan switched to bombing mode and armed his Mark-82s. He switched his release mode to bomb ripple. Rolling his fighter 100 degrees, he leveled off at fifteen-hundred feet and put his fighter into a shallow dive. Up ahead in his three o'clock position, he spotted Driller's aircraft pulling out of a dive, having dropped his bombs. A small shoulder fired surface to air missile suddenly streaked up from one of the enemy APC's, blowing the F-16 apart. Logan had no time to think about the loss, as the piper dot on his HUD passed over the lead APC. He pressed the pickle button. The Falcon shuddered and leaped into the air as it shed its four ton bomb load.

"You plastered the bastards," said Logan's wingman.

"That was for Driller."

"I'm taking ground fire! I'm hit," came over the radio.

Logan recognized the voice. It was Captain Tom Dickerson, Bravo flight leader. Logan could see the stricken F-16 about a kilometer off to his right wing. It was streaming smoke from its engine. "I can't control her, punching out!"

Logan briefly glimpsed the plane's canopy shoot off, immediately followed by the ejection seat carrying Dickerson. A couple of seconds later, the chute opened. The pilotless plane dived into the ground and exploded in a bright fireball. Logan had no time to stick around to see if Dickerson, who was being blown toward the enemy lines, made it down safe. He now had his own problem. His threat indicator chirped madly, indicating a ZU-23-4 radar controlled flak gun had locked on to him. Punching in after burner, he hit the chaff release as he put the fighter into a steep bank. Streams of 23mm anti-aircraft shells streaked by his right wing. Logan felt the plane shudder as several shells tore into his rudder and fuselage. Simultaneously, buzzers and warning lights began going off in the cockpit.

"I'm hit, I'm hit!"

"I'll get the bastard," said Wendy as she went for the gun. Before Logan could tell her to stay away, the ZU-23 was torn apart by a string of 20mm shells.

"Got the bastard!"

"Cowboy to Falcon leader. Can you make it back? I can see your rudder and vertical stabilizer. They look pretty chewed up," said Cowboy.

"I don't know how much longer I can keep this crate flying. I have engine warning lights and I am losing hydraulic pressure. Must have severed a line or two, I will try to keep her airborne as long as possible. Let's get out of here."

Having finished their bomb runs, the surviving planes formed around Logan's severely damaged aircraft. The formation turned southward taking them over the sea, leaving behind dozens of armored vehicles burning on the battlefield.

"How you doing, Falcon leader?"

"Not too good, Cowboy. She's shaking herself apart; I don't think I'm going to make it."

"It doesn't look too good from out here either. I can see the skin on your stabilizer ripping apart in the slip stream, what the hell! Falcon leader are you all right? I thought I saw an explosion from your engine."

Logan had felt the muffled explosion. His cockpit was starting to fill with smoke. Engine fire warning lights were going off in the cockpit. Logan hit his fire extinguisher. The plane suddenly lost power.

"I've lost my engine. I'm punching out!"

"We'll contact search and rescue. Good luck, Colonel."

"I'll stay with him until I see that he's okay," said Wendy.

Logan pulled his ejection handle. The force of the ejection pushed him into his seat as he rocketed free of the stricken jet. The next thing he felt was the jerk of the parachute canopy opening above him. Logan watched as his pilotless plane twisted and tumbled toward the sea. Only a black plume marked the spot where it hit the water. The sea quickly came up to meet him. He struck the water and went under. Releasing his chute, Logan fought his way to the surface and inflated his survival vest. Luckily, he spotted his survival dingy only a few meters away and quickly swam to it and climbed aboard. Turning on his PRC 90 emergency radio that every pilot carried in their survival vest, he contacted the F-16 orbiting above.

"This is Falcon leader, I made it down okay."

"Thank God Jack, I was worried stiff."

"I'll be okay as soon as search and rescue pulls me out of the drink."

"I can only stay a few minutes, I don't have much fuel."

Fifteen minutes later, Logan watched as Wendy's F-16 disappeared over the horizon. He was now all alone in the sea, several kilometers from the shore. Feeling hungry, he broke out one of his emergency high energy chocolate bars and began munching on the candy. His small survival dinghy bobbed up and down in the sea which was still choppy from the storm that had hit the area only a couple of hours earlier. To the best of his recollection, he was somewhere southwest of Thassos. Hopefully rescue would come quick. Chilled to the bone, he took off his wet flight suit and wrapped himself with one of the high-tech blankets that came with the rescue pack. He hoped he wouldn't have to wait too long for rescue.

Platamon River, Suilliman Armored Division
1237hrs, 21 May

The severely mauled forward elements of General Karakoglou's armored division huddled in a small defensive ring on the western side of the Platamon River awaiting further orders. Facing heavy enemy fire, the division had forced a crossing of the river and established a small bridgehead on the opposite bank. In the process, they had suffered a severe drubbing by an American air attack. General Karakoglou surveyed the carnage wrought on his armor by the Americans. His division had been reduced to less than 50% effectiveness. He was seething with rage. The fighter support he had been promised by command had never materialized. Without reinforcements, it would be almost impossible to continue the attack against the infidels.

"Sir, urgent message from headquarters," said Lieutenant Colonel Murat, one of his battalion commanders.

General Karakoglou quickly read the message. Colonel Murat saw the look of disbelief on the General's face.

"Bad news, sir?"

"We've been ordered to break out of this bridgehead."

The General saw the look of astonishment on the Colonel's face. Before Murat could say anything, he was handed the message.

"My God! It says sir, attack the enemy immediately and reinforcements will be forthcoming."

"I can read, Colonel."

"Excuse me, sir. From where are they going to get these reinforcements? The other two assaults against the Greek positions were only diversionary. We were the ones that spearheaded the main attack. Everything that we had was used up to force this crossing."

General Karakoglou raised his hand to cut off Colonel Murat. "The enemy can't be in much better shape. I suspect that they are in a much worse position than we are. With Allah's help, if we throw everything we have at them, they may break. Prepare your troops, Colonel. The attack begins thirty minutes from now."

"But, sir!"

"Colonel, you will obey your orders or you will be immediately relieved of command and shot."

"Yes, sir!" said Colonel Murat.

The whine of artillery shells passing overhead caused the two officers to briefly look toward the enemy lines, only two kilometers away. They could see the shells bursting among the Greek positions. "That should help soften them up and keep their heads down" said General Karakoglou as the tempo of shell fire began to increase.

"Now go and ready your men. Your tanks will be in the forefront of the attack. I must check on the rest of the division," said the General.

"And Murat. Good luck."

"Thank you, sir. We'll need lots of it to pull this attack off,"

But the General had already turned to leave and didn't hear the Colonel's reply.

Platamon River, 26th armored
1320hrs, 21 May

Mihalis sat in the loader's seat of his M-60 tank and prayed while the tank rocked from the explosions of near misses. He prayed that God would give him strength to continue. They had been fighting for their lives for most of the morning. The Turks had thrown the brunt of their assault on their sector of the line. Fortunately for them, a squadron of U.S. Fighter bombers had appeared in the nick of time and stopped the Turks dead in their tracks. The air strike gave the needed respite for Captain Kapsis to pull back what was left of the unit to the last of their defense positions.

Mihalis held his head as it throbbed with pain caused by the constant concussions of exploding shells. "They'll be coming again, Captain." It was more a statement of fact than a question.

"Yes, Mihalis. This will probably be it. Do or die."

"They've got to be hurting just as bad as we are, Captain,"

said the gunner.

"If they are, it surely isn't stopping them from coming at us again," said Mihalis.

The tank rocked from a near miss. "That was close," said the gunner.

"Yeah, too close," answered Mihalis.

After a couple of other near misses, the shelling began to slacken off. Captain Kapsis stuck his head out the turret to take a better look, but the whine of more incoming shells made him stick it back inside. "Damn, there was no explosion." He noticed a cloud of smoke.

"Oh God, a chemical attack. Put your masks on." The M-60 did have a filtering system to protect its crew from NBC (Nuclear, Biological and Chemical) attacks, but he was worried that after all the heavy fighting that they had been through, the integrity of the system was in question.

Looking through the tank commander's periscope, he noticed several soldiers without gas masks running by. Captain Kapsis quickly breathed a sigh of relief. "It's only smoke shells, but that doesn't mean we're in the clear. They'll be on us any minute. Are we loaded with SABOT?"

"It's done, Captain," said Mihalis.

"But how are we going to hit them if we can't see them?" asked Mihalis, ignorant to the ways of modern warfare.

"We don't have to see them, Mihalis. This is modern war. Our thermal sights will pick the heat signature from the target's engine."

"Thank God for technology," said Sergeant Nickolaou.

"Amen to that," said Mihalis. They were lucky that his unit had been equipped with the M-60s. Some of the older M-48 tanks brought out of reserve that were on the line had not yet been equipped with thermal sights and still depended on the old optical kind, he hated to be in those guys' boots.

"Multiple targets! Nine hundred meters at two o' clock. All units stand by to fire," said Captain Kapsis over the tactical net to the rest of his command.

"I see them," said the gunner. The Captain waited a few more seconds while the gun computer processed the target information to make sure they had a certain kill.

"Fire!"

"On the way!" said the gunner. The tank rocked from the gun's recoil.

"On target!" shouted the Captain as he saw the bright flash of the shell exploding on the enemy tank.

"Load SABOT!"

George shoved the fifty pound shell into the open breach.

"UP!"

"Two tanks, one o'clock, six hundred meters, aim left."

"Identified!" said the gunner.

"Fire!"

The enemy tank took the hit just below the turret and exploded in an orange ball of fire. At that same moment, the tank next to them erupted in flames as it took an enemy shell hit.

"There's too many of them!" yelled the gunner.

"Nickolaou! Get this thing out of here. We'll fight them on the run."

"Yes, sir!" said Nickolaou as he meshed the gas pedal.

Captain Kapsis keyed the transmitter and instructed his surviving units to make for the clump of trees two kilometers to the southwest.

"Load, SABOT! Target, twelve o' clock, three hundred meters," yelled the Captain as he visually spotted an enemy tank coming out of the smoke screen.

"Identified."

"Fire!"

The enemy tank stopped dead in its tracks, thick smoke pouring out of its hatches. The Captain gasped in horror as he spotted another enemy tank emerging from behind the one they had just knocked out.

"Load SABOT," screamed the Captain.

"Oh God! He is turning to fire," said Kapsis, realizing that their luck had just run out.

Just as George shoved the heavy shell into the breach, their tank was rocked by an explosion.

"We're hit!" screamed the gunner in obvious pain.

"Get out before we roast in here," screamed the driver.

George grasped the handle to open the gunner's hatch. Their tank had filled with smoke and he could feel the heat from a fire burning somewhere inside the vehicle. He had managed to open the loader's hatch and partially crawl out when the tank was rocked by another explosion. The last thing George remembered was being flung through the air by the force of the explosion.

Platamon River, West Bank
1355hrs, 21 May

Standing in the open commander's hatch, General Karakoglou observed the battlefield through a pair of binoculars. The scene of carnage was littered with the hulks of dozens of enemy and Turkish armored vehicles. Despite having suffered almost crippling losses, his armor had broken out of their bridgehead. At this very moment, his units were pouring through the breach that they had opened in the Greek defense line.

"Driver, take us closer," said General Karakoglou to the tank driver.

"Yes, sir," he replied.

The General had wanted to personally lead the breakout. However, he had been overruled by the Force Theater Commander. He was instructed to direct the battle from a safer location behind the lines. General Guval told him that he had taken enough risks and his loss would leave the division leaderless at such a crucial moment in the battle. This was not in his nature. It was a coward's way out. A commander should lead his men into battle as the old Ottoman generals did. But orders were orders.

"Sir! The Brigade Commander requests to speak to you."

"Give me the radio."

The General plugged in his headphones and keyed the mike. "What is it, Murat?"

"Sir, we are encountering stiff resistance. My command has suffered very heavy losses. I need reinforcements now if we are to exploit the breach we have opened in the Greek lines. If we delay, they will surely close it!"

General Karakoglou sensed that total victory was in his grasp, he would not wait for his infantry units to catch up. Once the city of Kavala was taken, he would drive northwards and envelope and destroy what remained of the Greek army. Then the road to Thessaloniki would be wide open to him. History would see him as another Guderien or Rommel. Therefore timing was critical if he was to achieve his goal. Each passing minute, gave opportunity for the Greeks to organize and mount a counter attack.

"Keep pressing on, Murat. I will release the 33rd".

Murat was elated. With the help of the 33rd, they would widen the breach and cause havoc in the enemy's rear. It was possible that they would be in Kavala by nightfall.

"Thank you, sir. Victory will be ours!"

"I will see you in Kavalla, Murat!" Switching frequency, the General called division and issued the necessary orders to release the 33rd armored brigade. It had been held in reserve for an opportunity like the one that had just been presented to them. Within minutes the 33rd was on the move.

Alpha Co., 23rd Inf. Brigade, 10th Mt. Div., U.S Army

1405hrs, 21 May

Captain Howland rubbed his fatigue strained eyes. He had still not recovered from the jet lag brought on from his Trans-Atlantic crossing. Only forty-eight hours ago, he had been in a warm bed, making love to his girlfriend, Susan. Now, he was lying in a hastily dug fox hole atop a hillock, somewhere in northern Greece, near a river called the Platamon. And to make matters worse, a whole Turkish armored division could be barreling down on them. Well, this was the occupation he had chosen and he was now responsible for the lives and wellbeing of over one hundred and thirty soldiers in Alpha Company.

He thought back to the last forty-eight hours. With the outbreak of the war in the Balkans, the 10th Mountain division had been placed on alert. When they had received their warning orders for deployment, they rapidly loaded their pre-palleted equipment into the bellies of waiting C-17 transports and took off for Greece. Twelve hours later, having landed in Thessaloniki, Greece and without having a chance to rest and recover from jet lag, they quickly unloaded their gear, put it into waiting Hellenic Army trucks and took off for the front lines.

When they finally reached their area of operations, he had the troops quickly unload their gear. The unit had been directed to set up as a blocking force atop a small tree covered knoll indicated on the map as Hill 225. The strategic knoll overlooked the approaches to the city of Kavala. If the enemy managed to break through the Greek lines, they could only go one way to get to the city, through Alpha Company.

"Sir, message on the radio. The Turks have breached the Greek positions. Their armor is headed this way," said Sergeant Major Alphanso Perry.

"Shit, that's what I was afraid of," Howland mumbled to himself.

Everybody had heard the ferocious fighting that was taking place only a few miles away. Howland hadn't imagined that they would be taking part in it so soon. The Captain stared at the First Sergeant without saying a word. If there was one thing about the six foot, two hundred pound African American, twenty-two year army veteran, which Howland respected, was his ability to stay calm in stressful situations.

"Sir, did you hear what I just said?"

"Yes, Top. I was just thinking. Are the troops ready to go?"

"Yes, sir. They're ready to give 'um hell!"

"Sir, Alpha battery is on the line," said his radio telephone operator.

"They've spotted tracked vehicles heading this way."

"How many, Sergeant?"

"Lots. At least two companies."

"Tell them to hold their fire and keep out of sight."

"Yes, sir."

Unless they were spotted first, he would have his anti-tank batteries' hold their fire as long as possible. This way he could maximize the damage done to the enemy.

"Top, get on the horn and get us some artillery support."

"Here they come," yelled one of Bravo battery's gunners. Captain Howland rushed to the tree line only a few meters away to see for himself what was going on. What he saw made his blood freeze. At least twenty tanks and armored personnel carriers were advancing their way.

"Holy Shit, there is a whole armored brigade bearing down on us," said Howland, his confidence shaken and his voice quivering from fear.

"Sir, we can't wait any longer. They'll surely see us and we'll lose the element of surprise," said the First Sergeant.

"Sergeant Jordan, advise all batteries to stand by and fire on my command," said Howland to his radio man.

"Sir, no artillery support for at least fifteen minutes. The Greeks are pulling back their batteries.

"Thanks, Top. I guess we'll do it alone," said Howland.

Howland glanced at the advancing armor. It was less than seven hundred meters away. The time had come. "Jordan, order all batteries to commence firing."

"Right away, sir."

Howland heard his order repeated over the radio. Almost simultaneously, a dozen AT-4 and Dragon anti-tank missiles left their launchers toward the advancing enemy armor. With victory practically in their grasp, the Turks had become over-confident. They would now pay for their overconfidence by being caught completely by surprise by the American ambush.

Suilliman Armored Division, Kavala road
1420hrs, 21 May

Within thirty seconds, the lead elements of General Karakoglou's division had ground to a complete halt. The havoc wrought on his tanks from the anti-tank unit that had been hiding in the wooded knoll just ahead of his lead elements had been devastating. From his periscope, the General could see over a dozen of his precious vehicles burning. He watched in horror as his few remaining APC's stopped to let down their ramps to deploy their infantry. But they too became funeral pyres, struck by accurate missile fire coming from the wooded knoll. Victory was slipping through his fingers. Unless he acted quickly and regained the initiative, their attack would end in disaster.

"Wolf leader to all units. Enemy infantry in the knoll. Open fire with high explosive rounds and begin dispersing smoke. Advance on the infidel immediately! Allah, Akhbar! To victory!"

Receiving the guidance they needed, the surviving tank commanders quickly recovered from the ambush and implemented their commander's orders. Heavy tank fire began pummeling the American positions in the wooded knoll, forcing the gunners to go to ground.

Alpha Company Hill 225
Same Time

With high explosive shells raining all around him, Howland ran as fast as he could toward the company command vehicle.

He could hear the screams of the wounded mixed among the shell blasts. Reaching his HUMMVEE, he saw his radio operator sprawled against the vehicle covered in blood.

"Medic! Medic!"

"Forget it, sir. The medics have more important things to do right now," said First Sergeant Perry.

Howland stared at the corpse, never having seen a man killed in combat before. "But, Top."

"He's dead, sir. We're about to get overrun and if we don't do something really soon, we'll all end up like Jordan."

The senior NCO's last words seemed to produce the necessary effect to shake him into action. "What is our status, Top?"

"Lieutenant Harvey last reported that his position was about to get overrun by the enemy. That was just a few minutes ago. I haven't been able to reach him or anyone else from Alpha battery, sir."

"Does the radio still work?"

"I think so, sir."

Howland took the mike and began transmitting. "Ops one to all battery commanders. I need an immediate status report." Howland waited while everyone reported in.

"Damn it, Top. Bravo battery reported that it is almost out of ammo. They'll get overrun in the next few minutes."

"Pull everybody back to Delta's position while we still have a chance, sir. It's the highest spot in the knoll. We can a make a stand there."

"I think you're right. We don't stand a chance otherwise. There is just too many of them." Howland took the radio mike and issued the necessary orders for everyone to pull back to Delta battery's position.

"It's done, sir. Let's get moving, the enemy will be here soon," said the First Sergeant.

Taking their remaining Dragon III anti-tank rocket from their HUMMVEE, Howland and the few surviving members of his command section took off running toward Delta battery. Halfway there, they heard the sound of heavy small arms fire coming from the vicinity where Bravo battery had been situated.

"We are in for it now, sir. They must be using dismounted infantry to clear out the area," said Corporal Watkins, the company's supply NCO.

"Look out!" Pushing the Captain aside, Perry let loose a burst from his M-4 cutting down two enemy infantrymen in their tracks.

"There must be more where those came from. Everybody, keep your eyes open. It's a few more hundred meters before we reach Delta, sir."

Howland heard the deep throated roar of diesel engines coming from the area they had just left.

"Tanks! Top, take the men and run for it. Give me the AT-4s. I'll stay here and cover you."

Maybe this guy might make a good officer and soldier yet, thought Perry. "Sir I think it's better if I stay" said Perry.

"No, Top. You're better needed there. Get moving. That's an order. Tell Lieutenant Lewis to hold out as long as he can inflict damage on the enemy and then get the hell out. Now move, you're wasting time."

Perry snapped to attention and rendered the Captain a sharp salute. "Yes, sir. It's been an honor to serve under you."

"Thanks, Top. I don't intend to commit suicide. I'll see you back at the battery."

"Okay let's move it!" yelled Perry. As Perry and the rest of the squad disappeared from view, he could hear the tanks coming closer. Arming the Dragon, he hid behind some tall underbrush and waited.

Suilliman Armored Div., Hill 225
Same Time

For the first time since hostilities had commenced, General Karakoglou began to feel a sense of apprehension about the whole war. His division had suffered heavily to achieve the breakout and now this ambush had cost him his last reserves. His troops were rapidly running out of steam. Still this was not what worried him. Entering the knoll, they came upon the bodies of American infantrymen that had been manning one of the anti-tank batteries. This was a bad sign. The Americans had been able to rush to their ally's aid much quicker than anyone had anticipated. He had been a fool to believe that Kemal's plan would work as originally planned. And now of all things, the Americans had entered the picture. If victory wasn't attained very soon, the whole war could be lost. Looking through his periscope, he could see his tanks advancing toward the center of the knoll.

"Driver, follow the lead tanks."

He would personally lead his weary men and capture Kavalla. After that, they would have to rest. What remained of his armor desperately needed maintenance. Breakdowns were becoming ever too common. Worst of all, his troops were running low on ammunition. The speed of their advance had caused the supply convoys to lag far behind and now constant enemy air attacks had further disrupted the system. It would be prudent, he thought, to halt the advance, refit and consolidate their gains. He would talk to General Kemal about this. Unfortunately, nothing could be done until they crushed the last bastion of enemy resistance holding up their advance to Kavalla.

The General's headphones suddenly came to life. "Echo one to Wolf leader."

"This is Wolf leader," replied the General.

"I am down to less than a company of tanks and we are almost out of ammunition. Enemy resistance is very heavy. Request to pull back."

General Karakoglou could not believe his ears. Everyone on the command must have heard the transmission. His troops needed leadership from their officers' not cowardice and defeatism.

"The spineless coward! I will have him shot!" he cried out in rage. Everyone in the tank was preoccupied with the General's raving and had not noticed the lone infantryman moving in the bushes less than a hundred meters away, until he raised his anti-tank missile to fire.

"Echo one to Wolf leader, I request instructions." Before he could reply, the General heard his driver scream a warning about a missile. It was the last thing General Karakoglou ever heard. The enemy missile that ripped through the tank, detonated amongst the remaining store of 120mm shells, instantly incinerating the General and his crew.

With the death of General Karakoglou, the division had become leaderless at a crucial point for the battle of Kavalla. The senior officer on scene that happened to be Echo one, the 33rd brigade commander, immediately took command and issued orders for an immediate withdrawal. The dazed survivors of Alpha Company who had just stared death in the face could not believe their eyes. The enemy was withdrawing and leaving them still in control of the approaches to Kavalla.

Thirty minutes later, the first tanks and personnel carriers of the Hellenic army's 24th armored brigade rolled into the knoll to relieve the dazed and ragged survivors of Alpha Company. Later that afternoon, the Hellenic army launched a counter attack against the mauled remnants of the Suilliman division. By sunset, the only Turks remaining on the west bank of the Platamon River were either dead or prisoners of war.

Hill 225

1550hrs, 21 May

"I found him, Sarge." yelled Private Babit. "I think he's alive"

"Medic! Over here." Perry ran over to where Babit was standing. Captain Howland was lying less than a hundred feet from a burning enemy tank and an empty AT-4 launcher was lying beside him.

"Move over!" said the medic.

"Is he hurt badly?" asked Perry, looking at Howland whose head and face was covered with blood.

"He must have got the son of a bitch," said Perry, looking over at the burning enemy tank.

The medic quickly checked Howland's vital signs and looked at his injuries that consisted of a deep cut on Howland's temple. Taking his canteen and some gauze, he washed the blood off Howland's face. The Captain stirred.

"I don't think he's hurt too badly. Head injuries usually look worse than they really are," said the medic.

Howland opened his eyes. "Oh, my head. What hap . . .?"

"Take it easy, Captain. You got clobbered on the head really hard, but you'll be all right."

"Top"

"It's me, sir."

"The men. How's the company?"

"We got pretty beat up, Captain, but we kicked their ass. The enemy withdrew and is now on the run. You got yourself an enemy tank, sir and a Purple Hart to go along with it," said the

First Sergeant. Howland smiled at the First Sergeant's words. He had passed the test of fire and had survived. The god of war had been kind to him this day.

Only years later, after military historians had pieced together the events of the battle of hill 225 from survivors of both sides, did Howland find out that his one shot had changed the course of the war.

Kesan Command Bunker
1600hrs, 21 May

General Kemal lay tossing and turning on one of the army cots that he had put in his office. He hadn't had much rest since the war had started. Even now while asleep, his subconscious mind would not let him have any peace of soul. He dreamed that he was hovering high above the church spires of a walled city somewhere in central Europe. The city was under siege, he could hear the roar of the giant cannon that had been bombarding the infidel bastion for weeks. Fluttering above the thousands of tents spread before the city walls was the star and crescent banner.

The General, from his high perch above the city, immediately recognized that he was witnessing the 1683 siege of Vienna. The Ottoman Empire, revitalized under the leadership of the Koprolougu family, had sent out its armies once again to threaten the very heart of Europe. Only one city, Vienna, stood between the Turkish Ottoman army and the rich Christian cities of the west. Bombarded and starved for weeks, the city refused to surrender to the mighty Kara Mustafa Pasha, Supreme Commander of the Ottoman forces. Unfortunately, the mighty Ottoman army spread before him had become too complacent. It was ripe for disaster, drunkenness and whoring among the troops had become commonplace. From the Turkish camp below him, the General suddenly heard screams and the sounds of musketry. He could see smoke and flames spreading throughout the camp.

"No! No!" shouted General Kemal. He had to stop the disaster that was about to befall the Ottoman army, a disaster it would never entirely recover from. Far below him, the Turkish camp had become a scene of death and destruction. The Christian forces under the command of Leopold I, the Hapsburg emperor, had caught the Ottoman army by complete surprise. Before the day ended, the siege of Vienna would be lifted and tens of thousands of Turkish soldiers would never again see the shores of the Aegean Sea.

"No please, this cannot happen. I must do something to stop it."

"Sir, wake up. You're having a bad dream," said Colonel Azoglou, shaking the General awake.

"What? Where am I?"

"Sir, You're in your command bunker in Kesan."

The General opened his eyes. "Oh, you were right Ahmet; I was having a bad dream. Or perhaps it was a premonition of things to come."

"Sir, I have bad news from the front."

"Tell me!"

"Sir, our forces have been halted just outside Kavalla. General Karakoglou is missing and some reports say that he was killed assaulting a position defended by Americans!"

"Damn It! He was my best commander,"

"That's not all the bad news. The enemy has launched a counter offensive. Our forces are retreating across the Platamon River under heavy aerial and artillery bombardment."

Kemal thought back to his dream. Maybe it was a premonition. History was somehow repeating itself.

"Also sir, the Bulgarians are massing additional troops on the borders."

He flew into a rage. "I knew they couldn't be trusted. I will teach them! I will teach them all a lesson that they will never forget!"

For the first time in his life, Colonel Azoglou began to fear the man whom he had considered a lifelong friend and mentor. "My friend, all is not yet lost. It is true that we have suffered some serious reverses, but we can pull the army back to a more secure defense line. The President of the European Union is offering to broker an immediate cease fire, and peace talks to be held in Brussels," said Ahmet.

"What! I never believed to hear this coming from your lips Ahmet. We will not talk; we will attack and destroy the infidels!"

"With what? The Americans are supplying the Greeks with men and material. We don't have any armored reserves left. We have no allies, the Macedonian army has for all aspects been destroyed. Hoxa is dead and the Albanians are suing for peace. On Limnos, our forces are barely holding on and without a major resupply with men and material, they'll be forced to evacuate or surrender within the next 48-72 hours! At best, we'll be lucky to hold on to what we have."

"We will destroy them with the fiery sword of Allah, you fool! Not all our missiles were launched during the opening attack. I gave orders that ten missiles be saved, just in case we needed them later. These missiles have been loaded with the deadliest nerve gas that we possess and placed on mobile launchers. If the front isn't stabilized soon, I will order their launching. Their targets will be Athens and Sofia."

Colonel Azoglou could not believe his ears.

"But, sir, that will cause the death of thousands, if not tens of thousands of civilians."

"You are correct. The warheads will detonate at an altitude of one thousand meters and release their deadly payloads. Our experts predict over a hundred thousand casualties."

The man is insane, he will destroy Turkey and everything we have worked for, the Colonel thought to himself.

"What of the Americans, sir?"

The General continued on with his senseless rambling. "It will be too late for the Americans to do anything. Once the enemy leadership is annihilated, we will attack with everything we have. Victory can still be ours!"

The Colonel wanted to tell him that they didn't have any

forces to attack with. But he genuinely feared for his life if he went against this lunatic whom he had once considered a friend. He had to do something to stop this madman before it was too late.

Chapter 9

Aegean Sea, South of Thassos
1540hrs, 21 May

"Anything on the radar, Takis?" asked Commander Vassiliou.

"Nothing. Just some of our fighters returning from air strikes, it's unbelievably calm," replied Lieutenant Takis Mavridis.

"Keep your eyes open. Their navy still has a few ships capable of giving us a run for the money. What's our distance from the emergency locator beacon?"

"About seven miles. We should be there in less than fifteen minutes."

Yiannis picked up his binoculars and scanned the horizon. The Hydra had been dispatched to Greece's second largest city, Thessaloniki, to pick up a team of Hellenic army tactical air controllers and deliver them to Limnos. He had been briefed that in the following morning, the U.S. army's 101st airborne division was going to drop on Limnos and help the Hellenic army secure the island. The air controllers were needed to help guide in the transports and call in air strikes if necessary. The closer they got to the island, the more Yiannis thought of Eleni and prayed that she was okay. He'd never forgive himself if something happened to her.

Having drifted with the currents southwards for most of the day, Logan had practically given up hope of rescue. That was until he spotted a ship headed his way at a high rate of speed. His spirits suddenly lifted. He hoped it was friendly and not the enemy. Ten minutes later, the Hellenic navy missile boat Hydra had pulled up alongside his dingy. One of the sailors threw him a line. Grabbing the rope, Logan pulled himself alongside the boat, grasped hold of a rope ladder the crew had lowered for him and climbed up to the deck. One of the crew offered him a hand and helped him to the deck.

"Thanks. I'm sure glad to see you guys."

"Welcome on board the Hydra. I'm Lieutenant Commander Yiannis Vassiliou, her captain. We are glad to be of assistance to you," replied the young naval officer who had helped pull him up to the deck.

"I am Lieutenant Colonel Jack Logan, Commander of the 526th fighter squadron, on loan to the Hellenic air force," he said offering his hand to Yiannis.

Yiannis took Logan's hand and gave him a firm shake.

"We are indebted to you, Colonel. You and your pilots have come to Greece's assistance in her hour of need. If it wasn't for your planes intercepting those enemy bombers the other day, we might now be at the bottom of the Aegean."

"Thanks, Commander, but I'm not too much use to anyone now, since I got my ass shot down by a flak battery over the Platamon."

"Nonsense, Colonel. Consider yourself lucky to be alive.

There will always be another day."

"I guess you're right, Commander. How soon before you can have me back at Thessaloniki?"

"Please call me, Yiannis. As for your question, that might be a slight problem. If you will please follow me, I will try to explain."

"Sure thing, Yiannis. And please, cut the formalities and call me Jack."

A few minutes later, both officers were inside the Hydra's combat information center where Yiannis briefed Logan of the Hydra's mission to Limnos.

"Now you see Jack why we can't take you back right away," said Yiannis.

"I see your point. Those transport pilots will need the forward air controllers to help guide them into the jump zone."

There was a knock at the door. "Come in!"

"Here's your coffee," said Lieutenant Mavridis.

"Thanks, Takis. Jack, this is my weapons officer and second in command, Lieutenant Takis Mavridis. Takis has had the experience of being shot down himself and living to tell about it."

Takis offered his hand to Logan. "I was a navigator and radar operator on an Albatross spotter plane. A Turkish air force fighter jumped us during the opening hours of the war. I was the only survivor."

"Consider yourself part of the lucky few, Takis."

"I was just explaining to the Colonel, we would be a little

late in delivering him back to his squadron."

"Bridge to Captain!" came over the ship's intercom. Yiannis picked up the phone and dialed the bridge. It was answered by one of his new officers, Ensign Svoronas, the acting bridge watch officer.

"Sir, we have sighted a small fishing boat adrift and low in the water. There seems to be people on it."

"I'll be right up," said Yiannis.

"Excuse me, gentlemen. The lookout has spotted a small boat that's adrift with people on it. If you like Jack, you can come up to the bridge."

"Sure. I always wondered what it would be like if I had joined the navy instead of the air force," said Logan.

A few kilometers away, George and the rest of the survivors from Piges were desperately bailing to keep the small fishing boat afloat. The storm that hit them had carried them far out into the Aegean. The small boat had survived the brief storm's fury, but had, in the course, sprung several more leaks. Marshall was the first to spot the high speed craft that was bearing down on them.

"Sarge if it's the bad guys, we've had it. We are out of ammo," said Marshall.

"I don't think we could do much against them even if we had more ammunition. This one's pretty big."

"Please God, give us a chance to see our families once more," whispered George to himself as he lifted the binoculars to his eyes. He relaxed when he saw the blue and white flag fluttering on the boat's stern.

"She's Greek!

Everybody on the small Kaiki began to cheer wildly. George took a small American flag that one of the airmen had brought along and began waving it over his head for the crew the boat to see. Yiannis, Logan and Takis entered the Hydra's bridge and saw Ensign Svoronas holding a pair of binoculars to his eyes.

"So what's going on?" asked Yiannis.

"Sir, one of them is waiving what looks to be an American flag."

"Can I see?" asked Logan. The ensign handed Logan the binoculars.

"By God, it is an American flag and that guy looks familiar," said Logan. "It sure is! It's Sergeant Pappas, one of the USAF cops that was defending Piges airfield. He's a Greek American and was acting as a liaison between us and the Greek air force."

"Piges fell early this morning to the enemy. I heard it on the radio," said Takis.

"Mr. Svoronas, notify the first aid station that there might be wounded coming on board," said Yiannis.

A few minutes later, the Hydra had pulled alongside the battered Kaiki. George noticed that one of the ship's fifty caliber machine guns was trained on the small fishing boat. Their commander wasn't taking any chances. A sign of a thorough officer thought George. One of the Hydra's sailors threw a line to George which he quickly secured to the boat.

"Thank God for the Hellenic navy arriving in the nick of

time. I don't know how much longer this thing would have stayed afloat," said George to one of the Greek sailors who had jumped aboard to help.

"Hey down there, identify yourselves." shouted Yiannis from the Hydra's deck."

"I am Master Sergeant George Pappas from the 86th Security Force Squadron, Ramstein Germany. I have eight others with me. We're all that's left from the defenders of Piges airfield," shouted George in perfect Greek.

"You are all welcome aboard." George was the first to climb the ladder up to the Hydra's deck.

"Permission to come aboard." he said, rendering Yiannis a sharp salute"

Yiannis returned the salute. "Permission granted."

"Would you please accompany me to the bridge? Don't worry about your people, they'll be well taken care of."

After everyone was helped aboard, one of the sailors cut the Kaiki adrift and the Hydra resumed her journey. George watched from the bridge as the small boat that had saved their lives quickly disappeared from view.

"So George, tell me. There were no other survivors that you know of?" asked Logan.

"No, sir. They shot all the prisoners. We saw them gunned down. We could do nothing to help them. And Cindy was the only survivor from the last plane out, which took a direct 122mm rocket hit"

"Thank God for that at least."

"Those murderers have to be made to pay for all their crimes," said Yiannis.

"How did you manage to slip through the Turkish lines?" asked Takis.

"A few hours after the fighter planes departed, the enemy began a large scale attack with armor and infantry.

"The base was overrun, but not without a stiff fight. The enemy suffered very heavy casualties. During the chaos, I gathered up whomever I could find. We found a HUMMVEE and fought our way to the coast. That's where we found the Kaiki. I will be the first to say, that God was watching over us today," said George.

"He had to be. Especially how you guys managed to destroy that enemy patrol boat," said Logan having heard the story from the other survivors.

"We could all use some of your luck when we reach Limnos. I'm sorry to say that you're not out of the frying pan yet," said Yiannis.

"Huh? What do you mean, sir?" Yiannis explained the nature of the Hydra's mission to George.

"So when do we get there?"

"Just after sunset. I know of a few coves along the way where we can hide the boat until the sun goes down. Even though the Turkish navy isn't out to sea anymore, we can't afford to get spotted."

"I almost forgot. You must all be tired and hungry after your ordeal. Would you all like something to eat?"

"Sure, Commander. I'm famished," said Logan.

"What I'd really like is a shower and a couple of hours of sleep," said George.

"No problem. You can use my cabin to freshen up and get some rest. I'll have a crewman throw your uniform in the ship's washer. It'll be ready for you when you wake up."

"Thanks, but I need to check on my people first."

"Don't worry George, I'll take care of that for you," said Logan.

"I've just left them. They're all taking hot showers and having something to eat," said Takis as he walked onto the bridge.

"Some of the crew have lent your men clean clothes until their uniforms come back from the boat's laundry. Your men can use the crew's bunks to get some rest. Cindy can use my cabin until we reach the island."

"That's very kind of all of you, Mr. Mavridis."

"It's the least we can do to thank all of you for coming to our country's aid," said Yiannis.

"Now go get some rest, Sergeant."

"What about you, Colonel?"

"Don't worry about me. I got plenty of rest floating in the Aegean all morning."

"Come, I'll show you to my cabin," said Yiannis.

The Presidential Palace, Sofia Bulgaria
1620hrs, 21 May

Everyone had already taken their seats when President Nickolovich called the cabinet meeting to order.

"Gentlemen, it has been a little over three days since the Turks began their bloody war of aggression against Greece. Initially, it seemed that they would be victorious. However, the American aid and tenacity of the Greeks, along with their recent successes on land and on the sea, have turned the tables on the Turks. It is a very distinct possibility that Turkey may even lose this war. What I propose is that we insure they do lose the war and that they are never again in a position to threaten anyone in the Balkans."

"And how do you propose we accomplish this, Mr. President?" asked the Minister of Agriculture.

"Our forces will attack them through Eastern Thrace tomorrow morning. I had instructed the Minister of Defense to prepare a plan just in case we did intervene in the war. Our armed forces are already on a high state of alert. All they need is the word from me to begin. General Gregorov, will you please continue with the briefing."

"Thank you, Mr. President. Gentlemen, the bulk of the Turkish army, east of the Platamon River is according to last reports still in retreat. Now is the time to strike while they are still disorganized. This is what I propose for us today. Tomorrow morning, at 0600hrs, we will begin offensive operations against Turkey. Our First Army will attack through

Western Thrace with the objective of reaching the coast just west of Alexandroupolis. This will drive a wedge between the Turks and effectively trap the bulk of their army between us and the Greeks. Once this is accomplished, the Turk must capitulate or face total destruction. Our second army will attack through Eastern Thrace, the objective being Tekeridag on the coast of the Sea of Marmara. This will be more of a feint to draw the pressure off the first army. Any territory that we seize can be used as leverage in any peace negotiations."

"What about the Greeks?" asked the Finance Minister.

"Our attaché in Athens is already in contact with the Hellenic general staff. Remember we are detaining over twenty thousand of their soldiers. We have begun returning their heavy weapons which we confiscated and they will join us in the attack."

"Excuse me, General," said President Nickolovich.

"One of the concessions that the Greeks will grant us is free trade zones in the ports of Thessaloniki and Kavalla. The President could see many of his ministers nodding their head in support."

"So Mr. President," said the Minister of Internal Affairs, the major coalition partner of his government and the person he would have to convince to support his plans.

"Bulgaria would have come out the winner either way."

"Yes, my friend, but at the price of a powerful Islamic fundamentalist Turkey as our neighbor. How long do you think before the neo Ottoman Islamists in Istanbul would have stirred trouble with the over one million Muslims in our country? Would we have been next? Now is the opportunity to crush them once and for all. Besides gentlemen, we can't allow this war to be prolonged any longer. It is costing the Bulgarian economy tens of millions of dollars a day in lost trade." The Finance Minister nodded his head agreeing with the President's last comment.

"You have a valid point there, Mr. President. My party will support your decision."

"Thank you, Igor. This will be a historic day for our country. Does anyone have any other questions before I adjourn this meeting? If there are none, I would like the Ministers of Health, Internal Affairs and the Foreign Minister to remain. This meeting is adjourned. May God grant our soldiers a speedy victory."

Igia Hospital, Athens
1705hrs, 21 May

Fahtme opened her eyes. She was inside what appeared to be a hospital room. So her earlier awakening had not been a dream after all. Her head felt like it was about to explode. Nonetheless, the pain helped clear her thinking. The last thing she remembered was that animal, Osman, raping her. Her father, she had heard someone saying had been murdered. She tried to sit up, but was unable to from all the tubes and wires connected to her.

"Miss, please don't move, you'll hurt yourself." Fahtme

turned toward the source of the voice. It was a young man wearing a police uniform.

"Where am I?"

"You're in Igia hospital in Athens. You were injured."

"Yes, I remember clearly now what happened."

"Just a minute, Miss. I was given instructions to call the doctor if you woke up," said the police officer as he got up to leave the room. Once outside in the hallway, he spoke into his portable radio alerting police headquarters that their star witness had awakened. Then he proceeded to get the doctor.

Twenty minutes later the chief of Greek military intelligence, Brigadier General Stamatis, and General Paraskevas, deputy commander of the Greek police, had arrived at Fahtme's room. They updated her on what had transpired during the time she was in her comma. "So you see, miss, it's vital that we have your assistance to help put a stop to this madness," said General Stamatis.

"What can I do to help stop this insane war?"

"You can help us relay the truth of what really happened to you and your father to your people. The earlier tape that we had made was refuted by Turkey. They claimed you were drugged and coached what to say. With your permission, we would like to bring the international news media here. I would like you to make another tape so we can broadcast the truth to the world about your father's murder. What do you say?"

Fahtme was seething with hatred for General Kemal and all he stood for. Not only did he have her father murdered, he had spilled the blood of thousands of innocent people on both sides.

"Yes, I will help you. My father would have wanted it."

"Thank you, I will make the arrangements," said the General.

"Let her get some rest," said the doctor.

"She is still very weak." When everybody had left the room Fahtme began to cry. Her father had been a simple man. His only wish had been that the two communities peacefully coexist side by side. Now she wondered if that would ever be possible again.

Kesan Command Bunker
1920hrs, 21 May

"Sir, here is the latest message from the front," said Colonel Azoglou, handing the sheet of paper to General Kemal. The General read the message and showed some visible signs of relief.

"So, we've managed to partially stabilize the front after falling back fifty kilometers."

"Yes, sir. The Greeks have stopped for the night to consolidate their gains. They've outrun their supply lines. They will probably resume their attack in the morning."

"This also gives us a chance to dig in and be ready for them," said the General.

"Ahmet, draft the orders to all commanders. Our troops will dig in where they are."

"Immediately, sir," said his aid as he picked up the phone and called the message center. Having given the necessary instructions, the Colonel hung up the phone.

"All done, sir."

"Thank you, Ahmet."

The Colonel turned to leave. "Oh before I forget, Ahmet. Is there anything new on the Bulgarian troop movements?"

"Not really. Except for the additional armor that they brought up this morning, everything is still quiet."

"Good. If all goes well, there may be no need to use our missiles after all."

"Yes, sir."

As he left the General's office, Ahmet prayed to Allah that all would go well tomorrow. If not, the Americans would be given the green light to proceed. He knew that he would be seen as a traitor by some, but he had to save his country from this madman he had helped create.

Limnos
2223hrs, 21 May

When the sun had finally settled below the horizon, the Hydra left her old hiding place at Agios Efstratios Island and made a straight beeline for the shores of Limnos. Approaching the blacked out island just south of the town of Plaka, Yiannis scanned the dark coast looking for their contact's signal. George and Logan were both on the bridge after having gotten some needed rest.

"I don't like this Yiannis, they should have been here already," said Takis.

"Hey! What's that over there?" said George pointing toward the shore where he had seen a light.

Everybody looked toward the beach. A few seconds later they were all rewarded by three flashes.

"That's it, the signal," said Yiannis. Yiannis acknowledged the flashes with the pre-arranged counter sign.

"Helmsman, bring us about. All ahead slow. Head for where the light came from."

"Aye, aye, sir."

A few minutes later, the Hydra had come alongside a rubber Zodiac containing three heavily armed men, whose faces were blackened with charcoal. One of the sailors threw a line and the Zodiac made fast to the Hydra. After the three men had come aboard, one of them, a short, but stocky man wearing officer's insignia introduced himself to Yiannis.

"Hello I'm Lieutenant Kostas Genetakos of the second Special Forces airborne company.

"Welcome to the Hydra. I'm Lieutenant Commander Yiannis Vassiliou, her Captain. This is Lieutenant Takis Mavridis, my second in command, Colonel Jack Logan and Sergeant George Pappas, U.S. air force."

"I'm pleased to meet you, gentlemen."

"Ah, so you are Commander Vassiliou. I've heard so much about you." Yiannis gave the Lieutenant a puzzled look.

"Oh, I must apologize, you don't know. Your fiancée Eleni, I'm sure she would want me to give you her best regards."

"Eleni, she's okay?"

"Why yes. She's at our camp, only a few kilometers from here, helping take care of our wounded." Yiannis was ecstatic.

"Thank God. I was so worried. Petros must have gotten her out of harm's way."

"Yes, he did. I found them wondering in the mountains a few days ago. We took them to our camp. Petros proved invaluable to us with his knowledge of the island."

"How's he doing?"

"I'm sorry, but I'm afraid that he was killed when we took out an enemy supply dump. He saved our lives by taking out an enemy machine gun nest."

"What about Anna, his wife?"

"She was murdered by enemy soldiers. Petros arrived back at the hotel in time to save Eleni."

"Damn this war. Damn those bastards! We were old shipmates. Petros had only retired a couple of years ago. He was looking for some peace and quiet and came back to his island."

"I know how you feel commander," said the Special Forces officer. "We all have lost a lot of good friends in this war."

"Anyway, let's get on with winning the war," said Yiannis, momentarily purging Petros from his thoughts.

"The forward air controllers will be ready to disembark in a few minutes and the medical supplies that you requested are being brought up."

"That's good news, Commander. We were air dropped some tents and supplies the other day, but we've run short on bandages and antibiotics. Oh, and don't worry about your boat, sir. You can stay anchored here as long as you want. This area of the island has been secured. The only Turks you'll find around here are dead ones."

"That's good to know. How far did you say your camp was?"

"Just a few kilometers from here."

"Great! I would like to come and . . . "

"Sir, sorry to interrupt you. We just received a priority message from fleet headquarters," said Mr. Faniou.

Yiannis took the message. After he had finished reading it, he handed it to Takis.

"Well, gentlemen. I guess we're not returning to Salamis real soon. We've all been ordered to stay here, including you, Jack. It seems we are to meet a certain American intelligence officer by the name of Colonel Robert Hess. He'll be dropping in with the paratroopers in the morning."

"I don't know him, Yiannis."

"I guess we'll find out more in the morning, Jack."

The forward air controllers had loaded their gear onto the Zodiac and were preparing to climb aboard.

"Stefanos, take them to shore and come on back. We're going to have more company tonight," said Lieutenant Genetakos to his sergeant manning the boat.

"Sure thing, sir."

"George, get your men ready. We'll be staying at the commando camp tonight," said Logan.

"Okay, sir. We'll be a couple of minutes, give me a chance to round up everyone."

"Takis, keep a crew at the guns. Rotate them every two hours. I'll be back in the morning. If anything happens, shove off and come back when it's safe."

"Okay, Yiannis. Give my regards to Eleni."

"Don't worry about your boat. I'll leave a few of my men on guard by the beach," said Lieutenant Genetakos.

"Thanks for the help. Takis, post five men as additional guards to augment the Lieutenant's troops. I'll be back in five minutes. I'm going to change uniform."

Kommotini, City Mosque
2255hrs, 21 May

For the past few days, both Mohamid and Osman had been basking in their success. Their operation had succeeded far beyond their wildest expectations. When the Turkish army had entered Kommotini, the two agents had proceeded to meet with the city's new military commander. He had been previously briefed by headquarters on the two agents whose identity was to remain secret. He gave them their new orders. Their mission would be to organize a local security force in the newly occupied prefecture, composed of all able bodied Muslim males living in the area. This would free the regular combat troops from occupational duties. The local Muslims did not agree with the new duties imposed on them. All they wanted to do was go back to their normal lives and farm their land. Mohamid and Osman had tried to solicit volunteers, but very few answered the call. Unable to get enough men willingly, they had been forced to use other methods.

The mood of the two men was now one of guarded optimism. The issue of the Muslim security force was beginning to cause friction between the locals and the Turkish army. Finding out that they had botched the murder of the Mufti's daughter didn't help matters much either. Fortunately, the propaganda people in Istanbul were able to convince everyone, that yesterday's broadcast of the Mufti's daughter had been a ploy by the Greeks. It was easily believable by anyone who viewed the broadcast, that in her apparent drugged state, she was coaxed into saying what the Greeks wanted.

"Gentlemen, there is a group of local citizens to see you," said the guard posted at their office door.

"Let them in," said Osman. They both noticed that the six men that had come into their office were all carrying arms. One of them, a Muslim cleric, was acting as their spokesman. Osman hoped that these were a group of volunteers for the new security force, though he doubted it when he saw the look on their faces.

"What can I do for you, gentlemen?" asked Osman.

"We have come to speak to you about an important matter," said the Imam.

"And what may that be?" asked Mohamid as he lit a cigarette.

"The matter of the Mufti's murder," said the cleric.

"What is there to say? I told you the infidels murdered him.

You saw the proof. What more do you want?"

"We will know more in a couple of minutes. It was just announced over Greek radio that the Mufti's daughter will be broadcasting live from her hospital bed. Since there is still no electricity in the city, we have brought one of our own portable televisions here for you to watch.

"Fortunately, there is no lack of batteries in the town," said one of the cleric's body guards as he turned on the small TV set.

"I hope you don't really believe the Greeks. They are losing the war. They will say anything.

"Silence!" The cleric abruptly cut Osman off as the picture of the telecaster from the eleven o'clock news came on the TV. After a quick brief of the day's top story, the defeat of the Turkish army at the Platamon River, the picture switched to Igia Hospital. The TV announcer related to his audience that the Mufti's daughter, who had barely escaped being murdered, had regained consciousness and would tell the world what really happened.

"They are lying," yelled Osman.

"I said silence. If they are lying, what do you have to fear?"

A few seconds later, the picture switched to a hospital bed showing a young woman with her head still swathed in bandages and several tubes connected to her body. Surrounding her were several high ranking government officials, police and military officers. The rest of the room was filled with reporters and TV cameras.

"I recognize her, that is Fahtme," said one of the men.

The cameras then switched to a man dressed in a doctor's hospital frock. He answered several reporters' questions on the extent of his patient's injuries and actually did a good job explaining to the viewer audience, in layman's terms, how she had survived the gunshot wound to the head. When the doctor finished, he gave his patient over to the reporters. The TV cameras switched over to Fahtme. In a weak, but steady voice, she began telling the world how General Kemal and his henchmen were responsible for the hideous crimes perpetrated against her and her father. At first, shock and disbelief appeared on the faces of those present in the room besides Mohamid and Osman. It was quickly replaced with anger.

"They are lying! She has obviously been drugged!" yelled Osman as he began to shake with fear.

"I told you to be silent!" said the cleric.

Fahtme ended with her asking the Greek Muslims to pray for peace and asking the Greeks to forgive what their people had done, because they too, had been victims of Kemal's ruthless plan. When she had finished with what she had to say, the camera switched to a young man wearing a turban. He was introduced to the audience as Fahtme's brother. He too spoke to the reporters confirming what his sister had just said was of her own free will.

"That pig is a traitor and a liar. He is collaborating with the enemy," said Mohamid.

"How dare you blaspheme the future Mufti, you murderous dog," said the cleric.

"He is not lying. I sent him to Athens to personally confirm his sister's story."

"You are lying, he was in Turkey."

"We also have our own intelligence network," said the cleric. When we first heard that Fahtme was still alive, we sent word for him to come to Greece.

"You are both liars and murderers! Both of you, from the very beginning have been just a little bit too willing to help us," said one of the cleric's followers.

"Yes, that is true," said the cleric. "How do you explain the Mufti's murder, my anonymous phone call and you two showing up in the square, telling everyone of the crime and ready to lead us against the Greeks?"

"We just happened to be passing by the Mufti's home and saw the police there. We then rushed to the square," said Mohamid.

"Stop your lies, you scum of the earth! You murdered the Mufti and made it look like the Greeks did it to start a war between the two communities. May Allah forgive me. I was a fool to fall for it, but I was overcome by emotion to think straight. The blood of hundreds if not thousands are on your hands!"

"No! No, we are Muslims just like you!" pleaded Mohamid, as he now trembled uncontrollably with fear.

"No you are not! You are cold blooded murderers and you will pay for your crimes," replied the cleric.

"No! You are all half-wits," yelled Osman. "Yes, we killed

the traitorous dog. He was a fool and a collaborator. You are too stupid to understand this. We have liberated you from the infidels and you are ungrateful."

"Yes, we have been very stupid," replied the cleric. "We were living fine with the Greeks, sharing the same freedoms as they. We should have all listened to the Mufti. He was a righteous human being who only wanted peace and coexistence between the two communities. Unfortunately, some of us were fools enough to believe in your General. He is evil, sent by Satan to destroy Islam."

"You are all traitorous fools and deserve to be the lapdogs of the Greeks," said Mohamid.

The cleric glared at the two men with hatred in his eyes.

"You are both murderers and rapists. You will be tried and punished for your crimes."

Osman laughed. "You really are a fool, old man. Who will judge us, the Turkish army?

"We are the law here. It is you who will be tried for treason," added Mohamid.

"Both of you will be tried by a council of the community's elders. This is true Islamic law."

"I don't think so. Guard, arrest these fools." No one moved.

"I said arrest these idiots!"

The guard, a local Muslim, did not move. "See, you are now alone," said the cleric.

"You will die first, old man" said Osman as he opened his desk drawer and pulled out a pistol. Before Osman could bring the gun fully to bear, the guard fired a burst from his submachine gun. The bullets hit Osman in the chest and spun him around. His last act before falling dead to the ground was to fire a shot. The bullet struck the cleric in the fleshy part of the arm passing right through. Several of the men rushed to the aid of the Muslim holy man.

"I am all right; it's only a flesh wound. Take this other pig away. Enough sin has been committed in the house of Allah for one day."

"What will we do with him?" asked one of the men.

"He will be immediately tried by our elders, as I promised. We are not killers like them. He will have a fair trial."

"No, please. I didn't do it. Osman shot the Mufti. Please, I'm innocent," cried Mohamid.

"Take him! Justice awaits," said the cleric. Several of the men grabbed Mohamid, gagged him, tied his hands and put him into a canvas sack as not to be seen by the roving Turkish patrols. They then took him out of the Mosque and threw him into the back of a horse drawn wagon. The next morning, a Turkish patrol found Mohamid's body dangling from a light pole. His penis had been cut off and stuffed in his mouth. He had a placard hanging on his body that said:

"I am a rapist and a murderer."

Limnos, Special Forces Encampment

2345hrs, 21 May

After walking for more than an hour through rough hilly terrain, Logan, Yiannis, George and the rest of the group were nearing the Special Forces encampment.

"We're almost there. It's just over this ridge," said Lieutenant Genetakos.

"Man, I am glad we're almost there," replied Logan.

"We pilots aren't used to taking these long nature walks."

Yiannis laughed.

"We sailors aren't either, Jack. But I would walk to hell and back right now if Eleni was there waiting for me. A few minutes later, they were challenged by a rough looking sentry. His face was blackened with soot and his helmet and rifle were covered with camouflage netting. The Lieutenant gave him the proper password and they proceeded on.

"What hole did he come out of?" asked George.

"I am glad these guys are on our side," said Logan.

"We have arrived. This is our new camp, we just moved here the other day when we secured this section of the island," The commando encampment was situated in a small wooded ravine on the side of a steep hill. Several tents had been set up and covered with camouflage netting that blended in with the trees. The encampment was virtually undetectable from the air.

"You guys did a pretty good job of hiding it," said George.

"We have also positioned Stinger gunners on several high spots overlooking the encampment just in case we have any unwanted visitors," said the Lieutenant.

When they entered the encampment, they were met by the

senior officer in charge, Major Christakos. Yiannis introduced himself and everybody in the group.

"You can't believe how happy we all are to see you. Just your presence here means we're winning the war."

"The war isn't won yet, Major, but neither are we losing anymore," said Yiannis.

"And I would like to thank our American friends who came through for us in our time of need," said Major Christakos in accented English.

"We have heard of your valiant defense of Piges airfield from one of our dispatches. We are proud to be fighting side by side with such gallant soldiers," he added, giving his hand first to Logan and then to George.

"Thank you, Major. Sergeant Pappas could tell you more about it, he was there. He and the few men you see here fought their way to the beach and managed to escape in a small boat."

"Oh," said the Major as he now looked upon George with renewed interest.

"A Greek-American. Do you speak Greek?"

"Yes, Sir," answered George in perfect Greek.

"I would like to set the record straight on Piges, sir. It wasn't gallant in any way. It was plain slaughter. I lost over thirty-five men. The few of us that you see here were the lucky ones, the only survivors. All the rest were shot after they had surrendered! I left over thirty-five men back there."

For a moment, the Major did not say anything; he just looked at George thoughtfully.

"I can appreciate exactly how you feel, Sergeant. Command is a terrible responsibility in time of war. We came here with two full companies of soldiers. When and if we ever leave here, I too, have a lot of letters to write to wives and parents. I see their faces in my sleep. We have signed so many treaties and conventions supposedly outlawing weapons of mass destruction and guaranteeing the safety of civilians and prisoners of war, but everything was for nothing. I believe it was one of your Generals that said, "War is hell." He was correct in every aspect."

"I hope when all this is over, those guilty of war crimes and atrocities will be judged for their crimes," added George.

"A good thought, Sergeant. Unfortunately, the big fish always manage to get away," replied Logan.

"Hopefully tomorrow, we'll manage to net a few when your countrymen arrive," said Major Christakos.

"What shape is the enemy in?"

"Well, Colonel, except for those still surrounding the airport. They're in a defensive posture trying to hold on to what they've taken. They're hold up in Mirina and several other small towns. They don't venture much inland anymore. They have to be very short on supplies and ammunition."

"Hardly any is getting through to them. We control the sea lanes in and around Limnos," said Yiannis.

"That's true. They are getting desperate. Nevertheless, like a trapped animal, they're still dangerous, "said the Major. "From what we can gather from people fleeing the occupied areas, their soldiers are mainly living off what they can loot from the civilian populace. They are treating the local populace very brutally."

"How many are there left on the island?" asked Yiannis.

"Probably 5000-7000, an understrength division, very few heavy weapons."

"Not too many. The 101st should be able to deal with them," said Logan.

"I'm sure you are all hungry and would like to get some rest for tomorrow. We'll be moving out very early. The jump will be at 0600hrs. Sergeant Alavanos will show you where to sleep," said Major Christakos.

"Sounds like a good idea. Some food would be just what the doctor ordered," said Logan.

"Excuse me, Major. There is someone I know here, my fiancée," said Yiannis.

"You must mean Eleni. She was a godsend for our wounded. She should be in the hospital tent." He pointed in the tent's direction.

"Thanks," said Yiannis as he took off toward the tent. Reaching the tent, he pulled the flap open. He saw her in the dim light provided by the one battle lantern hanging on the center tent pole. She was leaning over a wounded soldier, wiping his brow with a towel. Yiannis slowly went to her side. She looked up and for a moment, she just stood there looking at him.

"Yiannis!" She jumped up, wrapped her arms around him and smothered his mouth with hers.

"For a moment, I couldn't believe it was you. I heard that people were coming from the mainland, but I would never have imagined one of them would be you."

"Oh Eleni, Eleni, my darling. I lived all these days with the fear that something dreadful had happened to you. I would never have forgiven myself for bringing you here."

"It wasn't your fault. Who would have ever dreamed of a war breaking out? I owe my life to Anna and Petros, God rest their souls. Poor Anna, she was raped and murdered by those animals. Petros was killed blowing up an enemy supply dump."

"I know Eleni, Lieutenant Genetakos told me."

"So much pain and suffering," she said as she wiped the tears from her eyes and looked at the wounded soldiers lying about the tent.

"You're safe now. It will soon be over. Tomorrow morning, American paratroopers will come to liberate the rest of the island." Just then the tent flap opened and a tired looking, medium height, but well-built individual dressed in battle dress utilities with a stethoscope around his neck walked in.

"It's the doctor," said Eleni.

The doctor walked up to the both of them and held out his hand. "Hi! I'm Lieutenant Theoharis Bosinakis and you must be Yiannis. Eleni has talked so much about you." Yiannis took the younger man's hand.

"I'm pleased to meet you. I hope they were all good things."

"Oh, I envy you Commander. She is a great girl and a caring individual. She is a natural born nurse. I would have never managed here without her."

"It must have been very difficult caring for the wounded," said Yiannis.

"Yes it was, especially in the beginning. We weren't set up to handle serious casualties. It got better when we moved here to this location and with the air drops of medical supplies, we have been able to save more men. Eleni can tell you all about it. Why don't you two go to my tent and get some rest? I can manage here," said doctor Bosinakis.

"That's very kind of you, but we couldn't. You're the one that looks bushed, doctor. Why don't you go get some sleep?" said Yiannis.

"I can manage, Commander. Sergeant Koukis, my orderly, will be here shortly to give me a hand. I'll catch some rest on the cot over there in the corner. Now go get some rest. Tomorrow will be a very busy day, especially for the medical corp."

"Well thanks for your kind offer, Doc. Where is your tent by the way?"

"I know where it's at," said Eleni with a look of mischief in her eyes.

"Well good night, Doc. See you in the morning," said Yiannis. Hugging Eleni by her waist, they both headed for the tent and for some needed rest.

Chapter 10

Limnos

0605hrs, 22 May

Everyone at the Special Forces base camp was awakened during the early morning hours to the rumble of explosions coming from the direction of Mirina. The detonations had lasted for several minutes. It was unknown what had caused them, but Logan had speculated that it might have been a high altitude B-52 or B-1 bombing raid. The air force would want to soften up the target area before this morning's air drop. If they had been raids, more would follow. He wished he was back in the cockpit leading one of these air strikes.

A couple of hours before daybreak, the forward air controllers had departed the camp for the drop zone. The drop would take place in the center of the island, in a narrow strip of flat land, a few kilometers from the small town of Atsiki. Thirty minutes after the FAC team's departure, Yiannis, George, Logan and a platoon of soldiers under Lieutenant Genetakos's command left the camp for the drop zone.

Before leaving the camp, Yiannis used the commando's radio and contacted the Hydra to check on her situation. Takis had assured him that all was in order. He had used the occasion to fill Yiannis in on their latest orders from Athens. The Hydra had been instructed to stay at Limnos until further notice. That was perfectly fine with him. He would be close to Eleni.

After a grueling march, they finally reached the jump zone area and were greeted with the sounds of sporadic small arms fire. "Damn it! It must be the FAC team in trouble," said Logan.

"The shooting is coming from over that direction," said Yiannis, pointing towards the area where the gunshots had originated from.

"We should give them a hand. The planes will soon be overhead," said George.

"I'm with you," replied Lieutenant Genetakos. Taking a squad of his men, along with George and four of his Security Forces troops, armed with Grenade launchers, they took off down the trail. A couple of minutes later, the Lieutenant raised his arm for everyone to halt and take cover.

"Look over there, about two hundred meters to the left, in that thicket."

"I don't see anything, Lieutenant."

"Trust me, George, they are in there. They've gone to ground."

George heard the click of a rifle bolt going forward, coming from the direction of the thicket.

"I think you are right," said George after couple of shots rang out from the thicket.

"George, take two of your men and see if you can lob a few grenades into there."

"Gotcha, sir."

George signaled to both Airman Franklin and Jefferson to

quietly follow him. Crawling slowly through the rough brush on their hands and knees, they reached a spot that gave them a clear field of fire.

"Okay, guys. Make this good. I want you to hit the thicket the first time."

"Don't worry, Sarge, we're the best," said Franklin.

They both loaded their M-203s' with high a high explosive 40mm grenade and aimed toward the thicket.

"Fire!"

The two grenades shot out of the tubes and arched toward the enemy soldiers. Before the rounds had even landed, the two airmen had begun reloading their weapons with high explosive grenades. The grenades exploded in the thicket, showering the area with shrapnel.

"Give them another, just in case," said George. Jefferson raised his weapon and fired. As the smoke of the last grenade began to clear, Genetakos and his men charged the thicket. It was unnecessary; the four man enemy fire team was already dead.

"Who are they?" asked George, pointing to a small group of soldiers walking toward them.

"It's just the FAC team or what's left of it," said Logan who had joined George along with Lieutenant Genetakos and his team.

The three Greek soldiers approached the Americans. One had obviously been wounded in the arm, but not seriously.

"Are you guys okay?" asked Lieutenant Genetakos.

"We were ambushed," said the squad leader, Sergeant Major Alexopoulos.

"Tom and Harrilaos were killed outright. We should now be okay though. We have to set up our radios; the planes will be here in fifteen minutes. We all need to be extra vigilant, I have a bad feeling there are more enemy soldiers around."

"I'll take my men and move out a hundred meters and establish a three sixty security zone," said Lieutenant Genetakos.

"George, stay here and guard the FAC team and their gear."

"Okay, Lieutenant."

"I'll also stay here with the Colonel," said Yiannis.

"That sounds like a terrific idea," replied Logan who was now holding a rifle taken from one of the dead enemy soldiers. The FAC team had quickly set up their gear and portable radio station. "Are you ready to transmit, Sergeant?"

"We will be, Colonel, as soon as I finish stringing this antenna. Almost done. There, we are ready." replied the FAC team senior NCO.

"Antonis, crank her up."

The Corporal turned on the radio and tuned it to the pre-arranged frequency. Sergeant Alexopoulos took the mike and began transmitting in heavily accented English.

"This is Blue Dog to Red Eagle, over." They were answered almost immediately.

"This is Red Eagle, we read you loud and clear, Blue Dog," replied the aircraft commander of the lead plane carrying the paratroopers. "We are twenty minutes out. What are the conditions in the drop zone?"

"This is Blue Dog. Winds five knots, temperature 17 degrees centigrade. Landing zone is hot. I repeat hot. Enemy patrols are in the area, over."

"I copy, Blue Dog. I have ten friendlies along to help clear the area. Please direct them where you want them to drop their load, over."

"Roger, Red Eagle. See you in a little."

Sergeant Alexopoulos immediately switched frequencies and contacted the fighter bombers that were supporting the air drop and gave them their target coordinates. Seven minutes later, ten Hellenic air force A-7H Corsairs zoomed in out of the east. Five broke off and began dropping their ordnance. Cluster bombs mixed with five hundred pounders exploded loudly in the small valley. The other five planes orbited overhead, in case needed.

"Good drop and thanks a lot, guys. That should keep their heads down for a while. We'll call you if we need some more help. Blue Dog out."

Limnos, the Hydra
0625hrs, 22 May

Takis put down the coffee cup, he was starting to get the caffeine jitters. It was his fifth for the morning. The caffeine only worsened his anxiety. He sincerely wished his friend Yiannis was back. Except for the few minutes of sleep he had stolen in the CIC plot, he had stayed awake at his post on the bridge for most of the night. For the past hour, they had heard sporadic shooting off in the distance. With daybreak upon them, the Hydra would surely be visible to anyone approaching the cove. Just as a precaution, Takis had kept the ship's cannons manned and a man at the anchor chains, in case they had to make a quick getaway.

"Sir, I'm picking up a large formation of aircraft coming in from the east. Distance forty kilometers," said Lieutenant Evangelos Kourtis, the Hydra's acting Electronic warfare officer.

Kourtis had come aboard the Hydra just before their departure from Salamis to serve as the boat's second EW officer. He was an older man, visibly overweight, who had retired from active service several years prior. Now with the war, he had been recalled to active service.

"Thanks, Vangelis. Those must be the American transports and their escorts." He had heard the sound of aircraft and bombs going off, several minutes before. As a precaution to avoid attack from friendly aircraft, he had the Hydra's ensign run out. The large blue and white flag fluttered in the morning breeze from the flagstaff on the Hydra's stern. The flag was clearly visible from the air.

"Sir," hollered one of the Hydra's lookouts. "The shore guards are signaling that they've spotted an enemy patrol."

"Have the guns stand by to fire and get everyone back on board on the double. If they have any anti-tank weapons, we are in deep trouble. Hoist the anchor we're getting out of here."

"Yes, sir." replied the watch officer.

The Hydra's shore guards had already jumped into the Zodiac and started the engine when the enemy patrol from a distance of a few hundred meters opened fire with a machine gun. Several rounds hit the Zodiac hurling a sailor into the water and wounding two others. The few commandos that were with the Hydra had preferred to remain on shore and began engaging the enemy patrol. Takis gave the command for the Hydra's cannons to open fire. The missile boat's 35mm cannons roared out, peppering the shore line with high explosive rounds. The machine gun was quickly silenced. When the Zodiac reached the Hydra, the wounded men were quickly helped aboard.

"Helm, get us out of here!" commanded Takis. The Hydra's engines roared to life, the loud diesels muffling the noise of the enemy grenade launcher firing. The 40mm grenade arched toward the Hydra and struck the boat amidships spraying it with shrapnel, killing and wounding several sailors. The Hydra's gun returned fire, killing the rest of the enemy soldiers.

"Get a medic down there on the double," screamed Takis when he saw the carnage done by the enemy grenade.

In a couple of minutes, the Hydra was safe and out of range of the enemy fire.

"Where are we going, sir?" asked Mr. Panou, the helmsman.

"We'll stay offshore for a while until things settle down. I have to go check on the injured,"

"Hey, look up there. There must be over thirty transport

planes," yelled one of the bridge lookouts.

Everybody looked up toward the west. "It's the 101st Airborne," said Takis with a big smile. "And they're right on time!"

Limnos, the Jump Zone
0639hrs, 22 May

Logan and the rest of the joint Greek-American team watched in awe as the big C-17 transports came overhead and quickly filled the sky with blossoming parachute canopies. "Ain't that a beautiful sight," said Logan.

"It surely is," answered Yiannis.

"I am sure it isn't fun for all those soldiers, swinging in their chute canopies like sitting ducks,"

"Some of the bastards survived, Sergeant" said Lieutenant Genetakos as he watched several of the parachutists go limp as they were hit by enemy ground fire.

"There's not much we can do now. Our men are too close to them to call in air strikes."

"No, Colonel, but we can sure lend them a helping hand."

"My men and I are with you, Lieutenant."

"Let's go, but leave a few men to protect the FAC team, in case a few strays come back around," said Logan.

Fifteen minutes later, after mopping up several enemy troops and another machine gun nest, they come in contact with the lead elements of the 101st. The well trained paratroopers, within minutes of landing, had formed up into their respective squads and began securing the drop zone area. The scene of their link up with the Greeks was reminiscent of the 1945 meeting of the Soviet and American forces at the Elbe River. Both American and Greek soldiers hugged and shared bottles of Ouzo and wine that several of the Greek commandos had carried with them for the occasion.

While Logan and the rest of the team sipped on a bottle of wine that was being passed around, a paratrooper approached them and held out his hand to Logan.

"Obviously from the flight suit you're wearing, you must be Colonel Jack Logan," said the older man who was sporting Colonel's eagles on his shoulders.

"I'm Colonel Bob Hess, Deputy Chief of Staff for Intelligence at the Pentagon."

"Lieutenant Colonel Jack Logan at your service, sir," he said, feeling rather lightheaded from the few swigs Ouzo he had swallowed.

"This is Commander Yiannis Vassiliou of the missile boat Hydra."

"I'm very pleased to meet you. I read about your attack on the Turkish convoy. If it wasn't for your bravery, the island might have fallen."

"Thank you, sir. However Lieutenant Genetakos and his men deserve the real credit. They remained here and fought the enemy."

The Colonel took the young officers hand. "Thanks Lieutenant for securing the drop zone for us."

"I wish we could have done better, but the bastards were hiding from us."

"Nonsense, you and your men did a great job."

"And this is Master Sergeant Pappas. He was Flight Sergeant of the Security Force ABGD fight that was guarding Piges airfield. The rest over there are what is left of his team," said Logan.

George saw the Colonel's eyes open wide in disbelief. "Last I heard just before we were in the air was that everyone back at the Pentagon thought that you were all taken prisoners when the airfield was overrun."

"Well I hate to disappoint everybody back in Washington. There are no prisoners at Piges. We are it. Everybody else is dead. They were all butchered after having surrendered. We barely managed to make it to the coast and find a boat. We were picked up at sea by Commander Vassiliou and his crew."

"My God! No one could have imagined this would have happened. It was vital to get the planes and technicians away first. At the worst scenario, the brass figured you would have been taken as POWs to a holding camp. The Turks used to be our former allies for God's sake."

"Well, tell that to the families of all those murdered at Piges. My conscious is clear," said George.

"You don't know whom you're dealing with, Colonel," said Lieutenant Genetakos. "These people are the fundamentalist fanatics and see all Christians as infidels, unbelievers. They have totally gone back to their old eastern ways."

"In other words, Colonel, a good Christian is a dead Christian," added George.

"Well Sergeant, thanks for enlightening me. Nevertheless, I do know whom and what we are dealing with. And that is the reason I'm here."

"Sorry, sir. No disrespect meant," said George.

"None taken, Sergeant. Well, now to a more pleasant aspect. Colonel Logan, as of 0001hrs, this morning, you have been promoted to full bird Colonel."

"Oh," said Logan, quite surprised.

"And here is an extra pair of shiny eagles that I happened to be carrying just for the occasion," said Colonel Hess as he handed them to Logan."

"Why, thanks. I don't know what to say."

"From what I've heard of your exploits, you've earned them, Colonel."

"Well that calls for a toast. Colonel Hess, please do us the honors first," said Yiannis as he passed Hess the Ouzo bottle.

"Congratulations on your promotion, Colonel and here's to victory," said Hess as he took a healthy swig and passed the bottle to Logan. "Well now that the celebration is over, we have a war to win, gentlemen."

A few minutes later, they were all joined by several ranking officers and NCOs that made up the headquarters element of the 101st. After introducing all those present to the newcomers, Colonel Hess requested to speak to Logan privately. When they were out of earshot, Hess turned to Logan. "I guess you're wondering why I'm here?"

"I have to admit that I'm rather curious about why I was ordered to meet with you in the first place, instead of returning to my squadron," replied Logan.

"I can understand your feelings, but my mission here is of the utmost importance. Failure can cost the lives of tens of thousands of people. What I'm about to tell you is classified Top Secret."

Logan was caught by surprise. "But Turkey is losing the war."

"Exactly, and they're getting desperate. We have learned from a very reliable source that their leader, General Kemal, is planning to commit a final act of madness."

"What is he planning to do?"

"Suffice for now to say that it may change the total course of the war." Logan did not ask further. He knew that he'd be told when the intelligence officer deemed it appropriate.

"We tried to take him out early this morning with aircraft armed with special bunker busting munitions, developed during the Gulf war. In fact, it was your squadron that participated in the strike."

He now definitely had Logan's undivided attention. "We know that he's staying at his underground command post in Kesan, Turkey. Kesan is only forty kilometers from the border. The bunker is built into the side of a large hill and the approaches to it are heavily defended by layers of missile and anti-aircraft batteries."

Logan did not like what he was hearing. The Colonel was obviously leading up to something.

"We thought we knew where all the air ducts and the entrance to the bunker were from satellite photos. Unfortunately, we were wrong. The Turks have ingeniously camouflaged the bunker. They have built false entrances and air ducts to confuse our reconnaissance efforts."

"What happened with the air strike?" asked Logan, not knowing if he wanted to hear the answer...

"I was informed just before the jump, via secure voice link, that it was a complete failure. Those planes that managed to get through the air defenses, did not hit the target. They hit the decoys. There were losses."

Logan felt like he was kicked in the stomach.

"How many planes?"

"I don't know the full details, yet. When I do, you will be the first to know. That's one of the reasons I'm here. Just in case the raid did fail. Our options now are limited. We don't have the time nor the air assets in place to risk repeated strikes on the bunker. Kemal has to be taken out on the next strike."

"So what do we do next?"

"We are awaiting word from our man inside about Kemal's plans. In the meantime, we plan a commando style raid to hit the bunker. One part of the team will try to open a corridor through the enemy's air defenses for our planes. The others will find and illuminate the bunker's entrance with a laser target designator. This will ensure the precise delivery of the special munitions on to the target. Hopefully, our contact will give us the exact location of the bunker's entrance and air ducts before the team departs. That's all for now, Jack. I will give a detailed briefing when my Greek counterpart arrives from Athens."

"Sir, what if the raid fails?"

"Then, only one other option remains to ensure the bunker's destruction." The Colonel did not have to elaborate. Logan knew what the option was, a tactical nuclear strike.

Kesan Command Center
0800hrs, 22 May

General Kemal sat in his private quarters, which were sparsely furnished in comparison with the ones he had in Istanbul, contemplating his next moves. As he had feared, the Bulgarians had entered the war, attacking at daybreak on two fronts. Word had also arrived that American airborne forces had landed on Limnos. Things were looking very bleak. To make matters even worse, his bunker had been raided just before dawn by American fighter bombers. The attack had failed and the Americans had paid a price. He had just personally finished interrogating the American female aviator his soldiers had brought in. He still couldn't believe their audacity and using a woman pilot, only increased his rage. They had paid dearly for their stupidity, losing three aircraft in the attempt.

Kemal thought back to the interrogation. The woman was very beautiful. Hanging there naked before him had caused him sexual arousal. An emotion that he had kept suppressed for many years because of his commitment to the cause. She had refused to answer any of his questions, giving him even more reason to cause her pain. He had to learn if the raid had been an attempt on his life. And if so, how did the Americans know he was at the bunker? Was it possible that there was a traitor somewhere among his staff? Soon he would work on her some more. He smiled at the thought of how he would have fun with her. His thoughts were interrupted by a knock on the door.

"Enter!"

The door opened and his aid Ahmet entered the room, holding several sheets of paper. "Sir, I have the latest battle reports that you have requested?"

"So how are things on the front?"

"Sir, all the information is here in these reports," said Colonel Azoglou, not wanting to be the bearer of bad news.

General Kemal stood up from his seat and glared at his aid. "I asked you to tell me! What is the matter here? Is everyone a defeatist traitor?"

"No sir."

"Then brief me, or I will have you sent to the front line as a common soldier!"

Colonel Azoglou thought for a moment that might not be a bad choice after all. At least he would be away from this madman. Unfortunately, he had more pressing things to do if this monster was to be stopped.

"Excuse me, sir. Of course I will brief you. The news is bad. The Bulgarians have attacked on two fronts. In western Thrace, they are attempting to drive a wedge between our forces. If they succeed," and the colonel thought it very likely that they would, "our army will be trapped between their army and the Greeks who are advancing from the west. Our backs would be to the sea. In Eastern Thrace, they have already captured Edirne and are driving toward Tekiridag and the sea. On Limnos, the Americans have landed what we believe to be the 101st airborne division. Our forces there are retreating toward Mirina. Our senior commander is advising surrender to save needless bloodshed."

"What! Surrender? That is out of the question. I want the traitor shot and replaced immediately. Do you understand?"

"Yes, sir." He wouldn't even bother arguing with this raving lunatic. Kemal was beyond reasoning. Neither would he issue the order to have the commander shot. Ahmet knew the officer personally. He could vouch for his bravery and professional competence. The battle for Limnos had, in fact, been lost days ago.

The General had calmed down and turned to his aid. "Ahmet, I have been betrayed by everyone. One thing remains to be done to reap my revenge on the infidels. We will launch our Saladin missiles at the enemy capitals at 0600hrs tomorrow morning. Now leave me. I must have some rest before I interrogate the prisoner again. She is a feisty one, but she will talk."

"Yes, sir," said Ahmet as he turned and left the General's quarters. *I must get word out immediately, thought Ahmet. This mad man doesn't give a damn about what will happen to Turkey. He must be stopped tonight, before he gets a chance to carry out his plans.* Ahmet then thought of the prisoner and the General's sudden interest in her. He had seen the look in his eyes when he mentioned the prisoner. He suspected that in reality the women didn't know anything of value. The General just wanted to vent his sadistic pleasures on her. Kemal will kill her if he didn't do something. But what could he do? He thought about it, as he headed for the Bunker's entrance and to his vehicle which would take him to the meeting point he had set up to relay the new information to the Americans.

Limnos
1220hrs, 22 May

Thanks to the help of Lieutenant Genetakos' men, the drop zone area had been secured by the 101st with only a minimum amount of casualties. Immediately afterwards, the 101st's headquarters element radioed orbiting C-130 transports and requested delivery of their cargoes that consisted of the Humvees, light field guns and other supplies that the division needed. The C-130s quickly lined up behind each other and swooped in low over the valley. Flying just a little above stall speed with their rear ramp doors open, each plane, in turn, executed a shallow dive toward the drop zone. Reaching the intended delivery area, the pilot of the first transport pulled the plane's nose up abruptly. The palleted equipment, made up of four 105mm field guns and ammunition, rolled out the back ramp. A drogue chute, deploying at the last second, acted as a speed brake slowing the pallet's fall and preventing it from smashing as it hit the ground. The rest of the planes followed suit.

With most of their heavy equipment delivered, the Americans began pushing westward toward Mirina. The enemy, suffering from a lack of supplies and ammunition, began giving ground. By late morning, the Americans with Greek forces picked up along the way, had reached the island's airport and linked up with the troops there. Together, the Greek and US forces pushed toward Mirina. By nightfall, they would be at the town's outskirts.

Toward the end of the morning, a joint allied command headquarters was temporarily established in a large two story house in Atsiki, a small town located in the island's interior. The owners had gladly given up the use of the home to their liberators. Around noon, several Greek officers had arrived by helicopter from Athens. One of them was Colonel Papalexis, dispatched personally by General Makarios, director of the Hellenic Central Intelligence agency. Upon his arrival, Papalexis immediately requested a meeting with Colonel Hess and his counterparts to discuss the latest on Kemal's mad scheme. Logan, George, Major Christakos and Lieutenant Genetakos had been also invited to attend the meeting.

The participants gathered in the house's spacious living room, waiting for both Hess and Papalexis to arrive. In the center of the room was a large dining table with several maps of western Turkey adorning its surface.

"Gee, I wonder what's up. Why did they want us all here?" asked George.

"We'll find out soon enough. Here they come," said Logan who had not revealed any details of his previous conversation with Colonel Hess to anyone.

The two officers walked into the room followed by a heavily armed American military policeman who closed the door behind them and took his post outside. "This must be serious," murmured Yiannis.

Colonel Hess was the first to speak. "Gentlemen, first let me give you the good news. At 0600hrs this morning, Bulgaria entered the war on our side. Their army attacked the enemy on two fronts. It looks like the main Bulgarian drive is toward the port city of Alexandroupolis. If they can accomplish this in the next forty-eight hours, they can trap the bulk of the Turkish army between them and the Hellenic army advancing from the west. Then it would be only a matter of a short time before the Turks are forced to surrender or face eventual annihilation.

"That's great news," said Yiannis.

"Let me finish. This only complicates matters," said Hess.

"What I will now brief you on, has been classified Top Secret by the highest levels of both our governments. Time is running short, so please keep your questions for the end. Now, would everyone please bring their chairs up to the table?"

The Colonel opened his brief case and pulled out several photos and passed them around the table.

"Gentlemen, what I have here are photos recently taken by a U.S. KH-11 reconnaissance satellite of the Kesan command bunker. The bunker is located near the town of Kesan, approximately forty kilometers from the Greek border," he said, pointing to the location of Kesan on the map of western Turkey.

"After the destruction of the Turkish ministry of defense by American cruise missiles, Kemal has been using this bunker as his personal command center. We have recently learned from a well-placed source that Kemal is aware that he is losing the war, and is planning to commit a final act of madness. He is planning to launch ten missiles, filled with deadly nerve gas at Athens and Sofia, Bulgaria."

"Oh, my God. He'll murder thousands of innocent people," said Yiannis, thinking of his and Eleni's family living in the city.

"No commander. More like tens of thousands if he is allowed to carry out his satanic plan." Logan now understood the secrecy behind Hess. If word of this got out to the civilian population, there would be panic on a scale never seen before. Hundreds, if not thousands, would be killed trying to flee the doomed cities.

"The last word we received this morning from our source is that Kemal intends to launch his missiles tomorrow morning at 0600hr. Early this morning, USAF F-15 Strike Eagles, escorted by Colonel Logan's squadron, carrying special laser guided bunker busting bombs developed during the Persian Gulf War, attempted to raid the heavily defended bunker. The raid was a complete failure. The aircrews that did manage to make it through the heavy air defenses dropped the bombs on the wrong targets. You see, gentlemen, in order for these special munitions to be able to destroy the target, they have to be delivered with great precision. Normally, the bomb would enter either through the bunker's ventilator shafts or doors to be successful. I believe that everyone saw the film during Desert Storm of a bomb going through an air shaft and destroying an Iraqi bunker. Well, so did our enemy. When they built the bunker into the side of a hill, they camouflaged the outside entrance and air shafts by building several phony ones to confuse any would be raiders. Given enough time to bring additional resources to bear, we would eventually get it. Only we don't have the resources nor the time . . . "

"Why don't we go after the launchers?" asked Logan.

"First Colonel, we don't know exactly where they are and second they're on mobile launch platforms and are constantly moved around. Remember, Turkey isn't the Iraqi desert, there are forests and mountains. Those missiles could be hidden anywhere. We just don't have the time to look for them. Thus, gentlemen, we have only two options remaining in order to stop Kemal. I will now turn you over to Colonel Papalexis, Deputy Chief of Intelligence for the Hellenic general staff. He has just flown in from Athens to brief you on the joint operation that we have come up with to try and stop this madman."

Everyone turned their attention to the clean shaven, slim built officer, dressed in a brand new pair of starched battle dress utilities, standing at the head of the table.

"Good afternoon, I'm Colonel Papalexis," he said in accented, but understandable English.

"I will make this briefing short and to the point. We plan to take out Kemal in his bunker, one way or another. Our source has offered to reveal to us the location of the bunker's entrance and air ducts. An air strike will take place at precisely 0515hrs, tomorrow morning. Tonight, we will dispatch a twelve man element to Kesan to make contact with our man there. He will lead one team to a safe location close to the bunker. Once in position, they will use laser target illuminators, to paint the targets for the USAF Strike Eagles. Another team will be responsible for taking out a key radar network that controls the missile defense network. Hopefully, with some of their radar's out, the escorts will be able to punch a hole through the rest of the air defenses for the bombers to get through. If the air strike fails, twenty minutes later, there will be another raid. This time, by a single B-2 Stealth bomber. I don't have to tell you what it is carrying, gentlemen. The weapon will definitely take out the bunker and the surrounding area around it. The team on the ground will have twenty minutes to get far enough away from the target and take cover. We will not, at any cost, allow this madman to launch his missiles!"

No one said anything. If the air strike failed, they were all dead men. Kesan would be wiped off the face of the earth by the sword of Armageddon, nuclear fire and the team along with it.

"Colonel Logan, you will be in command of this team."

"What? I am no commando. I'm a pilot. I should be leading

the strike mission?"

Colonel Hess raised his hand to silence any further protests from Logan.

"Colonel, our source related that he would deal only with a senior American officer. You have been through survival school and are familiar with escape and evasion tactics. Those are the only skills you need for this mission. We have no time to waste. You're it."

"Well, in that case, I accept."

"Thanks. Colonel, please continue," Hess gestured to Papalexis.

"Lieutenant Genetakos, for this mission you will pick six of your best men. Sergeant Major Alexopoulos and two of his men will be going along. The FACs are familiar in the use of the Laser illuminators," he said as he turned and faced George. George had a feeling of what was coming next.

"Sergeant, I can't morally order you to go on this mission, especially after what you and your men have just been through. I can ask you to volunteer to act as an interpreter. Even though the Lieutenant understands basic English, we don't want to risk making any mistakes."

"Sir, I would be honored. It would be a chance to personally pay back the bastard that was responsible for what happened at Piges. Though, I do have one request."

"Name it, Sergeant."

"I would like two of my men to come along. One is an excellent shot with the grenade launcher and the other is handy with a machine gun."

"I don't know, Sergeant. Lieutenant, what do who think? Are his men up to it?"

"Colonel, I can vouch for them. I have personally seen them in action. Besides, they took on an entire armored division at Piges. They are definitely up to it."

"Okay, Sergeant. You can take two of your best men along."

"Now, may I continue, please?" Everyone remained silent. Their eyes were glued on the Greek officer.

"At 1900hrs, a specially outfitted Aegean Sea Hawk helicopter will be arriving from Athens to transport you to a location, twenty kilometers from Kesan. There, you will be met by our man who will take you to the bunker. Commander Vassiliou, this is where you will be coming to play. Once the mission has been completed, the helicopter will take off and rendezvous with the Hydra at a pre-designated location, several miles off the mouth of the Evros River. The Hydra will be carrying specially equipped floatable hundred liter fuel bladders to refuel the helicopter for the return trip. They can be tossed into the water and towed to shore. We don't really know how well the area is being patrolled by the enemy. A report from one of our subs this morning indicated that everything was quiet in that specific sector, although that can always change."

"We can handle it, sir."

"I'm sure you can, Commander. You are to avoid contact at all costs, if possible. Once the helicopter has been refueled, the

Hydra will return to Limnos. Gentlemen, if we fail, it will mean the first use of a nuclear weapon since the end of the Second World War. We don't know what the reaction will be from the other Islamic states which possess nuclear weapons. They may, in fact, rally to Turkey's side and the war will then spread, possibly involving the further use of nuclear weapons by both sides." No one in the room wanted to think of the terrible consequences of failure. The use of chemical weapons had been horrible enough. Using nuclear weapons was something one could not even contemplate.

"After the meeting, will all the officers please remain? Colonel Hess will give you the frequencies that will be used during the mission. I will now turn you over to Colonel Hess for questions," said Colonel Papalexis, visibly relieved at having finished his part of the briefing.

Colonel Hess took the floor. "Gentlemen, I'm ready for questions." Logan raised his hand.

"Yes, Colonel."

"How do we know that our contact can be trusted?"

"We don't have much of a choice, Colonel. He's the only guy we've got right now. As an act of good faith, he gave us some very reliable information on the results of the last raid. The Turks captured one of the pilots downed in the raid. They are holding the pilot at the bunker right now. Our man will attempt to get the prisoner moved to Istanbul, if possible. I will tell you more after the briefing. I know you are curious as to whom the prisoner is. Now, are there any other questions?" No one said anything.

"Since there are no questions, everyone take a ten minute break, and then I want to see all officers. Remember what you have heard is Top Secret, you are to speak of this to no one."

Everyone got up and left the room for some fresh air, except Logan.

"Sir, can you tell me who the captured pilot is?

Hess thought about it for a few seconds. "Yes, I don't suppose it can do much harm. Besides, you are their squadron commander. It's Captain Wendy Barnes."

Logan felt like he was just body slammed. A look of shock momentarily registered on his face, but he quickly regained his composure. It did not go unnoticed by Hess, but the intelligence officer chose to remain silent.

"Is she injured?"

"Not as far as we know," said Hess, omitting the part of what he had found out concerning her treatment in the bunker.

"Thanks for letting me know," said Logan as he turned for the door needing some fresh air. Now he had a personal reason to go on the mission. There had to be a way to get Wendy out before tomorrow morning's raid.

Kesan Command Bunker
1430hrs, 22 May

Wendy had lost all track of time of how long she had been hanging suspended from the bunker's ceiling. She looked down at her body which was covered with bloody welts and bruises caused by the numerous beatings she had received at the hands of her captors. Besides the pain she felt from her beating, her urge to urinate was reaching a critical stage. If she wasn't taken down soon, she wouldn't be able to hold her bladder back much longer. She hoped she wouldn't have to give the bastards the satisfaction of having to urinate on herself.

As she hung there, Wendy reflected back to the raid. Everything had gone wrong from the beginning. The air defenses around the bunker area had been very heavy. They had lost a plane to a SAM on the approach to the target area. Then to make matters worse, they had hit the wrong targets. She had been shot down on the run out. Her plane had taken a burst of triple A fire which had sheared off part of the wing. She had only seconds to punch out before the plane slammed into the ground. Upon landing, she was immediately captured and taken into the bunker.

Several minutes later, she had been brought before a high ranking officer. She knew that she was in trouble by the look of fear that this officer generated on the faces of the soldiers guarding her. Her intuitions were quickly justified when she saw how his eyes gleamed with hatred when he looked at her. The officer introduced himself as General Kemal, Commander and Chief of the Turkish armed forces and began asking her questions. He had wanted to know if he, in fact, had been the target of the raid. In accordance with the Geneva Convention, which Turkey had been a signature party to, she had only given him her name, rank and social security number. Her answer had produced a hard slap across her face that had made her ears ring. Kemal had repeated his questions, but her refusal to answer, only infuriated him more. Kemal then switched tactics with her. She had been dragged to the room where she was presently in, stripped naked by his soldiers and beaten with wooden canes as Kemal watched much to his pleasure. That had been several hours ago.

Wendy heard the sound of a key turning and the door of her prison opening. *Here they come again. I don't know how much more of this I can take, she thought.* Kemal and two soldiers walked in. One was carrying a bundle of clothes and the other was carrying what appeared to be food and water. Kemal stood there for a moment savoring the sight of her nakedness.

"Take her down." The two soldiers immediately lowered her and untied the ropes.

"Put on some clothes and have something to eat. I will be back," he said as he turned to leave the room.

Wendy, momentarily forgetting her nakedness, rubbed her sore shoulders and arms. "Thank you," she said as she quickly put on a fatigue shirt, several sizes too large for her. When she finished dressing, the guards put a set of handcuffs on her and left the room. Savoring her momentary privacy, she rushed to the toilet which was in a corner of the room and quickly relieved herself. Finished, she sat down next to the table, the only other furniture in the room and began eating the food the guards had brought her, which consisted of Pita bread, cheese and olives. Not having eaten for over twenty hours, the food had tasted good to her. With her stomach full and exhausted from the lack of sleep, Wendy dozed off.

The sound of a key being inserted into the lock jolted her from her short nap. Opening her eyes, she saw the man who had been conducting her interrogation, General Kemal.

"I hope the food was to your liking, that was all that was available at the moment," he said.

"Oh yes, it was good, thank you."

"Good. Maybe now we can reach some sort of understanding. You are a very brave woman, braver than many men that I have known. I can make your stay here very comfortable," said Kemal, caressing her cheek.

Wendy jerked her head away.

"My, a feisty one, such spirit. One could take much pleasure in taming you. Unfortunately, time is running short. Bitch! You will tell me what I want to know, or you will wish that you were never born," said Kemal.

"Tell me! Why were you sent here to bomb this bunker? screamed Kemal in a fit of rage.

"I told you. I don't know anything. I only flew escort."

"You are a lying whore!" he said, slapping her hard across the face, cutting her lip.

Wendy tasted blood. She spit in Kemal's face. "Kiss my ass you bastard!" she screamed back at him in defiance.

Wendy expected Kemal to hit her, but he just stared at her in shock. For the first time since her captivity she felt fear.

"You infidel whore, you dare insult me. I will show you

what a real man is!" He lunged at her. Surprised, Wendy crashed to the ground. Kemal fell on top of her. He grabbed her shirt and tore it from her body. She tried to fight him, but was unable to because of the cuffs she was wearing.

"No, please, don't." A sharp slap across her face quickly knocked most of the fight out of her. When Kemal had finished, Wendy just lay there staring at him, seething with hatred.

"Did you like it, bitch?"

"I will kill you, you bastard."

Kemal laughed. "You still have some fight in you. Good, I will be back," he said as he slammed the door behind him.

As she lay there all alone in her cell, she first thought of her father, then Jack Logan and began to cry.

Chapter 11

Limnos

22 May, 1725hrs

By midafternoon, except for a couple of enemy pockets that were in the process of being mopped up, most of the fighting on the west side of the island had subsided. Takis, who had been waiting offshore with the Hydra, had received a priority radio message from the allied command center to return immediately. His instructions ordered them to proceed without further delay to a small fishing village located on the eastern end of Moudros Bay and rendezvous with commander Vassiliou and other allied personnel.

Upon reaching their destination, thanks to her shallow draft, the missile boat was able to dock alongside the small wharf used by the village's few fishing boats without incident. There she was met by a supply truck which included both Yiannis and Logan as passengers. Both men immediately went aboard to brief Takis and prepare the ship for the upcoming mission. While walking up the deck plank, Yiannis noticed the scorched and scarred section where the enemy grenade had struck the ship. "Welcome aboard, gentlemen, come on right up," yelled Takis from the Hydra's bridge.

When the two officers reached the bridge, they were met by Takis at the door. "It's about time you returned, Yiannis. I was just getting to like this job," said Takis with a big grin on his face.

"What happened?" Yiannis asked before Takis could say anything further.

"Enemy 40mm grenade did it. We ran into a little trouble early this morning with an enemy patrol. That's why we left our earlier anchorage."

"Any casualties?"

"Two sailors killed and four others injured with minor shrapnel and bullet wounds. We got the bastards that hit us though," added Takis.

"Well I guess it could have been worse. At least you brought her back almost in one piece. Maybe you'll make a captain, yet," said Yiannis trying not to think of the dead sailors and the letters he would have to write to their families.

"What do you think, Colonel?"

"You guys can keep your boats. Just give me a good old airplane any day. At least they don't make me sea sick," said Logan with a chuckle.

"Did you see Eleni?" asked Takis.

"Yes and she's fine, though she did have a very rough time. I'll tell you about it later. Now we have a lot of work to do."

"What's up?" asked Takis.

"Let's go to the CIC, we'll brief you there." The sound of singing and cheers made the three men turn around and look toward the shore.

"Why it's a welcoming committee," said Logan. The small

fishing village which had been abandoned by most of its occupants during the initial stages of the Turkish invasion had suddenly come to life. Several dozen villagers had come to the dock, carrying Greek flags and bottles of wine. A few of them, in various stages of intoxication, were singing the Greek national anthem and cheering the Hellenic navy for their liberation.

"I guess they're happy. They do have something to celebrate about," said Logan.

"If we don't get moving soon, they won't be this happy tomorrow," said Yiannis.

"Well, I'll be seeing you two, hopefully when all of this is over," said Logan as he was shown to the boat's gang plank.

"Yeah, Colonel, and the victory party will be on me when this war is over. Excuse me, I have to go check on a few things, and help get the boat ready."

"Well Yiannis, here's where we part, for the time being. You'll have a lot of work to do between now and your departure. The fuel bladders should be arriving any minute."

As if on key, they heard the motor of an approaching vehicle.

"Be careful over there. Remember, we all have a party to go to when this is all over. Good luck." Yiannis watched as Logan walked down the gang plank and entered a waiting jeep that would whisk him back to headquarters.

The White House Oval Office
1130hrs (EST), 22 May

Just when it looked like he had weathered this crisis, things had gone completely to hell. The President of the United States was in a serious dilemma. He would be the first President since Harry S. Truman to authorize the use of a nuclear weapon. Never known for his rapid decision making, President Davis sat alone in his study and pondered over the moral and political implications of the use of the bomb. Not even his wife could help him on this decision. It was solely his. If Kemal was allowed to launch his missiles, thousands of innocent allied civilians would perish. There was no guarantee the Patriot air defense missiles could shoot down all the incoming ballistic missiles. Even if one got through, thousands would die. If he did give the order for the bomb to be dropped on the bunker in the town of Kesan, thousands of helpless enemy civilians would also perish.

The dropping of the bomb could also touch off a general nuclear conflagration if other nuclear armed Islamic states flocked to Turkey's aid. Would he go down in history as the man who initiated a nuclear war that killed millions? Well, it was the chance that he just would have to take. The American people had elected him as their leader. Hundreds of their sons and daughters had perished as a result of this madman's actions. He would not let wanton aggression go unpunished. The President's thoughts were momentarily interrupted by his intercom buzzer.

"Yes?"

"Sir, I have General Coleman on the line," said his secretary.

"Patch him through, Sarah."

"Go ahead, General, any good news?"

"Mr. President. We just received word from our man in Istanbul. The mission for tonight is a go. Now what about our backup plan in case the mission fails?"

"That's some good news," said the President, suddenly feeling a heavy load come off his shoulders.

"General, as for the backup plan, Operation Crusader is a go. Call me when you need the necessary release codes."

"He does have balls. I don't care what the others have to say about him," mumbled the General to himself when he heard the President's answer.

"Thank you, Mr. President. I'll pass on the necessary orders."

Hanging up the receiver, the President, a southern Baptist and a religious man, opened his desk drawer and pulled out a copy of a worn bible. He opened up to the chapter on Revelations and began reading.

Northeastern Aegean
2010hrs, 22 may

After finishing the loading and securing of the fuel bladders, Yiannis and his crew began the task of preparing the boat for the perilous voyage into the enemy's back yard. A couple of hours later, the Hydra was sailing into the northeastern Aegean. When they were well clear of the island, Yiannis briefed his crew on the assignment. He told them they were sailing deep into enemy territory and that the mission would be dangerous. Although almost defeated, the enemy still had sufficient forces to easily blow the little missile boat out of the water. It was imperative that they not be discovered. Their rendezvous with the helicopter had to succeed. Failure would mean their friends and comrades would remain stranded in enemy territory to be hunted down and killed. Yiannis had feared that when he told the crew of the impending chemical attack on the capital, it would panic the crew members having families living in the city. Instead, it brought a feeling of rage and a renewed determination to bring about the rapid defeat of the enemy.

While the missile boat sped northward through calm seas, both Yiannis and his second in command were bent over the bridge's navigation chart table which had a large map of the Northwestern Aegean. Yiannis was worried as he measured off the distance they had already traveled. In another hour, they would be in the enemy's back yard. They were sailing practically blind. Their radar was on passive mode to prevent the enemy from picking up their electronic emissions.

"I don't like this Takis, we're sailing into harm's way and we don't know what's in front of us."

"We'll be arriving in three hours. Let's hope that Intel was right about everything being quiet in that sector."

"If they are wrong, with our radar down, we'll be sitting ducks."

"Mr. Kourtis, how's it look out there?" asked Takis.

"I'm not picking up any emissions if that's what you're asking. However, that doesn't mean that there isn't anyone out there. They could be running quiet like us. We won't hear or see them until they're right on top of us."

"Thanks, Mr. Kourtis," said Yiannis.

"I suggest we double the lookouts. They're the only eyes we got right now," said Takis.

"You're right, Takis do it."

"Will do," said Takis as he left the plot.

Yiannis thought of Eleni. She had gone through a lot these past few days. She had come down to the dock in a jeep, provided by Jack Logan, to bid him good-bye. Jack was a great guy for taking the time to think of him, at such a time. Eleni's good-bye had been tearful. He could not tell her what the mission was, but she knew it would be dangerous. Both their families were in Athens. If by some chance the mission failed and Kemal launched his rockets, at least Eleni would be safe where she was.

"All accomplished," said Takis as he entered the plotting room.

"Good work. Now I need a cup of coffee."

"Sounds like a good idea to me. I'll go fetch us one," said Takis as he turned to go to the galley.

Yiannis looked toward Limnos which was beginning to fade in the distance. Everyone's hopes now rested on the commando team.

Limnos, Moudros Tent Field Hospital
2035hrs, 22 May

Eleni watched jealously while Cindy changed the bandages on Sergeant Theodoros Peratos' wounds. She could see that Cindy had the look of love in her eyes as she tended to the handsome soldier that had saved her life. During the early morning when the fighting had started, Theodoros had eagerly joined Lieutenant Genetakos's men in clearing out Turkish pockets of resistance. He had gotten himself wounded in the thigh by several grenade fragments and transported to the first aid station, all covered in blood. Cindy almost fainted when she saw him and after recovering from the initial shock, she had burst into hysterical tears and only stopped after the doctor had assured her that her Sergeant's wounds were only minor. When Theodoros had awakened, he had discovered that he now had a very pretty private nurse to attend to all his needs. Not that Eleni minded. Cindy still carried out her workload in the hospital tent caring for the rest of the wounded.

"Be careful with those scissors, Cindy. You don't want to cut off anything vital," said Eleni jokingly.

"Definitely not," said Cindy as she stroked Theodoros' bandaged thigh area.

"Ouch! I'm going to pop my stitches," said Theodoros.

"I guess we can wait a few days."

"I finish army in four months. Maybe we go to America together," said Theodoros.

"Sure, I'd love that. And you can meet my parents."

"Maybe they won't like Greeks. My English is very bad," he said rather worried.

"They'll love you, especially after I tell them what you did for their daughter. Besides, your English is fine and I will teach you more."

"Come on, Cindy, I did nothing special. Anyone would have done same thing," said Theodoros in his thick accented English.

"I didn't see anyone else jump in the water. Besides, I think I have taken a liking to good looking dark complicated men. Now rest and get better for me. I have to tend to the other wounded."

At least Cindy's man was now safe and out of harm's way, thought Eleni. She worried terribly about Yiannis. She suspected that he was going on a very dangerous mission and it had to do something with the helicopters that had arrived from the mainland. They had brought some special equipment that had been loaded onto the Hydra. Now Jack, George, Lieutenant Genetakos and some of his men were preparing to go somewhere in them. She prayed that they would all return safe and in one piece.

Over the Northern Aegean
2235hrs, 22 May

Logan looked out the hatchway window at the dark sea rushing by only fifty feet below them. *It would be a great time for the auto pilot to fail, he thought.* At this height, there would be no chance for the pilot to recover. They'd smash into the water at over 130 knots, with maybe a small fuel slick on the surface of the water to mark their grave. Nonetheless, it was necessary if they were to remain undetected by enemy radar.

So far everything had gone as planned. A Chinook C47D cargo helicopter had arrived from the mainland during the evening, bringing the fuel bladders that were loaded onto the Hydra. The Aegean Sea Hawk helicopter that would take them to Kesan had arrived just after sunset. The Aegean Sea Hawk was a special modified version of the U.S. Army's Blackhawk that had been ordered by the Hellenic navy in the mid-1990s. This particular one was painted dark black and was outfitted with a 20mm chain gun in its nose and a Penguin ship killing missile mounted on each of its pylons. Logan hoped that none of the weapons would have to be used during their flight to their destination. If they did use them, the mission would most likely be compromised and they would have to turn back.

"Sir, would you like some hot coffee?"

"Sure, George, thanks."

"The pilot said we should be reaching our landing zone in about thirty minutes."

"I hope our person is there to meet us."

"If not, we're in deep shit, Colonel." The helicopter suddenly pitched up violently, causing Logan to spill some of the hot coffee on his hand.

"Ouch, that was hot. I'd better drink this coffee before I spill it all over me."

"Would anybody like a sandwich?" asked Lieutenant

Genetakos who was sitting next to Logan.

"No thanks, not me," said Logan.

"Me neither," added George.

"How can you eat in a time like this? I, myself, am too nervous."

"Better enjoy the food while you can. You don't know when you'll get another chance to eat. Plus you'll need the energy."

"He's got a point," said Logan, grabbing a sandwich."

"No, I'll pass," insisted George. Closing his eyes, he could hear the sound of the helicopter's rotor. With every beat, it took them closer to the enemy. He thought of his decision to volunteer for this mission. He wanted to pay the Turks back for what they did to his men at Piges. Well now it was too late for any second thoughts. The die had been cast.

Fifteen Kilometers South of Kesan
2310hrs, 22 May

Colonel Azoglou waited for the arrival of the allied commando team in anticipation by the duce and a half truck that he had borrowed from the Kesan motor pool. The Sergeant in charge of the motor pool had given him a funny look when he had asked to requisition the vehicle. Fortunately, enlisted men in the Turkish military do not ask officers, especially Colonels, too many questions. The truck was now hidden in a knoll of trees that overlooked a small, open field. The clandestine meeting with Brigadier General Aturk, commander of the secret police, had gone off better that he had ever envisioned. Aturk's reaction to the news of Kemal's impending poison gas attacks on the enemy capitals had been just as he had anticipated. The General had flown into a rage. Not only had Kemal gotten them into a war that they were losing, he would now destroy everything that they had worked for.

Once General Aturk had sufficiently calmed down, the two of them had contemplated several possible solutions in dealing with Kemal. Assassination was definitely out of the question. The bunker was guarded by Kemal's elite Islamic guard and no one was allowed near him with a weapon. Destruction of the bunker from the outside was nearly impossible. When the General had reached an impasse, Ahmet shrewdly proposed another solution. He told the General of his plan. Initially Aturk had been shocked at the audacity of the Colonel's treasonous plan, for a moment it had looked like it was all over for him. But then, a rare smile appeared on the face of the Chief of the dreaded secret police and Ahmet breathed a sigh of relief. The General had not only found the plan brazen, but it had also been to his liking. The infidels would do most of the dirty work of disposing Kemal for them.

Ahmet once more glanced at the time. The helicopter would soon be arriving. They had until 0500hrs to reach the bunker and get in place. General Aturk's military police would neutralize the missile batteries guarding the approaches to the bunker at 0430hrs. All they had to do was paint the correct targets for the bombers. It sounded much too easy for Ahmet's liking. He thought of the poor woman prisoner in the bunker.

Ahmet wished he could do something to help her. She did not deserve to die.

The thump of helicopter rotors made him look skyward. The helicopter had arrived. There was no turning back now. He was committed. Taking a small red lens flashlight from the truck, he left the cover of the trees and ran toward the clearing, less than a hundred meters distant. Reaching the clearing, he switched the light on and pointed it skyward, waving it up and down. A quick flash of red light came from the helicopter's cockpit. They had seen him. Less than a minute later, the large helicopter which he recognized as an Aegean Sea Hawk, had touched down. Even as the rotors were still turning, several heavily armed individuals jumped out of the machine and formed a three-sixty. One of the men called out to him in Turkish to put his hands up in the air and walk toward him, to which Ahmet complied. When he was only ten meters away, they told him to turn around with his hands still up in the air. Even before he had completed his turn, one of the individuals had jumped on him, knocking him to the ground. He felt several pairs of hands searching his body.

"You can stand. I'm sorry, sir but it was necessary to search you. We didn't know if this had been a trap."

"No, offense taken," replied Ahmet. "I understand. All this must seem very strange to you." Another man, an American officer wearing Colonel insignia, approached him and offered his hand.

"This is Colonel Logan, the mission commander," replied the

Greek soldier who had initially spoken Turkish to him.

"I'm pleased to meet you. I am Colonel Ahmet Azoglou, aid to General Kemal," replied Ahmet in perfect English. He saw a look of surprise register on the American's face.

"You speak English?"

"Yes, I do, thanks to your Defense Language Institute which I had attended in Fort Mead, Maryland many years ago."

"Good. Then we can dispatch with the interpreter. Tell me, Colonel. If you are, who you say you are, how do we know that you can be trusted?"

The American had been joined by another American, an NCO and a Greek army Lieutenant.

"Well Colonel Logan, as you can see, I am here alone. I think, gentlemen that we share a mutual goal of stopping the madman before he carries out his insane plot. Plus you don't have a choice. I'm the only thing you got going for you right now."

"He has a point, sir," said George.

"I also agree with George," Lieutenant Genetakos added.

"Before we start, what do you want out of this?" said Logan to Ahmet.

"Not to see my country destroyed. We would also like to be given honorable terms for cessation of hostilities."

"What! You people started this war. You have wrecked most of my country, killed thousands and have the audacity to ask for terms!" said the Lieutenant.

"Enough, we will not argue here. We have a mission to attend to," said Logan.

"I'm afraid the Lieutenant is right. I was hoping to get the best deal for my country," said Ahmet.

"Right or not, none of us here can dictate demands or make any promises to you. It will be up to the politicians in Washington and Athens to make the decisions. All I can promise is that if you help us stop Kemal, your country will not face further destruction."

"I don't have much of a choice at this point, American. I will do what I can to stop this blood-shed and save my country from any further suffering. If it is Allah's will, then so be it."

Logan turned to Lieutenant Genetakos. "Get the cammy netting over the helicopter. The crew and one of your men will stay here to guard it."

"That will not be necessary," said the Turkish Colonel. The sound of vehicles approaching from the west made Logan apprehensive.

"You've betrayed us. This is a trap!" barked Logan.

"No, please have no fear. It is part of the planned arrangement."

"It better be or you'll be the first one to get it" said Lieutenant Genetakos, pointing his submachine gun at Ahmet.

A minute later, several jeeps pulled up each mounting a machine gun or recoilless rifle that was manned with soldiers. A Captain, dressed in the uniform of the Turkish military police, exited the lead jeep and approached the gathered men.

"I am Captain Senn. My men and I are at your disposal," he said to Colonel Azoglou in English for everyone's benefit.

Ahmet was relieved. General Aturk had come through with his promise for assistance.

"Captain, you will leave two of your vehicles here to guard the helicopter and with the other, you will escort us to where I tell you."

"As you wish, sir."

"Colonel Logan, it is time to go. Will you and your men please get into the truck? It's about a forty minute drive to where we are going.

Logan thought about it for several seconds, even if it was a trap, they had no choice, they were now committed.

"Okay everybody let's get moving. Into the truck."

After everyone boarded, Logan and George climbed into the cab and sat next to Ahmet who had assumed the driver's seat. With the Military Police jeep leading the way, they took off toward the bunker.

Kesan Command Bunker
2400hrs, 23 May

Sipping on a cup of very sweet thick Turkish coffee, Kemal sat at his desk reviewing the latest reports from the front, which were not too encouraging. The only good news was the Bulgarian drive had been stopped. Unfortunately, he had used all his reserves in the process. Nothing remained to stop the combined Greek and American forces that were bearing down on Kommotini this very instant. Dispatches from that city related that the Muslims there had thrown in with the Greeks and were, at this very moment, battling what Turkish occupation forces remained there.

He had been betrayed by everyone, especially by that deceitful Bulgarian President. Nickolovich had personally given his word that his country would remain neutral, in exchange for certain concessions that he had willingly offered them. They would all pay dearly for their treachery. At 0600hrs, he would give the order to launch the last of his gas tipped Saladin missiles. Kemal seethed with anger at his own people's betrayal. He would ensure the Muslims of Kommotini also paid for their disloyalty. Along with the enemy capitals, Kommotini would be included on his target list. His anger made him think of his prisoner. Just before giving the final order to launch his missiles, he would use her one more time to soothe the devils inside him. Afterwards, he would give the arrogant infidel whore to his guards, to use as they like. Most likely she would not live long enough to waste a bullet on.

Eight Kilometers South of Kesan
0143hrs, 23 May

The journey to their destination was taking longer than anyone had anticipated. Wishing to avoid heavy troop concentrations, their escort had used the back roads. Unfortunately, most of these roads had been unpaved and the rains that had fallen in the region had turned them into rivers of muck. Luckily, the duce and a half had four wheel drive, but their progress had been agonizingly slow. Finally having reached the main crossroad, they were delayed once again. This time, they waited for a large military convoy to drive past.

Throughout the drive, Logan had thought of Wendy. There had to be something he could do to get her out without compromising the mission.

"Damn it. If it's not the mud, then it's something else," said Logan, perturbed at their new delay.

"Don't worry, Colonel Logan, we still have enough time."

Do we? Logan thought. He wondered how Wendy was faring in her captivity. He'd risk a court martial for deviating from the original mission, but he would ask Azoglou if something could be done to get her out.

"Colonel, I was told that you mentioned of a POW being held at the bunker."

"Yes, that's true. A female aviator," said Ahmet, not wanting to relate any further information about Wendy's condition.

"Is she in good health?"

Ahmet didn't answer. "Colonel, that pilot is a member of my squadron. I need to know."

Ahmet saw the look of concern on Logan's face. He could tell that Logan's interest in the woman was more than that of a commander.

"If you must know, Colonel Logan, the woman is still being held in the bunker. She has drawn the personal attention of General Kemal."

"Jesus, has she been tortured?"

"I'm afraid, so. Kemal personally interrogated her. He wants to know if he had been the particular target of the raid."

"We must do something to help her," said Logan.

"There is nothing we can do. The bunker is heavily guarded. Besides, as much as I hate to say this to you, she may be already dead."

"Wait! I have an idea," said George who had so far been silent. Both men looked at him.

"A couple of Lieutenant Genetakos' men are Pomachs from northern Greece."

"So," interrupted Logan.

"Silence, let him finish," said Ahmet.

"The Pomachs live in northern Greece. They were people that were forcibly converted to Islam during the early days of the Ottoman Empire. They are Muslims not of Turkish origin, but many of them are loyal to Greece and some do, in fact, speak Turkish."

Logan's eyes lit up. "I get your drift, George. These two guys speak Turkish. Maybe we can use them somehow to get into the bunker."

"That's exactly what I had in mind, sir."

"It just might work," said Colonel Azoglou thoughtfully. "Because of my close association with General Kemal, the guards never question my authority. It may be possible for me to get a few men, dressed as Military Police, into the bunker. I will tell the guards that the Military police will be transporting the prisoner to Istanbul for further interrogation. The complex is fairly large. The prisoner is kept in the opposite end from where

Kemal stays. It may just work. The only catch is if Kemal finds out before we get out. Speed will be very important. We must be in and out."

"We have to try," said Logan.

In the meantime, the heavy military traffic on the road had cleared up enough for the truck to continue its journey toward the bunker. Twenty minutes later, the truck pulled off the road into a field, a couple of kilometers from the bunker. Logan saw several vehicles parked in the field with their lights on, surrounded by heavily armed Military Policemen. Ahmet shut off the truck's motor, but kept the lights on.

"Well, I guess we're here."

"Yeah, George, and so is the welcoming committee," said Logan. The Turkish MPs' kept their guns trained on the group of Greeks and Americans while they dismounted the truck. Logan noticed a group of men walking towards them.

"I hope your friend hasn't had a change of heart," he said to Ahmet. General Aturk approached the two officers.

"You are late."

"Your men took us through the back roads which were almost impassable," he said to the General in Turkish.

"It was by my instructions. Nevertheless, you are here now."

"There has been a slight change of plans General," immediately explaining Logan's interest in freeing Wendy from the bunker.

"No, it is impossible," said General Aturk in English while looking at Logan.

"General, it would be beneficial to everyone's interest if the girl was freed," said Logan.

"How is that?"

"Your country is practically defeated and will be at the mercy of the United States and her allies. Many of Turkey's leaders will be tried for war crimes and crimes against humanity."

"I had nothing to do with Kemal's mad schemes."

"You are part of the Revolutionary Committee which approved Kemal's plan. General Aturk did not reply. He knew that Logan had a point. Logan knew that he had Aturk's attention.

"If you help me free the girl, I will speak on your behalf, on how you risked your life to help me free the prisoner. We have a plan that might just work," he added.

"I think I would like to hear this plan of yours." Logan relaxed; he had Aturk just where he wanted him.

Rendezvous Refueling Site
0330hrs, 23 May

The Hydra rolled in the calm Aegean swell less than a hundred meters off the small rocky isle, which had been selected as the helicopter refueling point. With her moorings ready to slip at a moment's notice if trouble appeared, Yiannis kept the crew at their combat stations as an additional precaution. With most of the fuel already offloaded, all that remained for Yiannis and his crew to do was wait for the arrival of the helicopter carrying their friends. Deep in enemy waters and their radar off, the boat was a sitting duck for any patrol plane or passing warship. Both Yiannis and Takis sat in the blacked out bridge eating sandwiches passed out by the ships galley.

"I don't like this one bit, Takis. We still have almost two hours to go till the copter arrives,"

"Luckily for us this piece of rock provides us with some radar cover. I hope they were right about the enemy patrols in this area."

"Me too, my friend, if not, we're screwed."

"You know, Takis. Life is just too short. I think as soon as all this is over, Eleni and I are going to get married."

"You can say that again," said Takis remembering his own experiences of the past few days.

"Sir, sorry to interrupt you," said the on duty radio man. "We just received a message from the team; they arrived at the objective without any problems."

"Thanks. Keep me informed on their status."

"Yes, sir," said the radioman.

"Well, Takis. Now comes the real waiting."

Chapter 12

Kesan

0400hrs, 23 May

"We must load up. It's time you get moving," said Colonel Azoglou. Logan glanced at the time. They had less than an hour before the fireworks would begin.

"Good luck," said General Aturk. "And don't worry, my men will take care of the missile batteries and cut communications."

"Thanks, General. Rest assured, even if I don't make it out, Lieutenant Genetakos will tell my government how valuable your assistance was. Not that it would matter, thought Logan. If the mission failed, Kesan and everyone around it would be turned to cinders. Except for George and the two Greek Pomachs going with him into the bunker, the rest of the team would stay with General Aturk's men. Logan, George and the rest of the team quickly swapped uniforms with some of the Generals' men. Looking like Turkish military police, they boarded the jeep and drove toward the bunker's entrance only a few minutes away.

Kesan Bunker complex

0405hrs, 23 May

As the General undressed, he contemplated what he had just put into motion. Only a few minutes ago, he had given the last set of instructions to his missile battery commander, to prepare the remaining Saladin missiles for launching. The missiles were mounted on mobile launchers and spread over a hundred kilometer area. This made the possibility of an air strike getting them all virtually impossible. Less than two hours remained before he would transmit the final order that would unleash the deadly poison filled rockets on his enemies' capitals. Yes! He would have his revenge and no one would be able to stop him.

The General wondered where his aid, Ahmet, had run off to as he opened his closet and reached in for a clean uniform and towel. His security officer had reported that Ahmet had left the complex several hours earlier. There was no place in the Revolution for spineless and sentimental idiots. At this moment, he had more important things on his mind. He would deal with that fool later.

Outside the Kesan Bunker
0415hrs, 23 May

"We're here," said Colonel Azoglou, stopping the truck.

"Well, I'll be damned. You can't tell anything is there until you're practically on top of it. No wonder they couldn't find anything from the air. I have to hand it to your engineers, Colonel."

"Thank you, Colonel Logan. It will be a pity such an expensive undertaking will go to waste," said Ahmet.

"It wasn't us who started this war."

"Yes, that is unfortunately true. Come, we must hurry. We

have less than forty-five minutes left before your planes arrive. They all got out of the jeep and headed toward the bunker's dimly lit entrance only a few meters away.

"Jesus. I can't believe we're really doing this," said George.

"Quiet. And do not say another word. I will do the talking," said Ahmet.

"What if they question us? asked Logan.

"Don't worry. As I've told you before, in the Turkish military enlisted men do not question officers."

"Let's hope they don't start now," remarked George.

The four men approached the entrance which was guarded by two soldiers manning a machine gun.

"Halt! Identify yourselves," said one of the guards.

"It is I, Colonel Azoglou, with a Military Police to escort the prisoner for further interrogation to Istanbul."

Both guards cringed when they heard the word interrogation. General Aturk's Military Police were well known for their methods of obtaining information. The guards, who personally knew Colonel Azoglou, did not question his identity, but procedure required that they check the others.

"May I see the identity cards of your escorts, sir?"

Ahmet stared the sentry down. "Don't you know who I am, Corporal Kourkout? Are you questioning my authority and integrity as a senior officer? I am in a very big hurry."

"No, no, sir. I was just following procedures. You may pass."

"Thank you," said Ahmet, changing to a more pleasant tone of voice.

"I will tell the officer of the watch what a good job you're doing out here," Ahmet added.

"Thank you, sir," said the sentry obviously relieved that the Colonel had not gotten too pissed off. He would hate to leave this plush job. From what he had heard from the others, the survival rate of an infantry man in combat was pretty short.

"Oh, one thing, sir. You must all leave your weapons outside. Except for the guards inside, no other weapons are allowed to be taken in."

"Yes. You are right." Ahmet turned to George and Logan who hadn't understood a word of what had transpired. Fortunately, the two Greek Pomachs, who had unslung their rifles, put them in a weapons rack that had been placed at the entrance for visitors. George and Logan took the cue from them and followed suit.

"Oh, sir. General Kemal had given instructions for you to report to him as soon as you returned."

"Very good, thank you," said Ahmet. *That was not good, he thought.*

The four followed Colonel Azoglou down the stairs to the entrance of main bunker complex. The sentry, one of Kemal's Elite Islamic guards at the bottom of the stairway, snapped to attention as Ahmet walked by. Entering the large complex, Logan was awed by its size. He had been in many bunkers and underground command centers, but this one had to rival or surpass anything he had ever seen before. Scores of computer monitors littered the numerous desk tops and large computer generated maps on huge LCDs lined the walls of the immense room they were in. The numerous personnel on duty efficiently went about their business, not paying any particular attention to them as they walked by. Ahmet motioned for them to follow him down one of the long corridors leading from the main operations room. When they were out of hearing range, he spoke to Logan.

"The prisoner is being held at the other end of this corridor. We must hurry before Kemal finds out we are here."

Logan checked the time. "We got thirty minutes before the shit hits the fan."

"Let's go," said Ahmet. They followed him down the corridor until they came to a door with a sentry posted outside. The sentry snapped to attention when he recognized the Colonel.

"We are here to take the prisoner. She will be transported to Istanbul for further interrogation."

"I'm sorry, sir. General Kemal's specific orders were for no one to see the prisoner without his specific authorization.

"Don't you know who I am? I just left the General's quarters," said Ahmet feigning anger.

"Sorry, sir. But those were my instructions. I will call my superior," said the sentry reaching for the phone that hung on the wall. Logan suspected that something had gone wrong when Ahmet had raised his voice. In the wink of an eye, one of the Greek Pomachs pulled out a commando knife that he had hidden in his boot and plunged it in the sentry's throat. The other grabbed the sentry before he could fall.

"Oh God. Please no killing!" said Ahmet.

"There was no other choice," said Logan. Opening the door they dragged the sentry's body inside. Logan wasn't prepared for what he saw. In the corner of the room was a metal bed with wires attached to it and secured to it was Wendy. Logan rushed to her side and began to untie her.

"Jesus! What have they done to her?" He said as he saw the bloody welts and large bruises that covered her body. He took her head in his arms.

"Wendy?" She opened her eyes and smiled.

"Jack, it's you. I must be delirious."

"No. It's really me. We're here to rescue you."

She began to cry. "He raped and beat me!"

"Don't worry, baby. No one will ever hurt you again," said Logan, wiping away some of her tears. Can you walk?" he asked as he handed Wendy her flight suit that was at the foot of the cot.

"I think so."

"Hurry, sir. We must get out of here. In the next twenty minutes, all hell is going to break loose," said George.

Ahmet was aghast when he saw what Kemal had done to the girl. This was against everything Islam stood for. The animal Kemal had to die.

"Let's get out of here," said Logan as he helped Wendy up. The door opened suddenly and one of the Greek Pomachs stepped inside.

"Sir, there's company headed this way."

"Shit! We were so close," said Logan.

"Oh Jesus," said Wendy. Don't let them take me again, Jack."

"Don't worry, I won't. Let them come in; we'll try to bluff our way out. No shooting unless you have to. George, stuff the sentry's body in that store room."

George and Ahmet grabbed the body and quickly stuffed it in the room's only storage locker. The Pomach sentry outside the door snapped to attention when he recognized General Kemal approaching, accompanied by four other guards.

"What is the military police doing here? asked Kemal .

"We were dispatched here to retrieve the prisoner and transport her to Istanbul for further interrogation."

"By whose orders?" screamed Kemal.

"General Aturk, sir."

Kemal was furious. Aturk was trying to usurp his authority by taking his prisoner and possibly using her as leverage with the Americans. But how did he find out?

"Where is my guard?" asked Kemal.

"Inside, sir, with your aid, Colonel Azoglou."

As I might have suspected, thought Kemal. That traitorous idiot Ahmet is collaborating with that other fool Aturk. He would show all of them who was in charge.

"Guards, follow me," said Kemal as he shoved the Pomach aside. Logan and the rest were not surprised when Kemal and his men barged inside.

"Well, what is it we have here, Ahmet? Could you and Aturk

possibly be up to something?" asked Kemal in a sarcastic manner.

"These men are here to escort the prisoner to Istanbul where she will be treated according to the rules of the Geneva Convention."

"I have not given any instructions for her movement. I make the rules here," beamed Kemal.

Even though Logan and George could not understand a word of what was being said, it was definitely apparent that all was not going well. More so, by the way Kemal's guards were pointing their submachine guns at them.

"Yes, you make the rules. That is obviously true. Your own perverted set of rules, Muhammad."

"How dare you speak to me like this?"

"How dare I? Look at what you have done to this girl. Is this the way of Islam? You are planning to kill thousands of innocent civilians, all in the name of God. Whose God? Yours maybe? You will bring about this nation's destruction."

Kemal was seething with rage.

"You ungrateful dog. After all I have done for you."

"No, my friend. It is you who is ungrateful. It was I who first introduced you to the brotherhood. And you betrayed everything that we had entrusted to you!"

"Guards arrest this fool! As for you. . .," he said to Logan and George, but before he could finish, the Pomach sentry who had been standing outside entered the room.

"Drop your weapons!"

"The Cavalry to the rescue."

"Yeah, Colonel just like the movies," said George.

"What? Americans? Here? "said a shocked Kemal in English.

"Were you expecting someone from Mars instead, you son of a bitch!" said Logan, picking up one of the guards submachine guns.

"Then with whom do I have the pleasure of dealing with," said Kemal sarcastically.

"Colonel Jack Logan, USAF,"

"Tie the guards up," said Logan to the two Greek Pomach soldiers.

"Give me your pistol," said Ahmet.

Kemal reluctantly handed it over to his former aid. "So Ahmet, you have betrayed your country to the infidel."

"No, I am trying to save what is left of my country, before it is totally destroyed by your insanity."

"Enough talk for now. It's time to get the hell out of here," said Logan.

"What do you expect to do now, Colonel Logan? You'll never leave this bunker alive."

"Shut up, Kemal. Now move it. If you do anything, I'll put the first bullet into you, myself. Do you understand?"

"Don't worry, Colonel. I will cooperate. You can take your little whore with you."

"You bastard," said Logan, but before he could take a swing at Kemal, he was stopped by George.

"You're a lucky son of a bitch, Kemal. If I didn't value my

men's lives, I'd kill you!"

"How sentimental, so typically American."

"Move it," said Logan, giving Kemal a push with the barrel of the submachine gun he was carrying.

They entered the main corridor which led toward the operations center and the bunker's entrance. Wendy, who was having difficulty walking due to the beatings she had received, was helped along by George. "I feel so weak," said Wendy.

"Just a little more, we are almost out," said George trying to give her some encouragement.

Entering the Operation Center, they headed for the exit. "You are a traitor, Ahmet. You will pay for your treachery," whispered Kemal.

"Shut up! And keep moving," said Logan. The guard at the exit snapped to attention when he saw the two senior officers. Before they could exit the complex, a klaxon on the wall suddenly sprang to life. Its cry reverberated throughout the bunker.

"Enemy aircraft approaching, ETA seven minutes!" was heard over the bunker's speaker system.

"It's the air raid," said Ahmet to Logan who became momentarily confused by all the sudden noise and activity.

Sensing an opportunity, Kemal made his move and lunged for Ahmet's pistol. A struggle for the gun ensued between the two men. It ended almost immediately, when a single shot rang out and Ahmet fell to the ground. Kemal leaped behind a desk. "Kill them, they're enemy impostors!" screamed Kemal.

Before the guard at the exit door could bring his weapon up to shoot, George riddled him with a short burst of fire. Panic and pandemonium broke out in the control room as technicians and other duty personnel ran for cover.

"Move it, there is the exit!" yelled Logan, while at the same time spraying the room with a burst of gunfire smashing many of the screens and computer monitors. The last person through the exit, a Greek Pomach soldier, pulled the pin on one of the grenades he had taken from Kemal's guards and tossed it inside, closing the steel door behind them.

A couple of seconds later the grenade exploded with a muffled bang. "I think that will keep them quiet for a while, Colonel," said the soldier who had thrown the grenade.

"Hurry up the stairs," yelled Logan.

"I can make it myself now," said Wendy, "thanks for the help in the there, Sergeant."

"Okay, take this pistol and my name is George."

"Thanks, George."

With weapons at the ready, they cautiously moved up the first flight of stairs and turned the corner for the final flight of steps to the top. "Take cover," screamed one of the Greek soldiers as they just started to turn the stairway corner. His cry was drowned out by a burst of automatic weapons fire that hit him squarely in the chest, toppling him down the stairs.

"We're trapped," said Logan. The air strike will be arriving in five minutes.

"Not another air strike? said Wendy. "The last one had

ended in disaster."

"I know. But this one will have some help. A FAC team is here with Laser target illuminators to ensure the planes strike their targets this time. Kemal has to be taken out. He's planning to launch missiles filled with nerve gas at Athens and Sofia, Bulgaria."

"He's definitely insane," she added.

"If we fail, a B-2 bomber will drop a nuke on this bunker exactly twenty minutes later. We've all been deemed expendable.

"Oh, my God!"

Another burst of fire echoed causing cement chips to fly in their faces. George returned fire. "What are we going to do, sir? There is no way to take those guys up there out," said George.

"Do we have any more grenades?" asked Logan. George and the Greek shook their heads. "Then we say our prayers."

Outside the Bunker
Same time

Lieutenant Genetakos and his troops had successfully accomplished their mission of opening a route through the bunker's air defenses for the incoming strike force. It had been relatively easy with the help of General Aturk's men who had entered the missile launch control centers unopposed and quietly shut down the systems. Except for a few remaining outlying batteries which would have to be handled by the escorting fighters, the bunker was stripped of its air defenses.

With the way opened for the bombers, the only thing remaining was for the FAC teams to take up their positions. The Lieutenant and his team had chosen the bunker's entrance for the planes' target. They had taken up positions behind some trees, a couple of hundred meters from the bunker's entrance.

"Sir everyone's in position. I have contact with the mission flight leader, they're five minutes out," said the controller.

"Thanks, any word from the Colonel Logan?"

"Not yet, sir."

Damn it! I should have gone instead, he thought. Suddenly he saw commotion and heard shooting coming from the bunker's entrance.

"That must be Logan," he said out loud. "They're trapped inside. I'm going to help them, but I have to take out that machine gun nest first. Jefferson, follow me with your 203. The rest of you, cover us!"

Taking along some hand grenades, he and Jefferson took off running toward the bunker's entrance. Luck was with them. The enemy soldier manning the machine gun, momentarily distracted by what was happening in the bunker, did not see Genetakos approaching until it was too late.

"Now, Jefferson!"

Before the enemy soldier could traverse the machine gun, the American sky cop fired his M-203 grenade launcher from a distance of fifty meters and scored a direct hit. The exploding 40mm shell blew the gunner right out of the emplacement. Pulling the pin on one of his grenades, the Lieutenant tossed it into the bunker's entrance and dove for cover.

Inside the Bunker
Same Time

Logan had almost given up hope when a loud explosion ripped through the narrow confines of the stairway. When the smoke cleared a few seconds later, he heard the voice of Lieutenant Genetakos. "Colonel Logan! Is that you in there?"

"Yes. We're coming up."

"Hurry, the air strike will be here any minute. We'll cover you."

"Everybody, run for it." Logan scooped up Wendy and climbed the stairs to the bunker's entrance.

"Let me give you a hand, Colonel," said Genetakos who met Logan at the top of the stairs.

"No, I can manage." The rumble of anti-aircraft guns in the distance made everyone hesitate for a moment.

"The planes, they're almost here."

"Run!" shouted Genetakos.

"You don't have to tell me a second time," said George as they all took off running toward the clump of trees where the rest of the team was waiting. Reaching the trees, everyone dove behind them for cover. The loud roar of the approaching planes could clearly be heard over the din of the anti-aircraft fire.

"Here they come. Fire up the laser designator," said Logan.

"Already done, sir. My aircraft is making its bomb run at this very moment," said the controller as he illuminated the bunker's entrance with the invisible to the naked eye laser beam.

The steel vault door that normally secured the bunker's top entrance in case of an air attack had remained open, its automatic locking mechanism damaged by the Lieutenant's grenade blast. Not that it would have really mattered in any case.

The Bunker
0500hrs, 23 May

Following the escape of the Americans, the bunker had for security reasons been completely sealed to the outside world. With the approach of the incoming air strike, Kemal who had survived the brief firefight without serious injuries had immediately taken personal command of all operations.

"Sir, our radars report that enemy fighter bombers are only a few kilometers away. No missiles launched against them!" said the on duty OIC who was an army major.

"That's impossible! Get them on the line screamed Kemal."

"Sir, I have a military policeman on the line at one of the anti-aircraft batteries. He says he takes orders only from General Aturk.

"What!" Kemal finally had realized what had taken place. The bunker was now practically defenseless to attack from the air. Traitors had opened the way for the enemy to directly strike at him. He would still get his revenge.

"Get me the Saladin battery commander on the phone at once! I must give the order to fire the missiles immediately."

"You have failed, Muhammad and now you will atone for your sins. Fortunately, the Turkish people will not suffer much further from your indiscretions," said Ahmet in a weak voice.

The General looked at his former friend who lay propped up against one of the bunker's concrete pillars, bleeding from a gunshot wound to the stomach.

"Go to hell you traitor. I will still have my revenge."

"Yes, I probably will, for helping create you. May Allah have mercy on all our souls."

"Sir, I have the Saladin commander on the line," said the command post's duty officer."

"See Ahmet, I will beat you! I will ultimately win!" The General rushed toward the phone. High up above, a USAF F-15 Strike Eagle released the specially modified four thousand pound Paveway bomb it had been carrying. The guidance system on the bomb's nose immediately detected the laser beam which was being directed at the bunker's entrance and set its flight path toward the beam's aiming point. At the same instance, several more bombs dropped by other Strike Eagles had picked up laser designator beams that were aimed at the bunker's ventilator shafts. General Kemal took the telephone receiver in his hand.

"This is General Kemal, launch. . ." Before he could finish, the first bomb had sailed through the bunker's open entrance way and exploded. The blast wave tore through the bunkers lower level, incinerating everything in its path. It was immediately followed by several other explosions. Tons of broken concrete and steel came raining down on the bunker's occupants, killing them instantly. With communications from the bunker abruptly cut, the Saladin missile commander was momentarily at a loss of what to do. A rational man, he felt relieved at not having to fire his missiles at cities filled with helpless women and children. He was not a murderer. Being a proper Turkish officer, he decided to wait for further orders from his superiors before going ahead with the launch.

Kesan
0510hrs, 23 May

"We did it, Colonel," yelled George loud enough to be heard over the din of the departing fighter bombers. High up above, a couple of the escorting F-16s did victory rolls to celebrate the success of the air strike.

"Thanks to you, Jack, thousands of lives have been saved," whispered Wendy, still in obvious pain from her ordeal.

Logan momentarily thought of Colonel Azoglou as he looked at the bunker's entrance which was belching out clouds of black smoke like an erupting volcano. The enemy officer had given his life so his former enemies could live. He was the real hero.

"This war's not over yet, Wendy." Logan looked at her. She was crying.

"What is it? Are you in pain?"

"That too, but I just realized that I really love you."

He took her in his arms. "Oh baby, I'll never let you go now that I've found you."

"Vehicles approaching," shouted George. Everyone quickly went for their weapons and took cover, not knowing if the vehicles' occupants were hostile or friendly. A jeep, followed by a large military truck, stopped fifty meters from their position. A Turkish officer whom Logan recognized as General Aturk got out and walked toward them.

"It's General Aturk," said Logan as he got up, brushed himself off and walked toward Aturk.

"Greetings, Colonel. I see your pilots did a good job. This a great pity, a lot of good men perished in there," said Aturk, noting Colonel Azoglou's absence.

"Yes they did, General. We never could have done it without your assistance and Colonel Azoglou."

"Yes, yes, I hope you remember to tell this to your respective governments."

"Rest assured. I will tell them."

"Sir, the backup bomber has received confirmation of the bunker's destruction and has turned for home," said the air controller.

"What bomber?" asked Aturk, his curiosity aroused by what he had just heard.

Logan at this point did not feel like lying. "One of our B-2s," said Logan. Aturk knew that the B-2 was a strategic bomber, used mainly for nuclear deterrence or..

"By the grace of Allah! You wouldn't have!"

"Yes, General, we would have. The American President would not have allowed Kemal to go through with his plans to kill thousands of innocent people. If this mission had failed, Kesan would have been destroyed regardless!"

A chill ran through Aturk's spine as he realized how close he had come to meeting his maker. They had all grossly underestimated the determination of the United States in helping defend its friends and allies.

"Well Colonel Logan, you all must leave before other troops arrive. It could get a little complicated if I would have to explain your presence here. This vehicle will take you to your helicopter. I have a lot of work to do if this war is to end soon. Till we meet again."

Logan saluted the General. "Yes, till we meet again, General."

Rendezvous Point
0635hrs, 23 May

Yiannis and his crew were ecstatic. A coded message had come in a few minutes ago from the helicopter, relating the news of the successful strike against the bunker. It also meant that the war would soon end.

"Sir, another message from the helicopter, this one in clear text, ETA approximately fifteen minutes."

"Thanks, Mr. Fanopoulos."

"That's good news. However, it's already daylight and we're only ten kilometers from the enemy coast with our radar off. We're sitting ducks."

"I know, Takis. Hopefully this small rock will shield us from any enemy radar. It's only a few more minutes till the helicopter gets here..." Their conversation was interrupted by a seaman who came running into the bridge.

"Sir, message from the island. They've spotted an enemy patrol boat, possibly a Dogan, headed this way. It's about ten minutes out!"

"God damn our luck! Takis start the engines in case we have to make a run for it. Right now they don't know we're here. Keep the radar off. The spotters on the island can keep us informed of the Dogan's position. We will pick them up once the threat is gone."

"That warship carries Penguin missiles and has a large gun," said Takis.

"I know. Nevertheless, they have to round the island before their radar can pick us up. By then, they'll be too close to fire their missiles. Those missiles need at least a couple of kilometers to arm. We'll be able to get in the first shot with our gun."

"That's risking it, Takis."

"I realize it. But we don't have any other choice. The helicopter will be arriving here shortly with empty fuel tanks.

"Sir, the patrol boat has turned. It's coming this way, and it's definitely a Dogan.

"Mr. Fanopoulos, signal the Sea Hawk and advise them of our predicament."

"Yes, sir."

"Takis! That helicopter carries Penguin missiles."

"You're right."

"Mr. Fanopoulos ask the helicopter for assistance."

"Will do."

"I hope they make it in time," said Takis.

Forty Kilometers North of Rendezvous Point
0640hrs, 23 May

Exhausted by their ordeal, most of the team had fallen asleep when the helicopter had taken off for the return journey. Wendy, who had to be carried for most of the way, had received first aid, but the team medic suspected that she was suffering from internal bleeding and immediately needed a hospital. After they refueled, they would fly to Thessaloniki where the nearest hospital was located. Logan was awakened by someone shaking him.

"Sir, we're nearing the rendezvous point. I have the Hydra on the line, they're asking for our assistance. There's an enemy missile boat heading their way," said Lieutenant Genetakos.

"Have they been spotted?"

"Not yet."

Logan got out of his seat and walked into the cockpit. "I know this chopper carries missiles. How long before we're in range to do anything," he asked the pilot.

"Another five minutes, Colonel."

"Let's hope that Commander Vassiliou can hold out till we get there."

"He'd better, sir. We don't have any fuel to go farther," said the copilot.

Rendezvous Point
0642hrs, 23 May

Yiannis had gotten the Hydra underway and positioned the boat in such a manner in order to get the first shot with their cannons. Once the enemy boat rounded the rocky point, Yiannis would give the order to open fire.

"Signal from shore, sir. The enemy will be in range in less than a minute."

"Stand by to fire all guns."

He knew their chance of hitting and critically damaging the high speed Dogan was minimal. Every shot had to count. Yiannis momentarily thought of launching a torpedo, but the highly maneuverable craft could easily dodge it.

Aboard the Turkish missile boat Mehmet II, her captain, a cautious man and one of the few survivors of the battle of Limnos, had kept his crew at general quarters from the beginning of the patrol. Even though their radar did not show anything in the area, the Greeks were known to use the small islands dotting the Aegean to mask their presence. They were now sailing through such an area and he didn't want to get caught with his pants down. As an added precaution, he had doubled his lookouts; they would not be caught by surprise.

"Enemy boat on the port bow!" screamed one of the lookouts. Captain Tsiller beamed with pride. His tactics had paid off.

"Open fire!" commanded Yiannis.

Almost immediately, the Hydras' two 35mm cannons spoke in rapid succession. Several of the shells could be seen striking the enemy boat which was less than a mile away. The Dogan's commander immediately took evasive action and returned fire. The enemy boat's 76mm gun was only able to fire twice before being silenced by several shell hits. The first 76mm shell barely missed the Hydra sending water and shrapnel cascading over the bow. The second shell struck the Hydra's port cannon, blowing it off its mount, simultaneously setting off its ready ammunition. The resulting explosion sent metal flying everywhere.

Yiannis and everyone on the bridges were knocked off their feet by the blast.

"I'm hit," screamed Takis. Yiannis could see a red blotch beginning to spread on the front of his friend's uniform.

"Get a medic!" yelled Yiannis, ripping off the first aid kit that hung on the wall. Taking out a thick bandage, he applied it to his friend's wound.

"Sir, damage control reports fire below deck."

"Do we still have power?"

"Yes, sir," replied the helmsmen. Yiannis could hear the remaining 35mm cannon still firing at the enemy missile boat. Looking out of the shattered windshield, he could barely see the Dogan through the thick smoke. The enemy boat was lagging a couple of kilometers behind them, its smaller caliber cannons blazing away.

"Yiannis, help me up," said Takis.

"Take it easy, Takis. You caught a load of shrapnel in your shoulder."

"Sir, Chief Chronis says we must slow down so that his men can bring the fire under control," said Mr. Faniou.

"If we stop, we're dead. He'll open up the distance and hit us with a missile or torpedo," said Takis.

Yiannis had only one choice left, even though he suspected it would be in vain. "Helmsmen prepare for torpedo attack."

"Aye, aye, sir."

The Turkish commander who was about to order the firing of a Penguin missile to finish off the Hydra, was caught by surprise when he saw the Greek missile boat turn and head toward them. Being an experienced officer, he immediately realized what the brave, but desperate Greek commander was going to do. He gave the order to ready his own torpedoes for firing. He would not waste one of his expensive missiles. In the meantime, the Dogan's 35mm cannon were beginning to register hits on the enemy boat as it closed the range. Confident of the kill, he prepared to give the order to fire.

On board the Hydra, it was like a scene from hell. Bodies and blood were strewn about the decks. Having taken several 35mm cannon hits in the engine room, the Combattante had slowed to less than ten knots. Yiannis was just about to give the order to fire the torpedo, knowing that the gesture was in reality futile, when the enemy boat disintegrated in a huge ball of fire.

"Jack, you did it!"

Cheering immediately erupted throughout the ship. They had been given a new lease on life.

"Helmsman, all stop!"

"What happened, Yiannis? Did we get them?" asked Takis in obvious pain, but happy to be alive.

"The Sea Hawk must've launched their missiles."

"Just in the nick of time, sir," said Ensign Kourtis.

"You're bleeding, Vangelis."

"Just a flesh wound, sir. I'll be all right."

"Sir, I have the Sea Hawk on the line," said the boat's radio operator. "They're asking if we need any assistance."

"Tell them thanks for the help. We have a few wounded needing transport. Otherwise, I think we'll be all right now."

"Yes, sir."

Yiannis heard the engine room intercom buzzer.

"Yes, chief."

"The fire is almost under control, sir. One of the engines has had it. I can only give you twenty knots."

"How long before we can get underway, Chief?"

"About fifteen minutes, sir."

"I'll be down in a few, Chief, keep up the good work."

"Sir, I have a message from Naval command Aegean. The Turks have asked for an armistice, effective 1200hrs. Headquarters advises all commands to avoid further action, if possible."

"Thanks, George."

Yiannis looked at his friend who was being put on a stretcher by one of the sick bay orderlies to be picked up by the Sea Hawk. They had survived. Two more of his men had not. Less than a kilometer away, the burning Dogan was beginning to settle under the waves. *That could have been them, he thought.* The message had come too late for that ship and some of his crew.

"Navigator, when the Chief says we can start engines, set a course for Thessaloniki. We need to get the rest of our wounded to a hospital and the boat in a repair dock.

"Aye, aye, sir.

Kavala General Hospital
23 May, 1400hrs

Mihalis opened his eyes and realized that he was lying in a bed in what appeared to be a hospital. His hands and most of his lower body were swathed in bandages, but he felt little pain. To the left and right of him were other wounded men, also covered in bandages. The last thing he could remember was the enemy overrunning their position and the tank getting hit. Somehow he had survived the battle. The enemy must have found him and took him to the hospital. He was a prisoner of the Turks. In his drugged state, he tried to get up.

"Hey, what are you trying to do?" yelled someone in Greek.

Mihalis tried to get up, again.

"Don't get up. We worked on you for four hours trying to put you back together," said the man.

Mihalis looked toward the direction where the voice was coming from and saw an older person, dressed in hospital whites. He was probably in his early fifties. *Must be another Greek prisoner, thought Mihalis.* The person came over to Mihalis' bed and put his arm on him.

"Please son, lie down. You will rip your stitches if you keep moving."

"Where am I?"

"In Kavala General Hospital. You were brought in after the battle."

"Who are you? Are you a prisoner, too?"

The man smiled. "I am Colonel Lambros, your doctor. And no, I am not a prisoner."

"But the enemy? We were being overrun," said Mihalis excitedly.

"Take it easy. We stopped just outside the city with the help of the Americans. We regrouped and threw them back. They signed a cease fire this morning. We won."

Mihalis suddenly felt relaxed. "What about the rest of my tank crew?

"According to the medics that brought you in, you were the only survivor, only because you were ejected when your tank blew. You were hurt pretty bad. We dug out at least a kilo of metal from your body and you received some burns. Don't worry. You will fully recover. You really surprised us."

"How's that," replied Mihalis.

"When we identified you from your identity card and realized you were a policeman, we were shocked."

"I joined the tank as a loader just outside of Kommotini, after the city had fallen. I wanted to fight the Turks," said Mihalis.

"They must have been glad to have you."

"I was proud to have served with such a group of fine men," said Mihalis while thinking of Captain Kapsis and the rest of the crew.

"Well we contacted police headquarters in Athens and briefed them on your condition. They, in turn, contacted your family and told them you're okay. We were filled in on your exploits in Kommotini during the uprising. It seems you are a hero. When you are fit enough to travel, you will be air evacuated to Athens to be personally decorated by the President of the Republic for your gallant actions. Oh, and by the way, congratulations on your promotion to Lieutenant."

"Huh? Lieutenant," said Mihalis, genuinely surprised at the turn of events.

"If you need anything else, son, just ask," said the doctor, leaving to continue his rounds.

Mihalis felt a deep pain in his heart for the loss of his friends. They were really the true heroes. Nonetheless, he was happy to be alive. In those few brief days with them, he discovered a sense of belonging and had learned a lot of things about himself. He had passed through the trial by fire and had come out a better man. After he got out of the hospital, he would ask to be reassigned to Kommotini. There would be a lot of work to do there in helping rebuild the city. Besides, he was now a Lieutenant and a hero to boot. No one would ever dream of screwing with him again.

Metropolis Cathedral, Athens
1900hrs, 20 Aug

The Cathedral was filled almost to capacity with civilian and military dignitaries, there to attend the wedding of Greece's most decorated military hero, Lieutenant Commander Yiannis Vassiliou. The cathedral's interior, adorned with more than a dozen Byzantine style icons depicting various Christian saints, was beautifully decorated with different colored flowers. Both Logan and George were dressed in air force blues, with the Congressional Medal of Honor hanging from their necks. George had also been given a battlefield commission to Lieutenant for his exploits and reassigned to the Hellenic air force as a liaison officer. Both men watched as the Prelate of Greece gave Lieutenant Mavridis, the couple's best man, the two woven vine connected crowns to place on Yiannis and his bride's head. In traditional Orthodox custom, this symbolizes both the couple's spiritual and physical joining in matrimony.

"It's a very beautiful ceremony," said Wendy, who was sitting beside her husband and George. She was also wearing a dress blue uniform with Major's insignia, adorned with the Silver Star medal and the Distinguished Flying Cross.

"Our wedding wasn't as colorful."

"Yeah, but it was shorter," said Logan, getting a laugh from George, Cindy and Theodoros who sat next to them.

"Theodoros, will ours be just like this?" asked Cindy.

"Yes, my dear, a real wedding. Not like the ten minute one we had back at your parents."

"Shhh! It's almost finished," said George.

After the ceremony, both the Prelate and the Prime Minister gave a short speech by wishing the new couple good luck. Afterwards, Yiannis and Eleni passed under a military honor guard, composed of the Hydra's crew and a detachment of Greek Commandos, led by the recently promoted Captain Genetakos. Subsequently, the couple and their guests departed the cathedral. They all drove to Glyfada, a suburb on the coast, where the wedding reception was being held. Along the route, they passed the old Parliament building that was still under repair, having suffered heavy bomb damage during the war.

At the reception hall, the newly wedded couple sat at the table of honor surrounded by their closest friends and family.

"Well Yiannis, I told you I'd make it to your party," said Jack.

"Yes, you did. Though for a while there it looked like none of us were going to make it," he said thinking back to the events of only a couple of months ago and picturing the faces of all those that did not make it.

"It was very close." said George.

"Yeah, too close," added Takis.

"I hope all the bastards have been taught a lesson they will never forget. Even though we annexed Northern Epirus from Albania and got a piece of Eastern Thrace, the war cost Greece hundreds of billions in damages. I won't add the cost in blood and suffering. We should have marched right into Istanbul."

"I still think it was a mistake on the allied commission's part to let General Aturk remain in power, even though he pulled his forces from Cyprus and promises democratic reforms. I still don't trust him," said George.

"Yeah, and the Macedonians now have a military government in power. Their leader, General Mihalovic, seems like a good man. He has tried to mend fences with us by giving up all those responsible for Macedonia's involvement in the war to the United Nations to try as war criminals. I think he will come through on his promise for real democratic reforms in that country," added Takis.

"Maybe Macedonia might turn out to be an exception, but I don't trust politicians. Look what they did with Saddam Hussein in the first Gulf war. We could have been in Baghdad had they let the war go on for twenty-four more hours," said Logan.

"It took another war to get rid of him."

"You're right, Jack. The politicians screw up and leave it to the soldiers to clean up. I have a bad feeling we might be hearing from our friends again." said Yiannis.

"Come on, everybody. I don't want to hear any more about the war. Today is my wedding. Let's talk about happier things," said Eleni.

"Eleni is right," said Wendy. "Let's talk about the future, our future and our children's future," she said.

"I have an announcement to make. I'm giving up flying."

"But I thought flying was your life," said Logan genuinely surprised at his wife.

"Well, temporarily. Just for the next nine months," said

Wendy with a smile.

"Gee. You mean you're, I'm going to be..." said Jack, flabbergasted at the news.

"Ah ha," said Wendy with a mischievous look.

"To my new godson or daughter," said Yiannis.

"I'll drink to that!" George raised his glass in a toast.

After everyone had toasted the new father and mother to be, Takis stood up to make an announcement.

"Oh Yiannis, before I forget and since you will become my child's godfather and therefore family, we might have more in common than you think.

"Huh," Yiannis gave Jack a puzzled look.

"I spoke to my dad when I was home on leave. He's almost ninety one, but still in relatively good health. He told me about one of his exploits during the war. He was also a fighter pilot. While stationed in Italy in late 1943, he had participated on an escort mission to deliver gold to the Greek resistance. While over central Greece, they were jumped by German night fighters and shot down. It's a long story. Did you have a grandfather also named Yiannis Vassiliou who fought in the resistance?"

"Why, yes. He had also been a naval officer. While supporting a commando raid, his Sub was sunk by German Sub chasers. He swam to shore and ended up in the resistance to continue the fight."

"Well, I'll be damned," said Logan. "Both our families fought the Nazis side by side."

"I would like to hear this story of yours some time."

"Sure. I'll be glad to tell it. But now how about another toast to the bride and groom?" said Jack, raising his wine glass.

"To Yiannis and Eleni, may they be blessed with many children!" The toast was repeated throughout the reception room as everyone happily drank to the couple's future and temporarily forgot their recent unpleasant memories.

- Title: Operation Medina™: The Jihad
- Author: George Mavro
- Price: $27.95
- Publisher: TotalRecall Publications, Inc.
- Format: HARDCOVER, 6.14" x 9.21"
- Number of pages: 320
- 13-digit ISBN: 978-1-59095-747-9
- Publication: 2011

The Balkans and Mideast, a region very much in the news, is the setting for this action novel which takes place in the not too distant future. The secular pro-western government of Turkey has been overthrown in a violent revolution and replaced by an Islamic fundamentalist regime. Her fanatical leader, General Muhammad Kemal, has contrived a devious plan to restore the Ottoman Empire in the Balkans and unite the Islamic world under his evil rule. To accomplish this, Kemal will launch a devastating war with all the tools in his arsenal including Islamic Jihadist terrorists and WMDs. His first targets are US alley Greece and the few remaining American forces stationed in the region.

For his diabolic scheme to be successful, Kemal must eliminate any source of possible outside interference. To accomplish this, he sends a terrorist team to take out the USAF fighters.

A thousand miles to the south, a Palestinian terrorist sails a boat loaded with anti-ship missiles into Greek waters and delivers a devastating attack in the Mediterranean. The next morning, Turkey and her allies launch a devastating surprise attack against Greece.

With the Greeks facing certain defeat, the U.S. President quickly dispatches to Greece, a fighter squadron and a small USAF Security force contingent for airbase ground defense. The USAF expeditionary force is under the command Lieutenant Colonel Jack Logan a veteran fighter pilot. Logan will be faced with the greatest challenge of his career; he must use every bit of his skills to keep his outnumbered command from being annihilated and help stop the enemy onslaught.